Pearl Clark

Easter sunday

27 is a beautiful sunshineing
day. The wind blows hard.

DISTRICT NURSE .

DISTRICT
NURSE

BY

FAITH BALDWIN

THE BLAKISTON COMPANY

PHILADELPHIA

This TRIANGLE EDITION is published
by arrangement with Murray Hill Books, Inc.

TRIANGLE BOOKS is a series published by
The Blakiston Company, 1012 Walnut St., Philadelphia 5, Pa.

Dedicated, in admiration,
TO

The V. N. A.

AND WELFARE NURSES EVERYWHERE

Life is like a city street
Where the waves of traffic beat,
Tears and laughter, shade and sun,
Old day ending, new begun . . .
Kiss and quarrel, dream and die,
Life's a street of passers-by—
You and I—you and I.

All characters and situations
in this book are imaginary
THE AUTHOR

DISTRICT NURSE

CHAPTER ONE

Sidewalks.

'The sidewalks of city streets; the sidewalks of any city; your city, mine. But not of any streets. Not the sidewalks of the manicured boulevards, the wide, tree-bordered avenues. Not the sidewalks which lie, relatively immaculate, before the doorsteps of the rich; not those lightly trodden upon by eighteen-dollar, bench-made shoes, desecrated by the crass, if functional behavior, of leashed and high-hat dogs; nor yet the sidewalks decorated by the spotless uniforms of Generalissimos in the Doorman's Army. Not these.

Just sidewalks, over which the same sky arches, but a sky made vocal with the hoarse shriek of the hurtling L's, just sidewalks built on a common soil beneath which, like as not, the clamorous mole, the subway, weaves and burrows its vocal path. Just sidewalks, littered with paper, with casual garbage, marked with the pressure of countless feet, hurrying feet, feet which go unshod, feet protected against heat and cold by the makeshift leathers of the poor. Sidewalks, endless highways, leading to birth, to death, to success and to failure; leading to the cold, crowded windings of city rivers, leading out to freer, wider areas, leading—*back*.

On the sidewalks, people.

Children, playing, quarreling, laughing; lovers kissing, and lovers parting. Babies, in their mothers' arms. Neat women, slatternly women, women old and young. Men. Sober men, and drunken men. Men who walk upright and fear not man or God; men who lie in gutters; men who creep past in the indifferent shadows of old walls. Boys, on roller skates. Pushcarts loaded with fly-specked fruit. A baby carriage filled with pretzels. Open markets. A group of boys smoking cheap cigarettes outside a stationery store. One goes in, and comes out, grinning. He is the first slot machine customer of the day. He has won.

Dogs, chasing each other, chasing their own tails. Dogs, consciously well fed, dogs lean, marked with mange, beset with fleas. Cats. Cats that sit on doorsteps and wash their complacent faces, cats that slink by, their apparent ribs quivering with the memory of heavy boots.

Cars, flashing past. Old cars, new cars, cars on

their way uptown. Cars with women leaning back against good upholstery, saying to one another, my dear, such *smells!* Cars that stop before tenement houses, the cars of bootleggers, of other traffickers in forbidden commodities. Right around the corner, see, there's a ramshackle flat house. But cars park there every day, Lincolns, Cadillacs, the cars of Uptown. Why?

He's a doctor—isn't he?—who owns the flat house. Isn't his own apartment on the top floor, crammed with antiques, some very good, some bad? What kind of a doctor is he? He has an uptown practice. They come here to him. A clever hideaway.

All women, who come.

Sidewalks, teeming with sunlight, sinister in shadow, the breeding place of life, of death, of tragedy, of romance.

Turn a corner. Here are houses which once looked out upon a quiet street, with shuttered and aristocratic eyes. The street is no longer quiet, many of the shutters hang, flapping, on rusty, broken hinges. But the houses remain, brownstone, somber, four stories, fallen on evil days, dreaming perhaps of past position. They have yards, still, in which the grass grows with a feeble tenaciousness, in which are broken asphalt walks and stunted trees striving toward the sun.

Some have little gardens.

In such a house, in the first floor back apartment, Ellen Adams lived with her mother and her sister Nancy.

It was a small apartment. Two bedrooms, a rather leprous bathroom, a kitchenette, a living room. The living room was large, comfortably furnished, high-ceilinged, bay-windowed, with a fireplace which, if it did not draw too well on windy nights, supported an unusually fine mantelpiece.

The breakfast table was laid, one sunny spring morning, in the bay window, as usual. Spring, in the city of sidewalks, heralded its coming by a warmer wind swirling among the strewn papers, by a fragile veil of dusty green on shrub and tree, by roller skates and baseballs, and by, of an evening, people leaving the unknown intimacies of their roofs to sit on stoops or drag their broken chairs to the sidewalk itself.

"It's a grand day," said Ellen contentedly, one blue eye on the clock. "Golly, that coffee smells good."

Mrs. Adams, immaculate, small, slender, with apprehensive eyes, a tight, petulant mouth, and very fine hands, looked up from her small, industrious clashing among silver and china. "Nancy's late again," she said.

"Here she comes," Ellen answered, walking over to the window. "Out of breath, as usual."

Smiling a little, she watched Nancy making her dashing way down the street. Nancy was twenty, to Ellen's twenty-four. Nancy was a blue-eyed brunette, in contrast with Ellen's honey-colored fairness. Nancy was teetering along on her high heels, whistling, and under her arm she had the papers, the giddy, youthful papers which she herself perused on the way back from work, the more sober news sheet affected by her mother.

It was after seven in the morning and Nancy was returning from her work at a Central Telephone Office, from the eleven P.M. to seven A.M. shift.

"Hie, Family," said Nancy a moment later, prancing into the living room, dropping her newspapers, casting her purse aside, flinging her small, ridiculous hat on a table. "Lord, I'm hungry!"

Nancy was always hungry. After breakfast, after hot coffee and rolls and cereal, and maybe an egg, she would clear away and wash the dishes, yawning. Then, she would be sleepy; then, she would be dog-tired. Then, she would settle her mother with paper or book or mending and wander into the bedroom which was hers by day and Ellen's by night, and wiggle her slim body out of its encasing garments, and pull down the shades and open the windows and sleep and sleep with the concentration of youth and health until late afternoon.

"How you can read—" began Mrs. Adams, as usual, picking up the papers.

She never got any further. Nancy interrupted, gaily:

"I can't, very well; that's why I like my reading mostly pictures. Ellen, did you get the marmalade?"

Ellen had. Mrs. Adams mentioned, mildly:

"Your father always read the *Times*."

He had been dead, these many years. But his opinions were still his widow's opinions, his newspaper, her newspaper.

They sat down at the table, after Ellen had brought the rolls, hot from the little oven. Nancy said, suddenly, with authentic admiration:

"You look like a million dollars, Sis. How you manage it, in that uniform . . ."

Ellen looked down at the dark gray of her dress. Her coat was over a chair, nearby. Her uncompromising hat. Her small black bag. She replied amiably:

"Thanks. And district nurses aren't expected to dress like Follies girls, after all."

"Okay by me, Miss Nightingale," said Nancy. "How are the errands of mercy, by the way? Any murders? You haven't given me the low-down for a year. By the way, will you be home tonight? Chick's asked me to go to the new Garbo picture."

Up at four, a cup of tea; dinner, early, with the

family; out to a show, report for work at eleven. Time between the show and work for a sandwich somewhere. That was Nancy's usual routine.

"I'll be home," Ellen told her, "but why don't you stay in once in a while? You haven't gotten rid of your cold yet, you know."

"I certainly have. I don't know which was worse, the cold or your treatment," Nancy told her. "Mustard paste and hot baths, blankets and boiling lemon juice. And I haven't grown any skin on my chest yet as it is."

"You don't take care of yourself," Ellen told her absently, borrowing her mother's paper for a moment, running her wise, gray eyes over the headlines.

"Don't be professional, darling," said Nancy, starting to clear away.

Ellen rose and looked down at her mother. She was a slim girl, looking taller in the sedate, severely cut uniform than she really was. Her lovely, heavy hair, paler than gold, warmer than silver, was uncut and curled about her broad temples. There was faint, glowing color under the clear skin, and her generous, pretty mouth was healthily red, curving easily into smiling or the lines of pure compassion. There was strength in the firm set of her square, small chin, more than a hint of stubbornness, and perhaps, quick temper.

A moment later and she had kissed her mother and waved a casual affectionate farewell to Nancy, who was out in the kitchenette, slinging dishes loudly and haphazardly into the sink. Nancy yawned. " 'Bye," she said, "don't catch measles or take any wooden money."

"Aren't you leaving early?" her mother called after her. Ellen's reply came faintly through the closing door.

"I have to stop at Joe's," she said.

A moment later she went down the steps to the street. Someone called to her from across the way. That was Mrs. Murphy, shaking out her rugs from the windows, in bland defiance of law and disorder. Ellen called back and walked briskly down the street.

It was a gorgeous day. She was going toward work she loved with a single, astonishing passion. Her mother had not had a heart attack in four months. The house she had left had always been her home; she had known no other. Once the Adams family had owned the house, had spoken with a certain controlled pride of their "neighborhood." Now, they rented an apartment in that same house and the neighborhood was not as it had been. Ellen sighed a little, remembering her childhood.

But things had turned out all right, after all. She had been able to go through training after

High School, had been able to do and do well the work she had always wanted to do, among the people with whom she had grown up. Nancy was happy enough in her own work. She wished Nancy needn't work on the night shift. But it was better so; better that one of the girls be always within call, within reach of the frail elderly woman around whom their lives were centered; Ellen at night, Nancy by day. It couldn't have been done any other way.

If Coral hadn't gone away. Ellen shrugged her slim shoulders in the dark coat and amended it to . . . if Coral would come back? No use thinking of Coral, lost to them for nearly a decade. But somehow Ellen always remembered her, in the spring.

She swung around a corner, stopping to speak to Ike who was out with his pushcart early. "You wanna nize pear?" Ike asked beaming. "I should tell you, these pears is swell."

No, Ellen didn't want a pear, thanks just the same. How was Ike's smaller Ike? All better? That was good. "You won't let him eat things off the street again, will you, Ike?" Ike grinned and shook his greasy head. "How'm I to stop him?" he asked sorrowfully. "Boys is always hungry. They eat what they can get, ain't it?" asked Ike.

Little use of talking about balanced diets to Ike, his grimy hands hovering over his pushcart. If he could be persuaded to cover the fruit, a piece of netting. . . . But he only shrugged and fell back on a delightful non-comprehension of English when such hygienic measures were suggested to him.

Ellen, smiling, hurried on to Joe's. Joe was just around the corner, in a basement. There he sat at his window and watched the feet of the world pass by. Watched the shoes, new shoes, old shoes, shoes run over at the heels, shoes smart and shoes dejected. Sooner or later they all came to him, the shoes.

Ellen produced a package.

"Hello, Joe—resole these for me?" she asked.

Joe was willing. He stood up, a short squat man in a leather apron, and took the shoes in hands more like leather than leather itself. "Sure, I feex 'em," he told her heartily. He turned from his bench and fumbled on a shelf. "I gotta Mees Nancy's here," he told her, one of a pair of evening slippers dangling from his finger.

"I'll stop back on my way home, Joe," Ellen promised.

Joe regarded the sturdy, scuffed shoes she had given him, with their heavy soles and low rubber heels. "You sure walka a lot," chuckled Joe.

"That's my job," said Ellen.

After she had left him he put the shoes away. Niza girl. Real lady. Nancy gooda keed, too. But Ellen. Joe was sentimental about Ellen. Had she

not come and helped the time the last bambino was
born? Sure, fine girl. Lookit her shoes now, worn
out running around trying to help people. Not like
the other sister, the one who had run away, how
many years ago, six years, eight years? Joe had forgotten her name, but he remembered her dark hair
with the red lights in it, and her impatience. . . .
"Aren't my shoes ready yet, Joe, for heaven's sake,
what do you do with your time?" He'd mended so
many of her shoes, stilt-heeled, flimsy shoes, battered
with dancing, in strange company, their heedless
way through life. . . .

Ellen made her way through the increasing crowds
toward the sub-station of the Visiting Nurse Association where she would presently make her reports
and get her calls for the morning. On the corner
she saw Herman, the small round son of the man
known to the neighborhood as Accordion Al. Herman
was trotting along at his father's side, suiting his
schoolboy pace to the stiff halting gait of his com-
panion's wooden leg. On the corner, up against Mrs.
Lippinsky's stationery store news-stand Accordion
Al would unfold his camp stool and sit down to play
and sing through the long hours, unmolested. He'd
been quite affluent once when he'd had the ferry boat
concession. Not now. Ellen stopped to speak to the
pair and as she went on she heard Al's husky, fairly
true voice lifted in that song he was always sing-

ing. Where had he got it? she wondered . . . it had a charming, rather melancholy melody and a simple lyric. Some day she must ask him. She hummed it now under her breath, hurrying toward the sub-station. How did it go?

> "Life is like a city street
> Where the tides of traffic beat,
> Tears and laughter, shade and sun,
> Long day ending, new begun . . .
> Kiss and quarrel, dream and die,
> Life's a street of passers-by——
> You and I—you and I——"

"Hello," said Jim at the door of the sub-station, lounging against it, broad shoulders a little slouched, hands in pockets.

"Hello yourself," replied Ellen, smiling at him, "how come you're up so early?"

"Big deal," said Jim solemnly.

They laughed together standing there in the bright, warm sunlight. Jim was taller than Ellen and very dark. His eyes were brown, heritage from a mother who had left her South European home to come to a far country and fall in love with a gay, hard-living young Irishman who had, not much later, deserted her. Mrs. O'Connor was dead now. Jim lived with his father's devout maiden sister, a block or two from Ellen. They had grown up together, they had attended the same schools, several classes apart. Ellen couldn't remember the time when, in the eyes of the neighborhood, she hadn't been "Jim's girl."

Jim's small real estate and insurance office wasn't far from the sub-station. He rented flats and lofts, he had a finger in the various neighborhood pies. A few years older than herself, part of her life, part of her background. "How about a movie tonight?" he was asking.

Ellen shook her head.

"Nancy's going out," she told him. "I'd rather stay home. Mother doesn't like us both to be out—and I'd rather not——"

"Sure, I know. How's Aunt Elizabeth anyway?"

He always called her mother, Aunt Elizabeth. He was almost one of the family. Hadn't Mrs. Adams, in those younger, healthier, more prosperous days gone in to Mrs. O'Connor the bitter winter night Jim was born, the night that the senior O'Connor couldn't be found until Adams himself, at his wife's urgency, had struggled into a great coat and gone the rounds of the saloons?

"She's all right," Ellen told him. "Only, since that last attack she's not been as strong, you know. We have to look out for her. There's a lot of flu in the district and her resistance is nothing to brag about."

Jim's dark face was concerned.

"I know, it's a rotten break," he said, and touched

her hand. "Suppose I look in on her today? I'm going by that way anyway. Got a tenant for the upstairs back, next door."

"You have? Mrs. Lenz will be out of her mind with joy," Ellen told him; "the flat's been vacant for ages."

"This isn't business, it's friendship," grinned Jim. He hesitated, looking away, "It's Dot Mather, remember her?"

Ellen nodded gravely. She remembered Dot. They all did. The district's most defiant bad girl. Remembered earlier days when her mother had said, "Ellen, I don't *want* you to play with Dot . . ."

"She's married," said Jim finally, waiting for the question which didn't come, "some lad from New Haven. Trouble shooter now with the telephone company. She wrote me to find her a place. I thought of Mrs. Lenz."

"But," asked Ellen, "will Mrs. Lenz——?"

"Why not?" countered Jim instantly. "She's married now, isn't she? And nowadays people can't be too choosy. Too many flats going begging, you know."

Ellen knew. Dot. She remembered how pretty she was, red-headed, wild as a hare, loose as ashes. She shook her head, frowning a little. Her mother would ––be annoyed. Not that it mattered. She was suddenly aware of the spring sunlight, and of Jim lounging beside her, close, intent. Suddenly glad for little Dot Mather. Crazy Dot, they had called her. Married . . . and happy.

"I've got to go in," she said to Jim, and looked at her wrist watch. Eight-thirty.

"Wait a minute . . . can I come up to the house tonight, then?" he wanted to know.

"Of course. Why not?"

She smiled at him, and the door closed behind her. Jim O'Connor walked off down the street. Went into his office whistling, thinking of Ellen. No one like her. He inserted his key in the lock of the door. A very big, very young man standing in the shadow of the house next door slipped in after him, agile, silent. Jim turned and the whistle died on his lips.

"Damn it, Fontana, haven't I told you never to come here?" he asked, irritated.

CHAPTER TWO

The Association sub-station consisted of a ground floor office with a tailor shop and a loft above it. Ellen went in and found herself the last arrival. She nodded to Jenny, the little stenographer, already rattling the keys of her machine, and spoke to Miss Renwick, the tall, gray-haired supervisor. The other nurses, seven in all, were busy getting out their reports and Ellen sat down to write up hers. The telephone rang incessantly, a fire engine clanged past, children shouted and ran. Ellen, writing her last report, laid down her pen and ran her slim fingers through her curling hair.

The calls were coming in, from Central Headquarters, from various doctors, from families direct, from a great life insurance company which called on the visiting nurse service to attend its policyholders.

18

"Nice quiet little dump," remarked Harriet Peters, a girl whose delicate and vivacious beauty could not be subdued by the Oxford gray of her uniform or the unbecoming hat. She was a recent recruit from private nursing and had taken her special training for the new work. She had come to the district sub-station full of enthusiasm but was finding life under the L very different from hospital and private home adventures. She pulled her hat down over her eyes and made a face at Ellen who sat near her. "It's a far cry," said Harriet, "from a Eugenie bonnet!"

"Florentine tams are the latest," remarked Carolyn Mathews in an abstracted and indifferent tone and went to get her calls.

Ellen got hers for the morning and started out. She and Harriet came out together, carrying their black bags, and stood for a brief moment in the glancing warmth of the spring sunlight.

"I thought," sighed Harriet, "that hospital corridors were hard on the dogs, but gosh, they aren't a patch on this east side, west side, all around the town business. Look here, Adams, didn't you call on Rosa Chiarelli last week?"

"Chiarelli?" Ellen knitted her fine brows. "No, wasn't that Mathews' case? Pneumonia, I think. I didn't have it. What's happened?"

"Nothing with her. She's all right again but three

of the babies are down with the flu," said Harriet, dispiritedly. "I was there yesterday. Rosa wanted to know why the other nurse hadn't come—the 'nice' one. That was a fine beginning. Still, I guess she's reconciled. Well, so long, or are you going my way?"

Ellen wasn't. The two girls parted and Ellen saw Harriet cross briskly to the other side of the crowded street dodging a slightly demented cat, three trucks, two motor cars, and a horse-drawn "Good Eats" wagon. Saw, too, the man who lurched out of a doorway and lurched back with the most curious, inebriated gesture of respect as Harriet passed him. The uniform may not be becoming, thought Ellen, smiling, but it serves.

Her first call, neatly tabulated on the slip Miss Renwick had given her, was some six or seven blocks away in a house to which she had not been before. It was up three flights and back. The house was frankly tenement. The spring sunshine had no power there. Dim gas jets flickered on the dirty landings casting eerie shadows. In each hallway, as she passed, was the disgrace of an open toilet. She went on upstairs, feeling her way, not touching the filthy banisters. Presently, she knocked.

Two rooms: littered with dogs, with cats, with stale food, with children. In the back room her patient, a flu case. A three-year-old child playing on the littered floor, a year-old baby lying sucking at an indescribable rag of a pacifier on the bed. Relatives all around. The doctor had been and gone, and had telephoned the call in to the sub-station direct.

Ellen had never seen this family. She spoke to Mrs. Zina quietly, took off her coat, produced her white apron from her bag and set to work. The first thing indicated appeared to be to get the windows up and the babies out; harder than it would seem, especially the windows. She was assured by a half-grown daughter that air, especially fresh air, would kill the *madre—la povera!*

Much later she left the house, left Mrs. Zina sleeping comfortably, relatively speaking, left the rooms as clean and fresh as was humanly possible, and had actually succeeded in persuading the half-grown daughter who at sixteen turned out to be the mother of the year-old child, that little Camillo would be a lot better off without the pacifier. She had made some notes . . . Zina out of work, the girl's husband out of work, too. Something would have to be done about that, thought Ellen.

The morning wore on. Another call, a long one. A third which was in the nature of prenatal care, advice and instruction. It would shortly be time to go back to report and to get her afternoon calls and to have some lunch. The last place she had left was a basement, a den. That human beings lived there she had had complete evidence but somehow now out in the open air, tainted as it was, it seemed almost incredible.

She thought . . . there's so much more to this than nursing, so much more. She thought further that it was not astonishing that so many women connected with work of this type turned almost fiercely radical, seeing what they must see, realizing how little they could do, important though their work was . . .

"Miss Adams!"

The girl spoke twice before Ellen heard. Then Ellen turned and smiled into a small and radiant face. Gilda Esposito, who lived not far from her and whom Ellen, from her not very great seniority, had watched grow up.

"Going back to the office?" Gilda wanted to know.

"Yes . . . walk along with me. How's Mike?"

Mike was Gilda's brother. Mike was fine, said Gilda. Gilda had a mouth like an opening rose and great black eyes. She wore a little spring suit, fourteen dollars somewhere, but she wore it as if it were a hundred and fifty somewhere else. A little tailored suit, blue. The hat with the cavalier feather was not suitable to the suit but it was suitable to Gilda and her eyes and her white teeth.

"And your mother?"

"She's all right. She talks about you, wants to know why you don't come to see us."

Gilda's accent was all of the city; not a lingering trace of South European in it. Had she not been born here, in this very district? She was an *American*.

Ellen had known the Esposito family for years; had in fact gone to school with Mike, where they had been in the same class. And shortly after her affiliation with VNA she had called at the house, where Mrs. Esposito had been one of her first patients.

"But I thought you were working," she said to the other girl.

"I was. I got a better job now," Gilda explained, "but I don't start till tomorrow."

Stenographic work, she explained further, in an uptown office. "Gosh, what a break!" triumphed Gilda.

Presently they parted and Ellen went on her way. A small boy hailed her from the curb; a fantastically dirty little boy with red hair and freckles, broken braces and patched pants. A little tousle-headed devil with a wide grin and three missing teeth. The perfect *Saturday Evening Post* cover, thought Ellen.

"Hi, Mis' Nois'," was Bill's elegant greeting.

"Hi, yourself," replied Ellen, no more formal than he. "Bill, why *aren't* you in school?"

Bill was hugging a ragged pup, with eyes something like his own in expression. The pup wriggled furiously. "This is me dawg, see," announced Bill, changing the subject with tact if not brilliancy. "Found him, down the alley. Me old man says I kin keep him. Say, Miss Nois', do I gotter have one of them things—you know . . . li—li—" He looked up in suddenly mute appeal, all eyes and outstanding ears and freckles.

"License? I'm afraid you do, if you don't want him taken up."

"How much?" asked Bill practically.

Ellen told him. The freckles actually paled.

"Jees'," said Bill simply. "Well, we'll see." He looked at the dog with a preternaturally old affection. "We're pals," said Bill, "me an' Old Timer."

"Bill, why aren't you in school?" Ellen persisted. But her eyes laughed. She could be sympathetic with a small boy, in springtime, she could understand perfectly why the droning voices of schoolteachers and the hard desks and the harder seats made no appeal.

"Aw, gee, Mis' Nois'," said Bill plaintively, "me old man come home soused agin last night, see, and I gotter run errands for Ma."

He gestured with a grimy hand. Old Timer, with a yelp slipped from his master's arms and took a wild turn on the sidewalk. Exhilarated by the sense of freedom, the noise and brightness and general excitement, he cavorted, stubby tail pointing skyward, out to the street. Bill swore, without apology, called, and whistled. Ellen stepped forward quickly. A car turning a corner, a fast car, a small open car. Another yelp—the squeal of brakes—Ellen's exclamation of fear and pity . . .

Bill was out in the street. There was in the moment a crowd, come from nowhere, which, the occasion once passed, would vanish into nowhere . . .

"Why, God damn youse," Bill was shrieking at the top of his small leather lungs, "you lousy bastard——"

"*Bill* . . . *!*"

Ellen was beside him, one hand on his shoulder. The pup was now back in Bill's arms, whining, snuggling a bruised nose in Bill's shoulder.

"Jees'," remarked an older Bill, "He ain't dead." And with that consolation spat in the gutter and strode away, disgusted.

Ellen turned the little dog over as it lay in Bill's frantic clutch. "He's all right, Bill," she said, soothingly, "just shaken up, that's all," and drew boy and dog back to sidewalk safety again.

But Bill was not reconciled.

"An' who the hell do youse t'ink youse are anyway," he acidly inquired of the driver of the car who, his vehicle now drawn up to the curb, was standing beside him, "tearin' t'rough the streets like dat and knockin' a guy's dawg fer a loop?"

The driver spoke for the first time. He said:

"Take it easy, old boy. I'm sorry. Here, let me see the pup." And before Bill could speak or demur his slightly mangy burden had been transferred to other masculine arms. "Looks as if I'd knocked him out for a bit," diagnosed the driver ruefully, "I'm *darned* sorry, old man."

"Don't old man me," said Bill. "Here give me my dawg, and scram, you sonuvabitch!"

"Bill!" expostulated Ellen, trying very hard not to laugh.

"That's all right with me," said the culprit. "Look here," and he turned to Ellen in something resembling real dismay, "can't I square myself, somehow?"

"Well," she hesitated . . . "there's a veterinary over on the Avenue," she suggested.

This was a very personable young man. A tall young man in a top coat, hatless, the sun shining on brown hair with a tendency to curl. Fine hazel eyes smiling into her own. A square chin, stubborn. A *nice* mouth.

Bill was muttering to himself, hugging the dog which he had again managed to recover. "Beat it," bade Bill out of the corner of his youngster's innocent mouth to the gaping crowd of boys and men gathered about him. "Scram!"

The owner of the car lifted his quiet eyes and

looked about him. "We do seem to have something on an audience, don't we?" he murmured.

The audience scrammed, obligingly.

"See here, Bill," said the man, "I'm a lawyer. Suppose we settle this affair out of court." He gravely produced and presented a card to Bill, a card which Bill after reading—perhaps—flicked over to Ellen with an expression of doubt. "Francis Bartlett" read Ellen, and underneath, a downtown office address.

"It's all right, mister," said Bill, a little ashamed of his outburst and living up to his unwritten motto which was distrust everybody until they act human then meet 'em halfway. "On your way. Me an' the lady can take care of Old Timer. She's a nois'," Bill explained.

"So I gathered," Bartlett said, grinning, "but can she nurse dogs?"

Ellen, laughing, disclaimed all veterinary knowledge. Bartlett put his hand on Bill's shoulder.

"Hop in the bus," he invited, "and we'll see this vet. I'll settle the damages. What's the purp's name?"

Bill told him, every freckle grinning.

"Swell dog," commented Bartlett blandly, in the face of all evidence to the contrary. "Got a license for him? No? Then we'll see about that, too."

"He's a good guy," said Bill gravely to Ellen, after a long moment.

Privately Ellen agreed with him. Bill was only eight but Bill had good judgment. He had to have, as a means of self-defense.

She couldn't do anything more. Not that she had done anything. She smiled at young Bartlett who was staring at her as if she were a visitor from Mars. She became oppressed suddenly with the sense of being in uniform. Hadn't he ever seen a visiting nurse before? She had started to admonish Bill in farwell, when "Jees'!" said Bill with explosiveness and dived into the waiting car. "Come along, Mister," shrilled Bill with Old Timer clutched to his chest, "and step on it!"

"Why?—how?—" began the bewildered young man, and then shrugging followed Bill's example and a moment or so later stepped on it. Ellen walked on smiling, hastening her steps. A sandwich somewhere and a glass of milk and she'd get her afternoon calls. She was late. That Bill!

The car had shot away. Across the street Ellen saw a tall, rather stooped figure. She laughed aloud. The truant officer! Trust Bill and his sharp little eyes.

In the car Bill was explaining.

"The truant ossifer, see?" he was saying.

Bartlett nodded, turning a corner, threading a careful way through screaming traffic.

"Don't like school much, do you, Bill?" he wanted to know.

"Jees', no," replied Bill simply.

Driving to the veterinary's, where it was ascertained that Bill's beloved pup had suffered no injury, and later on the way to get that necessary license, Bartlett learned a good deal about Bill and "me old man." Bill, it appeared, would like to "go to work." "Strong as any other guy," said Bill, doubling up a skinny little arm in order that his new friend might admire the stringy muscles. "Jees', a feller wastes a helluva lotta time in school!" mourned Bill.

"How tough was it loining to be a lawyer?" he demanded.

"Pretty tough," replied Bartlett gravely, explaining that considerable schooling was indicated. He agreed with Bill that schooling was the catch in a great many professions.

"That's right," said Bill, sunk in sober thought, "there's Pete—Pete McGregor. He was hangin' round pool rooms, see, and there wuz a gink from uptown gets into a knifing scrap. *His* old man's a doctor, see? Pete, he gets the guy out of the scrap and the doctor sends him to school or sumpin. Since, he's been loining to be a doctor himself," said Bill, "rides the ambulance from the City Horspital, he does. I axed him once, does it take a long time? 'Hell,' says Pete to me, 'it takes pretty damned near forever!'"

Bartlett chuckled. This was a great little kid. But there were other things on his mind. Honey-colored hair and gray eyes and a lovely red mouth curved to smiling. He asked, idly:

"That nurse—she's a friend of yours?"

"Who? Oh, her," said Bill, "sure, she's everybody's friend. She lives down here and woiks at noising . . . see?"

"What did you say her name was?" pursued the wily Bartlett.

"I didn't say," Bill answered, forthright. "Nois' we call her." His accent was indescribable, and he spat with accuracy into a pushcart creaking past. "Adams, though, that's her moniker. Mis' Adams," explained Bill, severely.

A little later Bartlett let Bill out at his own corner. "You're pretty white," said Bill. He shook his red head fiercely at the tender of money. "Ain't you'se done enough?" he wanted to know.

"For Old Timer," suggested Bartlett persuasively, "he'll need a—a nourishing diet after his accident."

He was solemn. Bill stared at him. "Well," said Bill, doubtfully.

A negotiable bit of paper exchanged hands. "If me old man sees it," mused Bill aloud, "he'll be knocking on Fontana's door for a quart of the best. Right off the boat," grinned Bill, "I don't t'ink. The ferry boat!"

A moment later and the car had departed. Bill stood on the curb, unconsciously wistful, hugging the now somnolent dog. "Jees', a white guy." Bill's chest swelled. A friend of his. Jees', he'd like to do sumpin for him . . .

Not long afterwards Bartlett, back at his office high up in a downtown skyscraper, was engaged in obtaining information on fair-haired girls in dark gray uniforms. "What's the matter with you?" growled the doctor on the other end of the wire. "You've heard of the NVA before. Need a nurse, is that it, someone to hold your hand and can't afford the registry during the depression . . . ?"

Bill was profane but earnest. Quite profane: Bill had taught him a couple of new ones.

Later he hung up the receiver and smiled fatuously at his secretary, a plain but susceptible woman. What, she wondered, had come over him? A pleasant boss, even a charming one, but not given to fatuous smiles . . .

Ellen, coming out of the sub-station with a sheaf of afternoon calls, looked with something like amazement at the car at the curb. A perfectly familiar car, somehow. A perfectly familiar young man, at least his face, if not his manner. He said, smiling,

"You'll think I'm crazy, Miss Adams, but——"

Bill had been talking, thought Ellen. She said, "Yes?" with a rising inflection, a little remotely. He came nearer to her, looked down, spoke with that engaging smile.

"I took a fancy to Bill," said Bartlett. "I mean it. I'm not trying to use him as an excuse to see you again although I am perfectly willing to admit that I wanted to see you again as much as I ever wanted anything. But Bill and that darned little pup of his, they got under my skin somehow. I—isn't there anything I could do for the kid?"

She answered doubtfully, her heart beating a little faster—"as much as I ever wanted anything," he had said in a perfectly matter-of-fact voice—"I—I don't know. If"—she tried not to laugh, somehow she wanted to laugh, somehow the world was very bright, very gay, she felt light-hearted, a little giddy, "if you could influence him—as far as going to school is concerned?" she wanted to know.

"Lord!" said Bartlett in consternation. "That's a good one. I rather sympathize with him, you see. Look here, Miss Adams, this work of yours, honest to gosh, it interests me. There must be lots of Bills mixed up in it. Have you had lunch?" he wanted to know abruptly.

Thanks, she had had lunch. Then he demanded where she was going.

On her next call, she told him; it was quite far away, she would have to go along now to get the trolley.

"Your carriage waits," he said and opened the door, and then, as she hesitated, he urged her and, laughing, said:

"I'm not a bad guy, honestly. Even Bill agrees. Can't I drive you there? It—I'm going that way," he said, lying and lunchless.

Ellen looked up at him. After all, it was spring . . . and . . . there wasn't any harm in driving with him that far. It would save time. She said sedately, "It's very good of you, Mr. Bartlett."

As she got in the car a young man passed by, idled by. A dark young man, a young man very much better looking than Frank Bartlett, lounging past, his eyes on the door of the sub-station, his hands in his pockets. A car started. The young man turned at the sound of the engine.

"Hey, Ellen," said the young man, waving . . .

"Hello, Jim," said Ellen——

The car drove off. Jim O'Connor stood there on the curb very thoughtfully.

CHAPTER THREE

Somehow, evenings, the Adams flat was pleasantest. Ellen, walking homeward through the cool, blue dusk of spring, looked forward to supper, to a brief lazy time afterwards, and to bed. She was both hungry and tired. On the way up the steps she remembered that Jim was coming. Well, she'd send him home early, she thought.

She stumbled over her landlord's small girl sitting on the steps sucking a lollipop, a roly-poly child, very solemn, with a genius for getting underfoot. The landlord's wife, Mrs. Meader, was leaning across her brownstone balustrade in conversation with Mrs. Lenz who also rented separate rooms and small apartments in the identical house next door.

"Evening, Ellen," said Mrs. Meader, fatter than

her child, a placid and helpful woman in whom Ellen had great reliance.

Ellen stopped a moment and Mrs. Lenz, harried and shrill, continued her dissertation.

"And I says to Jim O'Connor, '*that* girl in my house!' Butter wouldn't melt in his mouth. 'Give her a break,' he tells me, 'she's married now and going straight. Her husband's a fine young man.'"

"What does he do for a living?" inquired Mrs. Meader, with interest. What people did for a living, if anything, was always of major importance.

"He's with the telephone company. He's—he's a *trouble maker*, Jim said," Mrs. Lenz offered after a pause during which she refreshed her memory.

"A trouble maker!" Mrs. Meader's round blue eyes were like saucers.

"Jim," said Ellen, taking off her hat and leaning against the balustrade. "Jim meant 'trouble shooter,'" she explained tactfully.

"*Gott behüte!*" cried Mrs. Lenz, agitated, "trouble shooter! As if I should have a gunman in my house. That Jim, he's crazy, *ganz verrückt!*"

"No, no." Ellen was laughing through Mrs. Meader's clucks and exclamations. "That's not what it means at all." She elucidated earnestly and both women nodded.

"That's right," agreed Mrs. Lenz, her face clearing. "Jim did tell me something. Maybe I didn't listen, *nicht?* So much to do with the Andersons moving out and their place to clear and a sign to hang out, and now the back floor to get ready. And my Heinie not so good."

"What's wrong with him?" asked Ellen.

"Something with his stummick," replied Mrs. Lenz. "Nothing he keeps down. Not even the good coffee with milk or the beer."

"Anything he et?" asked Mrs. Meader helpfully. "Kids is always eating things that don't sit good on their stummicks."

"I'll come over and look at him after supper," Ellen promised, and Mrs. Lenz smiled at her wanly, in gratitude.

"About that girl now," she was beginning again, "Jim says her husband—and what a *dumkopf* he is —makes fifty-eight dollars a week. That's good money, but I don't know. He said to me, 'you can't be too choosy in hard times.' As far as I'm concerned," said Mrs. Lenz sighing, "times is always hard; but anyway, I said I'd take them. Next week they're coming. I don't know what Heinrich would have said"—Heinrich was the late lamented Herr Lenz—"but I've got myself and the *bube* to think of, ain't?"

Mrs. Meader nodded in agreement. Ellen on her way to the hall heard her say soothingly, through the open door, ". . . and don't be too hard on the girl. We all make mistakes, don't we?"

At their own door Nancy met her dramatically.

"Gee, you're late," she said, flushed from sleep, her blue eyes clear and rested, her pretty hair pinned into exact damp swirls on cheeks and forehead and held there by a net cap. "Supper's almost ready," she added.

That was one of the convenient phases of their arrangement; Ellen, coming home tired, might be assured of a warm supper, a table laid and ready. Later Nancy, dancing off to play before work, would leave Ellen to do the dishes. In the morning it would be Nancy's turn to wash up as it was Ellen's to get breakfast.

The lights were on in the living room casting kindly shadows over the place where the plaster was peeling, over the discolorations on the buff painted walls. The room was really most livable. Nancy and Ellen had seen to that. Mrs. Adams, her small feet on a hassock, sat bolt upright near a reading lamp with the last lending library book in her hand. There was a pleasant odor of broiled ham and coffee . . .

"You're late, aren't you?" asked Mrs. Adams as they sat down to the meal.

Ellen, her uniform changed for a thin wool house dress in the dark warm red she loved, nodded.

"I had eight calls," she answered, "some of them

long. And late this afternoon I found a youngster back in the alley, you know, Mother, where the stables used to be? An old polio case. Creeping," went on Ellen, her eyes sick, "on all fours. I took his name and went in to see his mother. I'll report him tomorrow and we'll see what we can do. One of the orthopedic staff will attend to it, get him to the clinic and all. He's new hereabouts or I'd have seen him before."

"Jim was in," said Mrs. Adams comfortably. She gestured toward a small pot of bright pink geraniums. "He's a very considerate boy," she told Ellen with what seemed an inappropriate severity.

Nancy laughed and Ellen flushed a little.

"Everyone knows," said Nancy, "he's ace high with you, Mother. Glad you haven't picked out any one for me. I *like* being single," said Nancy.

"It's not natural," said Mrs. Adams, "for any girl to like being single!"

"Why, Mother!" Nancy stared in mock horror. "Haven't gone modern on us or anything, have you?"

Mrs. Adams smiled reluctantly.

"Is that modern? I thought it was very old-fashioned," she replied, "but no woman, no true woman, is really happy until she has a good husband and a family."

"Boloney," said Nancy. "I like my twenty-eight per."

Most of it, with Ellen's salary, went toward maintaining the apartment. The girls bore the greater burden, although from the sale of the house and a little insurance Mrs. Adams had a small income. But on her twenty-eight a week as senior operator, minus what she paid in toward the family budget, Nancy managed somehow. And when she couldn't, Ellen managed for her.

Nancy, it seemed, had had a busy day's—or rather night's—work. The supervisor had been absent. Nancy as senior operator had taken her place. It wouldn't be long, said Nancy, rising to clear the table while Ellen relaxed, sat still and listened and rested, before she'd be a supervisor, too.

Presently Ellen was washing dishes, a great blue-checked apron about her slim waist, and Nancy, dressing in the bedroom, was whistling like a blackbird. She emerged in time to snatch a last plate or two and put them away. She wore, of course, the clothes in which she would later go to work, the green tailored suit and a fresh little blouse. And her funny becoming little tam was cocked over her eyebrow. The dark short hair released from its net and dry, all traces of the setting fluid gone, lay in flat, pretty waves.

Chick arrived, a lanky imperturbable young man,

wire chief of Nancy's exchange. Mrs. Adams approved of him, and he lounged beside her chair teasing her a little, while Nancy made a last dart with a powder puff at her pert nose and snatched up her bag. "Where's the lunch?" asked Chick grinning.

"I'll buy it," replied Nancy with dignity, "or if you feed me well enough after the show I won't have to."

The central exchange had its own immaculate kitchen where the girls were served their meals at cost; where, too, during the two fifteen-minute relief periods during every shift they could procure cakes and sandwiches and other delicacies dear to the hearts of youth. They might, of course, bring in their own lunches and make tea or coffee in the kitchen, a procedure usually indulged in by the night shift.

"I'll feed you," promised Chick, whose other name was Smith, and jingled the coins in his pockets.

The door closed behind them, Nancy's last wisecrack drifting through it. Mrs. Adams remarked mildly, "She's getting slangier than ever."

"Heinie Lenz," said Ellen, making no reply to this comment as there seemed no reply to make, "is sick. Bilious attack, I suppose. You can't teach Mrs. Lenz that a seven-year-old shouldn't gorge on beer and coffee. However, now that he's sick again I may be able to frighten her into giving him a suitable diet, for once. When Jim comes, if you don't mind, I'll run over there for a few minutes."

"I wish," said Mrs. Adams, "that these people would leave you alone. You work hard enough all day."

Ellen said nothing. A moment later she laid down the evening paper she had brought, as her mother asked:

"Is it true that Dot Mather has rented next door?"

"Jim told me he was going to ask Mrs. Lenz," Ellen answered, bracing herself.

"Mrs. Lenz must be out of her mind," Mrs. Adams remarked with indignation, "a girl of that type! She was the talk of the neighborhood. And then to come back, flaunting herself—and——"

"Please, Mother," said Ellen hastily, "half of that talk may have been rumor. She's married now and it's up to the neighborhood to give her a chance, I think. She never had one anyway. No father, a drunken mother——"

She stopped in consternation. The slow easy tears were slipping down her mother's small cheeks, sliding over the delicate fine skin flushed ominously with the color of danger.

"Mother—*please!*"

She went over to her, put her young strong arms about her.

"I shouldn't have said that . . . I forgot," wept Mrs. Adams. "I forgot Coral. I mean I forgot what has happened, what might have happened . . . I . . ."

It was always the same story. When her little narrow mind passed judgment, then she remembered. Ellen shook her a very little.

"Don't be a silly," she said gently, "Coral's all right. You know she is. And just forget Dot. She's had a hard time, it will be over now provided people let her alone. Listen, isn't that Jim?"

It was Jim. He knocked, his own special double knock. Ellen opened to him and he greeted her as if he hadn't seen her for a year.

Mrs. Adams was composed when he greeted her. "Sit down and entertain an old lady for a while. This bad girl has to go next door."

Ellen explained. "I won't be a moment," she said apologetically.

"We'll get along without you, won't we, Aunt Elizabeth?" asked Jim cheerfully. He took out a package of cigarettes. Mrs. Adams, from whom the sight of Nancy's many and Ellen's occasional cigarettes had been kept religiously, smiled tolerantly and moved an ash tray nearer Jim's elbow. Men, thought Mrs. Adams, were a little mad and absolutely indispensable. If they wished to lounge on the backs of their necks in chairs and drop ashes from their ridiculous tobacco on floors and furniture, well, that was a part of their special privileges.

"And hurry back," called Jim after Ellen. "I want to see what explanation you have for hopping into swell Buicks with wealthy-looking young men about the time you're supposed to go to work."

Jim *would* do that, thought Ellen, as she hurried out to visit a weeping Heinie. She'd forgotten that he'd seen her. Darn him anyway and the big brother attitude he took with her when her mother was around! With her—with Ellen—it wasn't quite as brotherly. She lifted her small square chin. As if she owed him an explanation. She'd probably never *see* Frank Bartlett again . . .

At the thought she found herself far from reconciled. This annoyed her and she walked briskly into the Lenz household and made herself unpopular with Heinie, who as a rule adored her, by suggesting certain starvation diets.

"How about castor erl?" asked Mrs. Lenz, hovering about Heinie's bed.

"Any pain, Heinie?" asked Ellen.

Yes, Heinie had a bellyache.

Ellen felt the little abdomen gently. She said: "I think you better call Dr. Travers, Mrs. Lenz. Just to be sure. No, no castor oil and no hot water bags," she went on, removing one which was merely tepid, "until you're sure it isn't something more serious than a hot dog on top of an ice-cream cone."

Later, leaving, she added, "And be sure and call me after the doctor goes."

Mrs. Lenz, subdued and worried, took her to the door. "I don't believe it's anything more than an upset," Ellen reassured her to the tune of Heinie's "Mom—mom—can't I see the evenin' funnies?"— "but it's best to be certain."

She arrived back in the living room. "You were gone half an hour!" Jim accused her.

"I know, I'm sorry. It may be an appendix," she said, sitting down in the big wing chair, "but I hope not. I told her to send for Dr. Travers."

She relaxed and smiled at her mother and Jim. It struck her that they looked rather grave. She sighed inwardly. Jim ought to know better, even in fun.

Now it started.

"Who was this man Jim saw you with, Ellen?" asked Mrs. Adams.

"A lawyer," said Ellen, "I'm going to get a divorce."

"I wish you wouldn't joke about such things," Mrs. Adams complained fretfully, "and where's the sense in trying to put me off? Just because I have to sit home all day, an invalid—is that any reason why

I shouldn't want to keep an eye on my girls—all I have?"

"I'm sorry, Mother," said Ellen but the look she shot at Jim, gray eyes dark with anger, was far from apologetic. He shrugged and spread out his hands. His dark quirked eyebrows were whimsical.

"Me, too. Didn't mean to start anything," he assured her.

"The man," explained Ellen, fighting to keep her temper, "is named Bartlett. He's a lawyer. He ran over Bill Maloney's dog this morning. I happened to be there. The dog wasn't hurt but Mr. Bartlett took it and Bill to the vet's. That's all. Later he came back to the office to see if there was anything he could do for Bill, he'd taken a fancy to the youngster. And as he offered to drive me to my first afternoon call I accepted. After all," added Ellen, her temper slipping, "I can take care of myself, Mother."

She repented immediately that she had said it. Someone else had said it before her, eight years before, in this very room. Coral had said it. And Coral hadn't taken care of herself—or had she? Would they ever know?

"It's not necessary to speak to me in that tone," her mother said. The tip of her delicate slim nose reddened and her eyes filled.

"I'm sorry," said Ellen once more, resigned—or outwardly so.

So was Jim. He talked gaily, wildly of other things. Little by little he coaxed Mrs. Adams back to normal with the neighborhood gossip which seemed to be practically in his pocket. The Hogans had been dispossessed. The Rosensteins were moving uptown. Sure, money was plentiful with them and why not? Didn't Rosy lend it to poor people; wasn't his interest rate highly illegal? The Drive, Becky had told him, her nose in the air. Lily Lane's young husband had left her. Gilda Esposito had a new job. And, "Do you ever see Pete McGregor any more?" asked Jim almost undoing his good work, "he nearly ran over me the other day, that is to say, his ambulance did. He was hanging on behind, more or less, waved to me and grinned. They weren't going anywhere, I suppose, but they were in a hurry. Well, it's a true saying if the accident doesn't kill you the ambulance will."

Mrs. Adams replied, presently, in a very small voice that Pete hadn't been to see her for over two years now. Ellen saw him, of course, in the day's work. He must be nearly through, said Mrs. Adams.

"Eight years," said Jim, "since that uptown doctor dragged him out of Greasy Mike's and sent him to Columbia, no, nearer nine, isn't it?"

Ellen kicked him viciously. She said, rising, "Let's get some music."

She turned on the radio, shifted the dials, lowered the loud blare which issued forth, and found the program her mother liked. Mrs. Adams listened and presently her strained small face relaxed into lines of contentment. Jim and Ellen were quarrelling over something as usual, in their half-laughing manner. Jim was a good boy. Ellen was a good girl, none better; Nancy, too, for all her flyaway airs. It was, she supposed, foolish of her to treat them as if they were children, schoolgirls, with Nancy earning her living since seventeen, and Ellen, going through High School and training, seeing life as young girls, perhaps, shouldn't see it. But that was a part of her profession . . .

Later Ellen made her mother some milk toast and weak tea and a rarebit for Jim and herself. They set up the card table and ate and drank milk. Ellen, pushing back her plate, winding a last string of cheese absently about the prongs of her fork, yawned frankly.

"That gives me the air," said Jim. "Gee, Ellen, you're a swell cook."

"Between mother and the dietetics course I ought to be," she told him, smiling. "Too bad, Jimmy, didn't mean to be rude but I'm half dead."

She went to the hallway with him, shutting the

door behind her. She sighed while he lighted a fresh cigarette and offered it to her with a grin. "Want a drag?" he asked.

She took one, too, smiling, and then handed it back. "I'll have to clean my teeth before I put mother to bed," she said ruefully, "and any change in the routine worries her. She'll say, 'Why don't you wait to do that till you're undressed?'"

"You and Nancy ought to break her into the fact that all the girls smoke nowadays," he suggested.

"Oh, she knows it. All but *us*. If she were well, it would be different. But we have to be very careful of her, Jim."

"Didn't Dr. Travers say——?"

"Yes, I know what he said. I'm a nurse. Pseudo-angina. She may live for years, of course, she'll live for years. But even if it doesn't—doesn't kill her—and it won't—we have to be careful. The attacks *hurt*, Jim, just as much as if they were dangerous. And I can't endure to see her hurt."

"No, of course not. How about Saturday night? Go on a party with me somewhere?"

She would, she said. She'd like to. He bent his tall dark head . . .

"Kiss Jim goodnight?" he asked persuasively.

She laughed. He was ridiculous. She got so angry at him, she wouldn't marry him, ever, although he'd asked her a hundred times. She wasn't in love with him. But she did love him in a way, part of her life, part of her background. And she'd kissed him before. A good many times. Not, you understand, seriously. Like this.

She reached up—he was so much taller—and brushed her cool red lips to his cheek, a smoothly shaven dark cheek. His arm went out and held her fast.

"That's all right for a starter," he muttered, "but . . . Ellen, I've been patient, you can't say that I haven't been patient. Couldn't you learn—I mean, won't you let me teach you——?"

But she was very strong for all her look of fragility. She twisted out of his grasp, laughing a little.

"Go home," she ordered, "and leave me alone. Perhaps I don't *want* to learn!"

CHAPTER FOUR

He was not, however, to be put off so easily. Which was unusual for Jim. For a good many years now he had kept their friendship balanced rather delicately between comradeship and sentiment . . . now and then, as when he proposed to her, the balance dipped. But usually she could handle him.

It couldn't be—just because he had seen her with Frank Bartlett? She'd known other men . . . other men had taken her around, liked her, one or two had more than liked her. Old Dr. Travers' son, for instance, now practicing somewhere in the suburbs for himself, as he refused to come down into the neighborhood with his father, and his father refused to leave it. She'd liked Mel Travers, had been even a little crazy about him, but his decision, "What's in a dump like this for me? I want to make money, want *human* patients. These people, I give you my word, Ellen, they're half animals," had ended it for her.

That was while she'd been in training, while he'd been an interne at the same hospital.

Now, the telephone rang in the apartment. She could hear it, through the door. She pulled herself away from Jim for the second time.

"Please be sensible, Jimmy. There's the phone, it must be Mrs. Lenz. Let me go."

He did so, reluctantly, trying, knowing himself more disturbed than usual, to laugh it off.

A moment later her mother regarded Ellen's heightened color with an appraising eye. She was answering the telephone, speaking quickly, with hastened breath. Mrs. Adams didn't, she thought, approve of hallway courtships. It didn't occur to her that her own girls must accustom themselves to courtship, in its more intimate sense, in hallways, motion picture theaters, buses, park benches. For when "company" came Mrs. Adams was always serenely seated in the living room save on those not very rare occasions when she was confined to her bed, in which case no company came.

It wasn't Mrs. Lenz, it was Dr. Travers. He was explaining in his slow, deep voice, always a little tired, that he'd been delayed . . . a delivery, he said. "Who?" demanded Ellen. "Anyone I know?"

The doctor chuckled. He supposed so, he said, she knew everyone. Mrs. di Carlo, then. Her fifth, and not as easy as might have been expected. "By the way," he went on, "I've a case for you. I'll call the office direct tomorrow. In your district, an Irish family, measles, three of them, and very sick; that is, the baby is very sick. Looks like pneumonia."

They'd attend to it, Ellen assured him; he'd phone the details, of course. And they'd get a night nurse, if necessary.

A grand organization, the doctor was thinking, wearily. They'd see that the night nurse was paid for, heaven knows the di Carlo family couldn't pay not even a dime, a quarter, toward the daytime visiting nurse herself.

"Heinie, you wanted to tell me about Heinie," Ellen's hurried voice went on.

"Of course, I'm an old fool. Told Alma Lenz I'd tell you. He's all right. Gastric, and why not? But you're a sensible girl, Ellen, God bless you."

"How's Mel?"

"Fine. Working into a nice little practice as Henderson's assistant. Buzzes all over the suburbs in a new car, holding the hands of the victims of the depression epidemic. The depression has upset more stomachs and caused more gastric ulcers," he said dramatically, "than speakeasies. It has also," he went on, "done away with a lot of private rooms and special nurses in the hospitals. However, that's neither here nor there. Mel's all right, I think he has a girl. I'm sorry that won't hurt your feelings, Ellen," said Dr. Travers.

Presently she hung up and turned to repeat the conversation from Travers' end to her mother. Mrs. Adams was fretful. "You didn't tell him how I was," she said.

"Yes, I did. I said you were just grand. He asked, of course."

Travers was their family doctor. He had ushered Coral and Ellen and Nancy into the world. He had watched their father leave it. He had been taking care of Mrs. Adams since her illness, since the first attack when the heart specialist had been called in, in consultation.

"Well, I'm not 'just grand,'" denied Mrs. Adams, offended. She rose and moved toward her bedroom. "I'll go to bed now, Ellen," she said.

This would be Ellen's last job. To put her mother to bed, to give her the sleeping tablet that was a blank, but Mrs. Adams didn't know that and relied, religiously, on her sugar pellet; to rub her back and to tuck her in and open the windows.

During the process Mrs. Adams returned to the subject of Frank Bartlett.

"I can't understand," she said, "picking up men in this way. *You!*"

"Oh, I didn't." Ellen was tired to the point of impatience. "Or, yes, I suppose I did. In my work I pick up a lot of people, I don't wait for introductions, you know."

"It was hardly your work," her mother reminded her, "a dog!"

Ellen laughed. "Well, never mind, I'll probably never see him again."

"You probably shall, if he came back to see you, the second time," her mother surmised shrewdly. "How did he know who you were?"

"Billy, I suppose. Billy knows everything."

"I'd just as soon," said Mrs. Adams, "that neither you nor Nancy struck up friendships out of—out of——"

"Mother, if you say 'out of your class' I'll scream," Ellen told her. "You know that's ridiculous. You, poring over a genealogy book dull afternoons and telling us time and time again about the Adamses, who they are, and why, to say nothing of the Westons, your branch, the whole history."

"I don't mean class," denied Mrs. Adams, with dignity, "and you know it. I hope I have proper pride in my stock and that of your father. I only mean class as far as—as circumstances are concerned."

"I don't think Billy's new friend is a Vanderbilt," Ellen assured her, deftly massaging the slender back with its surprisingly youthful skin. "Turn over a little, will you, angel? And after all, a visiting nurse may look at a lawyer, may she not? You had no objection to Elmer Jones . . . he was a lawyer, wasn't he? Or to Mel Travers. He's a doctor. And you haven't any to Jim, certainly, and he's a realtor, or whatever they call it, and he told me the other day that he was going to turn in his Ford for a Lincoln!"

"You know I didn't mean that," murmured Mrs. Adams sleepily, her lids heavy without benefit of sugar pill. "We have always known these young men. Strangers—are different."

"They needn't," suggested Ellen sensibly, "*stay* strangers."

Mrs. Adams was silent, half in dreams. Ellen roused her a little to settle her comfortably in the big bed, which she refused to discard and which broke Ellen's back anew every night. She pinched the white nainsook frill at her mother's thin sagging throat, raised her a little to give her her water and the "sleeping" medicine, tucked in sheets and blankets and raised the window.

Then she tiptoed out of the bedroom and went to her own. There she undressed slowly, deep in thought. Her mother had a fixed idea. It really *was* a fixed idea, it wasn't just a notion. Strangers . . . with money . . .

Coral had met such a "stranger." She'd never

brought him to the house. Met him in her first job.
It was he who persuaded her to give up the stenog-
raphy and try the stage. She had tried, and all her
mother's tears and her father's anger had been unable to move her. She had found her work. And then,
she had moved "uptown" with some other girls.
After which she had gone on the road. And finally
the man's wife had sued him for divorce, naming
her, Cora; Cora Carmen, she had called herself.

After that, silence; with young Pete McGregor,
who had been insane about her since their school-
days, coming to the house, white with worry, wild
with threats . . . That had been the beginning of
Pete's careless degradation, from which, through
rescuing a lad of his own kidney, if of a different
environment, he in his turn had been rescued.

While their father had lived Ellen and Nancy
had not dared to try to find Coral. Since his death,
two years after she had gone, they had tried through
every means open to them. To no avail.

Some day, she would come back. On that hope
their mother lived.

Prettier than either of them, Coral, thought Ellen
in just appraisal, with her dark hair and the red
lights, and her small slenderness, her very especial
dimple, near the corner of a too full mouth, with
her tremendous blue eyes, bigger and darker than
Nancy's.

Later, lying in bed, she found herself too tired to sleep. She always slept with one ear alert anyway, listening for the knock on the wall which so often came and which never failed to frighten her, to make her start up, sweat on the palms of her hands, her own heart beating painfully. Too tired, tonight, thoughts coming and going, arresting her attention, some of them.

There was, she supposed, no earthly reason why she shouldn't know Frank Bartlett, provided he made any effort to see her again. She had liked him. He attracted her. He was, he had to be, a very decent sort to take an interest in Bill, really to care what became of Bill. If he did care. Or was it an excuse? At the thought that it might have been an excuse she felt herself flushing in the darkness. That might cast doubt on his sincerity toward Bill, but, toward herself? He'd said, "I'm not trying to use him as an excuse to see you again . . ." But he'd gone on saying, quite matter-of-factly, not at all frivolously—what had he gone on saying? She didn't remember.

She remembered.

She didn't, of course, believe in love at first sight. She wondered how much she believed in love anyway, romantic love. She was slowly learning to look on life with eyes adjusted just a little differently from those of other girls, Nancy's eyes, for instance. In love itself one had to believe; in mother love, smothering, hurting, sacrificial, wounding, savage. In father love, too. In love of kindred for kindred. In love of man and wife, a building, dogged, patient sort of love. But romantic love?

Perhaps what they all started out with was just that. But down here, where the sidewalks came so close to a person's house, where intimacy was inevitable, but privacy impossible, it faded pretty quickly. Jobs and money, clothes and food, babies crying, diapers on a line, illness, stupidity, ignorance . . .

Where was your romantic love, then?

Uptown, perhaps, it lasted longer.

Did it? She had had some months of private duty before she came into the VNA, just for the actual practical experience.

She'd seen things—uptown.

Marriage, thought Ellen. Three kinds, really. One kind you read about and it sometimes happens, but is rare. Not rare in her own experience, for she had been brought up with one such marriage before her eyes, her mother's and father's; marriage which had managed to build itself up into a partnership. Her father had, of course, carried the main burden. But he and Elizabeth Weston had loved each other to the end, although that end had been embittered by their desperate warfare over Coral. And since his death had taken from his wife all that she had loved most, Ellen found it easy to forgive her mother much of her clinging petulance. When she had had strength to cling she had stood on her own feet, happy, busy, a little sharp-tongued, a little proud, a little resentful that the family fortunes had decreased instead of increased just as the neighborhood had fallen, encroached upon by the stealthy march of the sidewalks, as pitiless and single purposed as any jungle, instead of rising. But happy for all that, companioned. Now that that background strength had gone, she had turned weak . . . wavering.

The marriages one saw most often were the tolerated ones, thought Ellen further. You fell in love, you married, passion passed and love walked instead of using wings. You got used to it, to each other; indifferent, you got along.

Then there were the marriages that didn't last; that were not nourished either by sharing or by toleration.

Why was she thinking of marriage?

Jim, of course, asking her, sometimes not in words; generally in words, trivial, half laughing: "Look here, Ellen, haven't you been my girl long enough? Jim O'Connor's girl? Sure you are. Why not Jim O'Connor's wife? I'm doing well, I can look after you and Aunt Elizabeth too."

But she didn't want him.

He *was* doing well. He was, the neighborhood said, a good business man. He had to be to squeeze any profit from the wretched tenements and shacks and shabby stores he rented or for which he acted as agent; he had to be else his little insurance business couldn't, she thought, survive down here under the conditions she knew all too well.

Suddenly she sat bolt upright. Something had occurred to her; why hadn't she wondered about it before?

Perhaps Bartlett was married.

Well, what of it? she demanded of herself, and lay down again.

Most attractive men were.

Still, he hadn't *looked* married.

She laughed a little, aloud.

No, he hadn't looked married . . . hadn't looked at *her* as if he were. Not that married men hadn't looked at her before this with interest and a question and a wondering . . .

But it hadn't been that kind of a look, exactly.

She drifted into dreams, wondering why she was wakeful over—oh, over anything. Perhaps it was just because young Bartlett had been a new man. She didn't have much opportunity to meet new men. How did one? Working, every day, in the neighborhood familiar to her; going out little enough except with Jim or with someone she'd always known.

Nancy met more men than she, unconnected with her work, men met on parties or somewhere. But even Nancy didn't meet many.

"When it comes to meeting men," someone had said to her once, "why don't you consider quitting and going back into specializing?"

That was a legend, of course. Very few private nurses married their handsome and rich young patients, fiction to the contrary. Mostly they nursed them, left them, and went out with the internes at their hospitals, or their brother's friends, or heaven knew who.

And now she slept lightly, easily, breathing like a child. The little insistent knocking on the wall beside her thudded into her fleeting dreams like a crash of thunder.

Her slippers were here, her robe there. She got into them, practiced, still half asleep physically, but wide awake mentally. Had all this silly talk of hers and Jim's brought on another attack? The amyl nitrite . . .?

By her mother's bed, naturally, and also in the handbag she always carried. Ellen was in her mother's room now, quiet, capable.

"What is it, darling?"

"A bad dream." Mrs. Adams was half in tears. Coral. She had seen her "plain as day." "Ellen, she's in trouble."

Ellen sat beside her for a long time, stroking her arm, helping her to relax. Another of the sugar pellets. "You're all right," she soothed her as if the older woman had been a child.

It was nearly four o'clock before she reached her room again leaving her mother fast asleep. "Ellen, I saw her put out her hands to me . . . She was little, she wore her hair in the two thick braids, remember, they always curled at the end? She wore the plaid jumper dress I made for her . . . Remember, Pete's old grandfather said it was the Mc-Gregor tartan——?"

"Hush, darling, try and get to sleep."

"Oh, but where *is* she?" wailed Mrs. Adams. "If I only knew where she was. If I knew—if I knew she was dead. Dead and safe. With your father, Ellen."

People actually believed that sort of thing, thought Ellen, stroking her mother's arm, massaging the back of her neck where the nerves were so tense. Safe, Coral and her father. Because they were dead. But Coral wasn't dead—still, if she were?

She thought, I'd like to believe the way mother does. I——

So much evidence against it. Scientific. Philosophic. She thought of the hospital corridors at night, the light burning over the desk, people going out, the stretchers going by, the morgue. She thought of the people who wept and were not comforted and of the people who said, "He's gone, he doesn't suffer any more, he's happy, he knows *we'll see him again*."

Perhaps, after all, they were right.

Life, she thought, bleeding, fighting, struggling, terribly cowardly, terribly brave.

And presently she was back in her room again, sleeping deeply, sunk in sleep, drowned in it for the few hours left her until the new day began.

CHAPTER FIVE

Her mother was right. She did see Frank Bartlett again. On the very next day he telephoned her at the sub-station. "Call for you," said Jenny the stenographer with a wide grin. "Personal, I take it."

The conversation was brief. Ellen had her reports to make out and they were longer than usual. Bartlett, telephoning from his apartment, said, pleadingly, "You won't be sore at my calling up? Look here. I'm going to take young Bill to a ball game Saturday. We'd like to take you, too. Or do you hate baseball?"

No, she liked it, she said. But she couldn't come. She'd be working.

"Meet us," suggested Bartlett, "for dinner afterwards. We're going to make a day of it."

She had an engagement, she said.

Bartlett threw caution to the winds.

"But I've got to see you again," he told her. "I've —I've hundreds of things to ask you. Would you have dinner with me the very first night you can? May I come to your house and call for you?" asked Bartlett.

She hesitated, palpably. On the other end of the wire he waited, listening, wondering why he was so disturbed, so anxious, wondering why he was praying, a very little, to Lady Luck.

There was only one thing to do according to the rules of the household if she wanted to see him again. Did she? She knew that she did. So she answered, smiling:

"Suppose you come and have dinner with us, instead, Tuesday?"

"Gosh, that's great," said Bartlett. "I'll be there with whole carillons on. Where and what time?"

She told him and presently hung up. Jenny viewed her with marked amusement. "New boy friend?" inquired Jenny casually.

"No——"

"Be yourself!"

"Possibly," admitted Ellen and laughed aloud in sheer astonishment to find how very pleasant the thought could be.

On Monday Dot Mather, now "Mis'" Brown by virtue of a marriage license, came home to Mrs.

Lenz' back floor apartment. Her husband was seen, briefly, by the neighborhood, a plain pleasant young man, stocky as a pony. A good many pairs of eyes watched her come to the front steps with him that first morning, watched her wave him good-bye, regarded her trim girlish figure in the bungalow apron, the pert, painted little face and the eyes which were both frightened and happy. "He don't look so much," said someone, and someone else said, "Jees', what a bum break *that* guy got!"

Women going marketing idled away some of their precious moments walking past hoping to see "her." Some did. They all spoke to her carelessly. "Hello, Dot, hear you got hitched," they said. She was very much on her guard, defiant, chin raised. "Hello, Mrs. Lippinsky," said Dot buying a paper, three two-cent stamps, a pad and envelopes, and a package of cigarettes, "did you see my husband this morning?"

Mrs. Lippinsky looked her up and down. Mrs. Lippinsky had eyes like shoe buttons and about eight chins coursing downward toward a more than ample bosom. Mrs. Lippinsky folded her small, fat hands and replied, "Sure, I seen him." And that was all. But her tone was one of grave commiseration, whether for Dot or for young Mr. Brown no one could fathom.

Dot flushed under the careful layer of rouge. Mrs.

Lippinsky relented. After all she had to get her story out of this, not for nothing was her stationery shop known as the gossip clearing house of the neighborhood.

"Where you meet him?" she asked, leaning across the counter. "I heard he's from Noo Haven. Ain't been married long, hev you?" she pursued, and then, "Sooch a nize yong man he seems."

Dot said briefly.

"Yeah, he's from New Haven. Gee, the news travels, don't it? I met him there. I had a job in the town. No, we ain't been married long. Two months," said Dot, and her eyes softened, remembering.

A job in New Haven. She'd drifted there, a port of call. She'd been a waitress in a cafeteria, there's where she'd met Dan. He knew all about her, Dan did. Poor kid, he'd said, that first night when she'd told him, crying a little from self-pity, bad gin and something which resembled pure shame, "a girl has it damned hard," Dan had said simply.

Well, he'd married her and she had gone straight. She'd stay straight, too. She was crazy about Dan. The whitest guy—the swellest . . . She had for Dan no vocabulary of words. She had for Dan merely the vocabulary of love, love that expressed itself in service, in anxiety, in broken murmurs, in terror . . .

Going straight. She'd never really wanted to be anything else. But you had jobs and you lost them.

You were pretty and wisecracking and hard-boiled.
Men said you're a great girl. Men said you're the
berries. Men said how about a dinner and a show,
kid, and afterwards——?

She'd had a year of High School; even then she'd
been pestered to death, even then surrender was
easier than the other thing. Not so hot going home
to the sodden mother sprawled sloppily across a
table . . .

Jobs. Shop-girl in cheap shops, untrained jobs, all
of them. Bringing the money, what little there was
of it, home and being screamed at because it was no
more. Then an ambulance and a noisy ward and a
grave somewhere. And Dot was free, astonished to
find herself crying noisily. Poor Ma—oh, *poor Ma!*

After that just drifting till she found Dan.

Bad. Because of the wild warm blood in her veins,
because she loved laughter and music and bright
lights and something to eat and something to drink
and the brief escape of a show. Because she loved
silk stockings and cheap lace-trimmed teddies, sleazy
silk nightgowns, and heavy perfume.

Not for money, you understand, but for gaiety
and presents and good times.

Girl, alone.

Then New Haven and Dan. And now Mrs. Lenz'
back floor with the cute kitchenette and the gingham
curtains from the Five-and-Ten, and the silver and

napery and cutlery and pots and pans from the same place.

The neighborhood watched her go shopping for the things.

"Nu," said Mrs. Lippinsky and rolled the words on her tongue, "it von't last. Six months, I give it. Comes in here, bold as brass—'did you see my husband?'" quoted Mrs. Lippinsky in a high voice. The audience, all women, rocked with laughter. "Husband," replied Mrs. Lippinsky. "I'm telling you, I vonder. *Meshugge*, that one . . ."

"Do you suppose he knows about her?" someone asked, leaning on the counter.

"You should esk me about that," cried Mrs. Lippinsky, rolling her shoe button eyes. "I should know! But of course he don't know. Hush," warned Mrs. Lippinsky, "here comes my Shirley. I don't vant she should hear."

Shirley passed through, a dark slim flame, at fourteen. At thirty she would be like her mother. "Smart girl," said someone looking after her.

"At the head of her class she stends," said Mrs. Lippinsky pridefully, "and there's my Morty now. Always vit a book, my Morty. He vants to be a lawyer," bragged Mrs. Lippinsky.

Ellen came in to buy a paper before going home. She was tired. Her day had been long and hard. At noon Accordion Al, the song stilled on his ashen lips, had come stumping in, "Herman," he gasped, "he's burned himself!"

She'd gone. A scalding kettle of water; Herman chasing the cat about the table.

Now she was through, buying the evening paper. Mrs. Lippinsky greeted her heartily. Mrs. Lippinsky leaned over and said, "A shame, ain't it, dot girl, dot *bumiker* comes into your good neighborhood?"

The other women leaned closer. Jim, hurtling his sinewy self past the door having caught a glimpse of Ellen through the windows, stopped, quite still, waiting, smiling a little.

"Why?" asked Ellen, her clear grave eyes on the other woman's.

Consternation. Someone giggled.

Mrs. Lippinsky shrugged. Her chins quivered like a bowl of jelly, her vast bosom heaved, sea-like.

"You should know," she said indifferently, "you're a nois', ain't?"

"Dot's married," Ellen said after a moment, "and the only mistake she's made is to come back to a neighborhood where people haven't learned to be kind. God knows why," said Ellen wearily, "they all need kindness more than anything in the world. If it had been your Shirley, Mrs. Lippinsky——"

"My Shirley!" Mrs. Lippinsky drew herself up to her full height of five foot two and glowered angrily

at Ellen. Her small dirty hands gesticulated wildly,
"You should say dot to me, dot my Shirley . . .?"

Words failed her.

"Why not?" Ellen asked her quietly. "Or anyone
else's Shirley."

"My Shirley," shrilled Mrs. Lippinsky, "has a
momma and a poppa and a big good home. We loin
her to be good. She——"

"Dot didn't have either," said Ellen.

Ridiculously, she was near to tears. Poor Dot.
Poor everybody.

Jim stepped forward and put his arm through
hers. She hadn't seen him come in nor stand there
waiting. She looked up at him, the sweet, fine mouth
shaking a little.

"Come on home," said Jim, "you can't fight Dot's
battles. That's up to her."

Out in the clear evening air she said, trying to
laugh:

"I don't know why I get so upset. The girl's nothing to me. I've talked to her, of course, tried to be
decent. But she's suspicious of any advances, I suppose, holds me off. Only—why are people so darned
cruel, Jim? Yet they're kind, too. I've seen so much
down here of real neighborliness, of generosity.
When someone's sick or dies or starves. But in Dot's
case——"

"Forget Dot," said Jim with his man-of-the-world

manner, "it's a swell night. Haven't seen you really since Saturday. How's Nancy? If she's not going out tomorrow, how about us, huh?"

Tomorrow was Tuesday. Ellen remembered. The somber curve of her lips lifted to a faint smile. She answered lightly, "Sorry, Jimmy, I've a date, at home."

"With me?" He pressed her arm closer to his hard firm side.

"No," she told him, laughing, "company."

When she was at home again, she told her mother and Nancy,

"If people would only leave Dot alone. Can't see what they're doing to her? Making it so much harder. Why on earth she ever came back here with that nice boy . . .!"

"I wonder, too," said Nancy. "It's pretty hard to buck those few kind friends who knew you when."

The conversation was very distasteful to their mother. Mrs. Adams flushed and then said sharply:

"I wish you girls would have nothing to do with —that young person. If your father could know what this neighborhood has come to——" She added in homely parlance, "He'd turn in his grave."

Ellen was silent, Nancy shrugged. Nancy said, "That's no reason to give the poor kid a rotten break, is it?"

"Nancy, you don't know what you're talking about," said Mrs. Adams acidly.

"Be your age, darling, and let me be mine," Nancy said. "I know plenty."

Plenty. Did she? Ellen looked across at Nancy, viciously darning a stocking and muttering imprecations on all chiffon hosiery under her breath. Sometimes Ellen wondered, if only they could be more together; occasionally she felt that she scarcely knew the younger girl. But—in the circumstances they couldn't be together. She could only trust to Nancy. At that moment Nancy's blue eyes lifted and encountered Ellen's. She made a little face. "Sorry," she said under her breath. She knew that her mother hated her pertness, was afraid of it; knew that Ellen was sometimes worried about her. She smiled at her sister. Ellen smiled back, reassured. Nancy was— Nancy. Pretty fine under the veneer.

Now, Ellen braced herself, relying suddenly on Nancy to see her through, and said:

"Mother, I've asked Mr. Bartlett to dinner tomorrow night. I—Nancy's going out after, but I thought we could manage. I told him not till seven."

"Mr.—Bartlett?" Her mother's hands were eloquent. "Bartlett?"

She was being purposely stupid. Nancy commented, slanting a look at Ellen:

"Sure, why not? Your lawyer boy friend. That's

swell. Let's be reckless and have steak . . . and French fried . . . and a salad . . . and . . . Look here, how about an ice box cake from the bakery, made to order?"

"You know my views," Mrs. Adams said, trembling, ignoring all this "and yet you deliberately——"

She fought, or appeared to fight for breath. Then she asked unsteadily:

"How long has this been going on? How often have you seen this——" There was no word. She said "man," weakly; and waited.

Ellen said quietly:

"Please don't upset yourself, Mother, I haven't seen Mr. Bartlett again. He telephoned, asking me to go to a ball game with him and Bill, or to meet them later for dinner; on Saturday, that was. I had a date with Jim, so he asked me to have dinner with him, this week. I asked him here. I thought you'd rather."

Her mother said, bitterly:

"As if either of you girls really cared——"

"Pipe down, darling," said Nancy gently. "We do care. Ellen could have met her new beau outside, couldn't she? Instead, she brings him home, like a good little daughter, and sister, for our inspection."

"He's hardly a beau," Ellen said, smiling faintly. She rose and went over to her mother and sat down on the hassock by her feet. She put her arms across Mrs. Adams' neat lap and looked up into her face.

"He's nice," explained Ellen simply, "and I like him. I see no harm in my having friends here, even if," she smiled again, "even if they weren't brought up under the L. I'd like you to know him. I—I intend to see him," Ellen went on clearly, "and if you don't want him here, I'll call his office to-morrow morning and make some explanation, and meet him outside for dinner—if you'd rather."

"Atta-girl," applauded Nancy—but mutely.

Mrs. Adams surrendered.

"This home," she said dramatically, "is yours. You girls maintain it. I have nothing to say."

Ellen controlled herself; impatience, anger, pity, love—all these mixed emotions warred within her. None was apparent as she spoke again, touching her lips to her mother's thin hand.

"But I *do* want you to say something," she coaxed. "I want you to say, 'Good evening, Mr. Bartlett, we're very glad to see you.'"

"I hope," said her mother, softened but wounded, "that I have never failed in courtesy toward your friends."

Ellen knelt on the hassock and hugged her.

"Angel, don't be stiff as a little old poker with me. Of course you haven't. But I think you'll like him, and I know he'll like you. Who knows," cried Ellen, laughing, "but that we'll need a lawyer in the family circle some day?"

She hadn't meant quite that. She flushed, and laid her face against her mother's. Mrs. Adams put up a hand and reluctantly patted her head. Nancy said, grinning,

"I need one right now. I need someone to sue this Walkpruf Hosiery Company for me. Walk proof! It isn't even *sit* proof. I sit at a switchboard all night and do things with cute little gadgets. But do my stockings know that? They do not. They think I've gone for a five-mile tramp in the Catskills!"

"And now," said Ellen, getting up and procuring paper and pencil, "let's make a list for tomorrow's dinner and plan how we can shop." She looked at Nancy. "I hate like the dickens to put it all on you."

"Darling, be calm. I will arise in plenty of time to purchase the materials for our fiesta," said Nancy mincingly. "And you'll help cook it, just to do mother proud and show Mr. Bartlett what an elegant and housewifely little home he's about to enter. Make your list and go wash your hair. Yell when you need help. I lit the heater for you right after supper and we didn't use too much for the dishes. Make it snappy as I have to get to work before morning."

She added, as Ellen left the room: "The only time I wish you'd shingle that mane of yours is when I have to help rinse it and when I see that here-I-come-all-good-works lid of yours wobble around on the top of your bean."

Ellen went laughing into her room to undress. Later she bent over the basin in the bathroom and allowed Nancy's deft hands to rinse the suds from her hair. "Glory!" said Nancy, as she had said every time she assisted in this rite, "I don't blame you for not cutting it. When long hair comes back you'll be Miss Nineteen Hundred and Something. And if it never comes back, you'll still be It."

Later, she helped dry Ellen's hair by hand. There was still time before she left for work. Ellen's hair, almost to her waist, was marvelous. Heavy and almost straight, except where it curled about her temples in little tendrils, and at the golden ends. Her brows were a shade darker but her long lashes remained golden. Nancy regarded her and said suddenly, "I've asked you a thousand times to touch up your lashes, here's the thousand-and-oneth. One sweep of the pencil, and you'd be a knockout."

Ellen shook her head. She was almost smothered in the flow and sweep of her hair. "Not me," she said cheerfully. "I tried it once. I looked like nothing on earth!"

Her hair was almost dry. By the time Nancy had gone and Mrs. Adams had been put to bed, demanding a good many things, somehow, as a reward for her recent concession, it was quite dry, save where it curled, loosely and damply. Ellen went to her room and brushed it, with that graceful turn of the wrist seen only under such circumstances. Then she braided it in two heavy braids. Presently she regarded her glowing face in the mirror. From the sedate middle parting, her hair sprang strongly, pressed into wide waves by her clever fingers. Gold and silver, and gray eyes smiling, cheekbones touched with color. She thought . . . tomorrow night . . . and frowned and shook her head at herself. "Behaving," said Ellen, aloud, sternly, "like a schoolgirl . . . I wonder," asked Ellen wistfully, "if he'll be as nice as I think he is?"

"Probably not," said Ellen, and went to bed and turned her errant thoughts to Herman, crying with his miserable burns, and to Herman's fragile, frightened mother. Something ran swiftly through her mind, something connected with—was it only Herman? A snatch of song . . .

> "Kiss and quarrel, dream and die,
> Life's a street of passers-by.
> You and I—you and I——"

CHAPTER SIX

At seven o'clock Tuesday evening the steak waited the trick broiler which one set over the flame, and the deep fat sizzled in the frying kettle. The coffee was in the pot, ready to be plugged into an electric outlet. Rolls, on the pretty table, fresh and crisp. Radishes. The rose-colored pottery, the tall blue glasses. String beans, cooked and waiting; and the ice box cake from Larsen's. . . .

Ellen, coming home in a rush, had wriggled out of her uniform and into a house dress and set to work, but Nancy had done all the preparation for her. Together they persuaded Mrs. Adams into the pretty flowered voile which deepened the faded tone of her eyes and set off her pretty, gray hair. "Must look nice," they told her, laughing. "You're our show piece." She sniffed a little. "As if it matters!" she said. But she was determined to show the alien young man that he was entering, for the first and, she devoutedly hoped, the last time, a house of refinement. A *genteel* house, she called it in her old-fashioned way.

At seven promptly Bartlett arrived. He had flowers, a great sheaf of them, spring flowers, like sunshine, like the after-glow of a glorious sunset. He had candy, in a big purple box.

"This," he said, beaming upon the three women impartially, "is awfully good of you." He sniffed; not as Mrs. Adams had, previous to his arrival, but with appreciation. "Golly, something smells good. It's pretty darned nice of you," he told Ellen, "to take pity on a poor bachelor."

Afterward, Mrs. Adams remarked that he had laid far too much emphasis on the important word with which he had ended that sentence. Afterward, Ellen remembered.

He joked with Nancy, who took a fancy to him at once, and was courteous and attentive to Mrs. Adams. But his eyes were for Ellen, her house dress changed for a plain little green frock, which turned her gray eyes to emerald and made her look like spring itself, with the matchless hair curling about her forehead, caught in a loose, heavy knot at the nape of her very white neck. He insisted on

helping with the serving, got in the way, and admitted it ruefully.

Over dinner, Mrs. Adams managed to find out a
good deal about him. Yes, he was city born and
bred. No, his parents were not living. The only relatives he possessed were an aunt—"who disapproved
of me," he explained, laughing—and a couple of cous-
ins, in Indianapolis. Prep school, college, law school.
A usual routine. He'd been with a big downtown firm
for a couple of years and had recently gone in
for himself. There was no suggestion of struggle
in his story. The implication was that he had always
been sufficiently affluent to do as he wished. His
father, he explained, had been a lawyer before him.
One had the impression of an easy road and, aside
from the natural sorrow of loss and death, of a
happy enough time.

He was eloquent on the subject of Bill. He had,
he announced, adopted him, more or less. He was
trying to persuade him that school was a necessary
evil. "Sharp as a knife and quick as lightning,"
said Bartlett, with an absurd pride. "If he really
wants to 'loin' to be a lawyer, we'll have to see him
through somehow."

He had thought that Bill's grave boy-friendship
would be enough reward; but he realized that the
reward he sought was facing him across a small,
laden table; a smiling look, two eyes that altered in

color from gray to green. "What color *are* they, anyway?" he demanded, without realizing that he spoke aloud.

Ellen flushed and Mrs. Adams looked mildly astonished. The young man, presentable enough, was plainly a lunatic. Nancy giggled. She knew. Bartlett found himself reddening.

"I have," he explained hastily, "an appalling habit of thinking out loud." Nothing to do but carry it off with a high hand, he decided. He grinned engagingly, with the smile of a good child detected in some minor mischief. "Your eyes," he told Ellen solemnly, "I thought they were gray. But they're green."

"Cat's eyes," Ellen informed him, laughing. "It depends on what I wear. Sometimes I can fool people into thinking they're blue."

Well, that had gone over all right, although Bartlett was quite aware that, as far as Ellen's mother was concerned, he was in her home only on sufferance. She'd been courteous, hospitable even, but she was, he decided, a remote little lady. . . .

Chick came for Nancy. The two men met, decided they liked each other. Nancy was gone with a flirt of her hand at Bartlett and Ellen and a kiss for her mother. Off, heaven knew where, the two of them. "Maybe a movie," suggested Chick. "Maybe not," decided Nancy. "Let's go for a bus ride. I'm shut up all day, and I like to get my fresh air, even if it's only at night."

Ellen cleared away. She'd let the dishes go, she said. "No," Bartlett told her, "let's wash 'em. I'll help." He permitted her to tie an apron about his lean waist. They laughed a good deal, the two of them in the tiny kitchen. Mrs. Adams, under the reading light, read the same sentence over and over again and shuddered to hear the crash of china on the kitchen floor. One of her cups! She mourned it in an unusual silence.

"Tell me about your sister," Bartlett was saying. Ellen told him briefly. "She's training for a supervisor's job," she said. "She went to the company nearly three years ago. Likes the work a lot."

"It sounds awful to me," Bartlett said frankly, "cooped up all night plugging things and unplugging them." He had the attitude of the entirely non-mechanical man, Ellen told him. "She isn't cooped up at all," she denied. "Shows all you know about it! I've been through her exchange. Grand place, lots of light and air. The girls like their work. They've rest periods, a really lovely recreation room, a kitchen to cook in or from which to buy luncheons and between-time snacks. They have their days off, you know, like anybody else, with relief operators taking their places. Girls who want to work Saturday afternoons, get overtime, of course. It's something of a job, a twenty-four-hour service, but it's worked out remarkably well. Nancy gets two weeks' vacation, with pay. She's looked after if she's ill——"

"I'll bet a cookie," said Bartlett, polishing a glass and then standing off to regard his handiwork with pride, "that you don't let anyone else take care of her."

"Well, no, I didn't mean that, exactly."

They had finished their work. He said, persuasively, drawing her back gently from the doorway into the living room, "Couldn't we go bus riding, too? I've my car outside . . . "

"I can't leave Mother." She explained that, too, lowering her voice. He nodded, disappointed, understanding. But they had not been long in the living room when Mrs. Meader knocked at the door and came in, a little taken aback to find the Adamses entertaining company, "and me in my housecleaning clothes!"

She was, it appeared, full of news. She knew this and that. She hesitated. "I'll run in another time," she said, "but the baby's in bed and Pa's downstairs and Jimmy's off to night school, so I thought I'd stop in and visit with your mother."

"That would be awfully nice of you," Ellen said quickly, before her mother could speak, "as Mr. Bartlett has just asked me to go for a ride."

"Run along," said Mrs. Meader, beaming, "I'll set with Mother while you're gone."

And that was that.

They drove uptown to the Drive. Ellen took off her hat and let the soft spring wind ruffle her hair. "You don't mind, do you," asked Bartlett, "if I tell you you have the loveliest hair I ever saw? Don't ever cut it."

"It's my chief vanity," she admitted, laughing. "They tell me I inherit it from some Scandinavian ancestor and that it crops out every so often. No, of course, I don't mind, why should I?" and she looked at him with such friendly directness and sweetness that his heart skipped about six beats.

He lived, he told her vaguely, uptown, East Side, in an apartment. It was better, he said, than a hotel. He spoke of his work; he was, he said, particularly interested in criminal law. She'd like, she told him, to hear him try a case some day.

"Would you come, really, if I let you know?" he asked her eagerly.

"I'd love to, but I probably couldn't. I'm pretty busy," she reminded him.

"Tell me more about your job," he demanded.

She told him, as they went at a swift, but legal speed through the exquisite night. And her voice warmed, and there was a little catch in her breath.

He wondered, aloud, "Are they grateful? Is it worth it?"

Of course, it was worth it, she responded, in some indignation.

He hadn't meant that, he assured her, but "To save the lives of countless babies and children who will live only to grow up in squalor and misery which they can't overcome," he said, musingly, "I wonder? And to bring a woman through safely only to have her bear, year after year, more pitiable babies. I wonder again."

She didn't, she told him, feel that way at all about it. There wasn't a sick baby brought back to health who didn't have some chance, some opportunity. That's what she was there for, aside from the nursing part of it, to see that they got their chance, their opportunity. She and hundreds of women like her, all over the country.

"What," asked Bartlett, in some amusement, "are we arguing for? It's a grand night. Just the night to swear an eternal friendship. Do let's. Shall we?"

She shook her head. She didn't, she told him, like to swear. So many things happened.

But nothing would happen, he promised. They were at a crossing, waiting for the lights, and he held out his hand. "Come on," he bade her, smiling, "be a sport."

After a moment, she laid her strong narrow hand in his. "All right," agreed Ellen.

There was a gravity about the moment. Perhaps he hadn't intended it; perhaps he had. They looked at one another gravely, measuringly, and smiled.

The lights had changed. An indignant honking was going on behind them; they were oblivious. "Hey, you," said a large cop, strolling up, "where do you think you are, at the opera?"

"Sorry," said Frank Bartlett; but he wasn't. "Hello, Mike," said Frank, and the cop grinned.

"Sure, I didn't know it was you, Mr. Bartlett," he said. "On your way, on your way."

They were on their way, laughing.

Later that night, while Mrs. Adams was receiving in an unwonted silence her evening attentions, Ellen asked her with a secret timidity which astonished and annoyed her, "You liked him, didn't you, Mother?"

"Whom?" asked Mrs. Adams.

"Mother!" Ellen gave her a small firm spank on the shoulder, "don't be perverse."

Mrs. Adams surrendered.

"He seemed a very pleasant young man," she replied cautiously, with a complete air of "if-one-can-believe-all-he-says," an air of mental reservations. She added, "Jim looked in while you were gone."

That was like her mother, Ellen thought, exasperated. She would wait until now to tell her. Probably she had taken some satisfaction in telling Jim . . .

When Ellen was leaving her for the night her mother reached up her thin arms and drew her down to her, holding the girl's glowing young face close to her own faded cheek.

"My good girl," she murmured.

Ellen went back to her room, thoughtful, moved. Her mother was not demonstrative. She demanded a good deal, she gave no sign of having received. She must have been disturbed to have offered as much . . . disturbed or worried.

Well, there was nothing to worry about. When she came to know Frank Bartlett she would like him; she must, could she help it? Her prejudice against him was not really personal; it was allied to that fixed idea, that fatal, baseless terror which for over eight years had been an integral part of her. Ellen sighed, from pity, not from fatigue. She had never felt less weary, more wide awake in all her life.

Poor Mother. Poor Coral. . . .

At breakfast, Nancy was gay.

"We saw you," she mentioned, aside, to Ellen, "but you didn't see us. We were riding on top of the bus like the rest of the hoi polloi. You were speeding along, lost to the world." She laughed into Ellen's startled eyes.

"Why didn't you yell?" Ellen wanted to know reasonably.

"Child, the Avenue isn't the prairie," said Nancy pityingly, "not that you would have heard us if we had . . . "

Later, she announced for Mrs. Adams' benefit: "I like the new boy friend. He's a good egg."

Mrs. Adams regarded her with resignation.

"Nancy, where on earth you pick up such expressions—" she began, and then switched to an abrupt statement, "and I wish you wouldn't say boy friend. It's vulgar. Besides, Mr. Bartlett is only an acquaintance."

"And how!" murmured Nancy. Ellen looked up, her eyes dark.

"I expected to see him often, Mother," she stated, without any compromise, "I like him."

That was that, again. Mrs. Adams reddened, to the tip of her nose. She looked reproved and reproached and ate no breakfast after that. Ellen was, Ellen told herself, sorry. But it couldn't be helped. She *did* expect to see Frank. She *did* like him. And she wished she could somehow harden her heart and cure herself of this feeling of pity and remorse which troubled her every time she crossed her mother in the least degree.

She had given him her word, however. She would not dishonor it.

She kept her word. She saw him, with an increasing frequency. Sometimes they had dinner out. Once in a while on a Sunday, they went off in the car, when Nancy was at home. Once, when Mrs. Adams' cousin, Laura Farrell, came to spend the day and night with her, Nancy and Chick went picnicking with them, out in the country, and as Nancy had her night off, they stayed late, ate supper at a roadhouse and danced until ten o'clock and managed to get home, despite the heavy traffic, before midnight. Mrs. Farrell was there, yawningly ready to make up her bed on the living-room davenport. Mrs. Adams had not retired.

"You promised us you'd let Cousin Laura put you to bed," Ellen said.

"I couldn't have slept," said Mrs. Adams shortly.

Later, as the two girls lay awake in the double bed which they shared on those occasions of Nancy's free nights, Ellen said:

"I suppose we should have come home sooner——"

Nancy yawned.

"Mother's all right. And she loved having Laura fuss over her."

"But——"

A silence. Nancy was almost asleep. Then Ellen asked suddenly:

"Why under the sun does she dislike him so?"

"Frank? Oh, because he has money, and is footloose and—oh, you know why. *You* don't dislike him?" asked Nancy, and a thread of sleepy laughter ran through the question.

"No," said Ellen, "of course not."

"You—you like him a lot?" asked Nancy, no longer laughing. "Don't you, Ellen?"

Another silence. Then she answered:

"You know I do." She hesitated. She added, finally, "Sometimes I think he knows it, too."

"Well, naturally he does. He's just waiting . . . " Nancy's voice trailed off. Then she asked:

"Better than Jim, don't you?"

"Differently," said Ellen, after a pause. "Jim— oh, we've always known Jim. He's part of the family."

"He'd like to be," Nancy reminded her.

"Nancy, for heaven's sake, go to sleep. I have to go to work in the morning, even if you don't," Ellen reminded her.

Nancy, with a courteous alacrity, obeyed.

But Ellen wasn't as sleepy as she had thought on the long ride home, the warm night encompassing her, sitting close beside Frank, not talking much, unheeding of Nancy and Chick who, in the back seat, were beginning one of their interminable and not very serious quarrels.

Better than Jim?

Of course not—and yet?

Differently?

Very differently.

In what degree?

But she refused to pursue that subject to its dangerous conclusions. Turned her mind away. But a moment later told herself without astonishment and without fear . . . *I'm in love* . . .

Even if Frank loved her—and did he not? didn't he betray it, without words, without the committing finality of speech and touch?—what could she do? Her mother would never dream—never consent—that she and Frank——

But she was free to follow her heart.

No, she wasn't free. If her mother had been other than she was, she might be ready, for the sake of her own happiness, to cause her mother unhappiness. But she couldn't.

What was the use of thinking about that now? Nothing had happened. Nothing would happen, or if so, not for a long time. By then Mrs. Adams might be reconciled.

She would be seeing Jim tomorrow night. That caused her to frown a little in the darkness. Jim was becoming—difficult.

But when she slept it was not of Jim she dreamed.

When she reached the sub-station the following morning, Bill, astonishingly, was there to meet her. Bill was important and elated. There wasn't any school, not for long weeks. Golly, the summer was swell. Bill had a note for her. It was from Frank; Frank had "boined" down to Bill's early and delivered it into his own hands to give her. Why, she thought, tearing it open, why couldn't Frank have told her last night what he wanted—or telephone?

"Dear Ellen," wrote Bartlett, "I arrived home safely and found an urgent message waiting me. I have to go to Washington for a few days and will be gone before you get to work. I don't like to ring up your house and disturb you, so I'll give this to Bill. Save me the very first evening you can after I get back. I have something to ask you," he wrote. "And then there's Bill. Can't we get him to one of the fresh air camps? Or better, can't he be placed in someone's house in the country somewhere through one of the organizations, and let me pay his board? Think it over and see what you can do and we'll fix it up when I get back. Yours, Frank."

She folded the letter and smiled at Bill. Bill smiled back.

"Mr. Bartlett wants to know if you would like to have a vacation in the country this summer," she inquired.

"Jees'!" said Bill, paling till the freckles stood out in a strange brown pattern. "Jees', can a duck swim? Wotta guy, wotta guy!" said Bill.

CHAPTER SEVEN

Joe, the cobbler, looked up from his basement windows to the street above. He could see feet going by, old feet, young feet, feet which moved with reluctance, feet which almost ran . . . Those were Ellen's feet which passed, walking as if to an inner swinging march. He knew the shoes, he regarded them with creative pride. He turned from his contemplation of the passers-by to the task in his hands. "Mis' " Brown's shoes. Dot's.

Not the first time he had mended her shoes. But these shoes were different. They no longer trod strange streets, crooked streets . . . They were sober shoes, of a better material. She'd brought them in.

"Can I have them tonight, Joe?" she asked. And then, as he looked at her with his dark small eyes of a sagacious monkey, she had stammered a little.

"You remember me, Joe? Sure, you remember? Dot Mather that was? I'm Mrs. Dan Brown now."

Yes, sure, he remembered. *Si, si!* She could have the shoes by evening.

Ebbène.

He looked after her, as she left, shaking his head. *La povera.* He wished her luck. He was not young, he had nothing but an impersonal compassion for her and for girls like her, all over the world. The world was hard on women; women were hard toward women; they made things something less than easy for them; women and young men. . . .

Ellen, hurrying to work, felt a little dizzy with the heat. It had turned terrifically hot, and the sunshine, implacable, beat up from the pavements. In the street the asphalt had softened, there were hoof marks in it. Which, she wondered, was harder on the poor, the cold or the heat? The cold, she thought. People couldn't get warm, although they huddled together, crouched in doorways out of the wind, or stooped over ash cans in which burned paper and bits of boxes with a big ephemeral flame. Summer was bad, too, but the exodus to the beaches had begun, the subways filled with peevish half-sick children, with draggled women. The fire escapes were crowded with bedding, with babies in clothes baskets . . .

Bill would be taken care of. She'd seen to that.

When Frank came home he would find it all arranged.

When Frank came home . . .

She missed him terribly. A note, on the paper of a Washington hotel, had reached her. He would be delayed for a day or two, but he would be home soon, and would telephone . . . "Don't forget me, Ellen."

Nancy would take her vacation during the following month. It did not tally with Ellen's, so she would not go away, except, perhaps, for a day at the beach now and then. Neither girl had ever been able to go out of town for more than a day or so on her vacation, for some years. It was too much of a task to try and find a place in the country to which they could take their mother, even when their vacations coincided. Perhaps Cousin Laura would ask Mrs. Adams and Nancy down for a week-end; she had a little place on the water, a cottage, for the summer. If she did so Ellen would be free, for a time.

Meantime life went on. Sometimes Ellen wondered that the mere routine still held such drama, such appeal for her. Some days were woven in so monotonous a pattern. Opening windows, taking temperatures, giving bed baths, mixing mustard plasters, trying to bring something of cleanliness, light, health

into the crowded houses with their smell of food
and humanity, sickness and dirt. . . .

"I have something to ask you," Frank had written. If it were—*that*? But suppose it were, could she
give up her work, could she antagonize her mother,
could she cease utterly to carry the little torch of
her individual service into the dark, crowded places?

She found herself, later, leaving the sub-station,
with a busy day before her. She would not have time
to report at noon, she would have to telephone, for
several of her calls were on the very outskirts of
her usual district. And it was, she thought as the
day wore on and the brazen sky showed no signs of a
friendly cloud, too hot to hurry much.

Sick babies, for the most part, gastric upsets,
prickly heat, teething complaints. The calls had come
in, direct, fast and furious . . . "my baby sick" . . .
"my boy, very sick, send a nurse, *hurry*——"

The first cases of infantile paralysis were being
reported. Every summer cases, of course. But this
summer more. "If only," said the supervisor anxiously, "we don't find ourselves in an epidemic—
like that of nineteen-fifteen."

There were Board of Health Reports. And warn-
ings. And a lack of serum; and an unfortunate lack
of certain diagnoses. Already Ellen had sent doctors
in to two supposed cases, the nurses had reported
others. Yet people would continue to take their chil-

dren to the beaches, take them to parks, carry them
through crowds . . . It was out of all reason to believe that they would keep them at home. How could
they, home being what it was?

Something awfully wrong, thought Ellen, leaving
a dark and stifling tenement room, when people
have to live like animals, cooped up together, breathing the tainted air, eating the insufficient food, living
on top of one another, with not a chance to escape.
Uptown there were wide avenues and trees, apartment houses rose proudly into the cleaner air. There
were winds by night and shade by day. But down
here, the matter of a few minutes' drive in a car, it
was another world. Something awfully wrong, that
two such dissimilar worlds should be permitted to
exist.

She was walking down a long flight of steps, a
little sick with the heat, the odor of the place she
had just left. She heard just before reaching a landing, voices coming through a half-closed door;
women's voices, raised in anger.

Ellen was used to such ugly sounds, the worst in
human nature turned articulate. She was used to
the heavy voices of men tuned to accusation or curse;
accustomed to the weeping of children; to the more
hysterical tears of women; to the sound of blows.
Accustomed and yet not hardened.

A woman came through the door, slamming it behind her. A woman probably in her early forties, looking sixty. She wore something very nondescript over her bare body. Her hair straggled out from under a torn net. On her bare feet, men's slippers. She was still talking—to herself. Beyond the door, silence.

Ellen reached the landing where the gas jet flickered. The woman looked up, indifferently. She exclaimed, suddenly, "If it ain't Ellen Adams!"

Mrs. Markey. Once she'd lived in the flat over Joe's, the cobbler. A shiftless woman. When Markey had lived she had been well enough provided for. But she had never achieved any trimness of attire; she had been born sloppy, Ellen had thought, mentally and physically.

Ellen stopped to talk to her a moment, reluctantly enough, glancing at her wrist watch as she did so.

"I didn't know you had moved here," she said.

Mrs. Markey shrugged her shapeless shoulders.

"It ain't what I'm used to, of course," she stated, "but after Markey died, what else was there to do? He'd even let his insurance lapse," she complained, with an undying rancor. "I go out cleaning."

Her face was swollen, her eyes reddened. Ellen said quickly, "But Gladys——?"

Mrs. Markey's face darkened. A word escaped her; an unpleasant word . . .

"Gladys?" She laughed. Her laughter was more unpleasant than the epithet. She jerked a thumb over her shoulder. "She's in there. Come in," said Mrs. Markey, "and see for yourself. Come in."

"I—I have some other calls to make," began Ellen, but Mrs. Markey had her arm, was pulling her to the door.

"Perhaps," said Mrs. Markey, "you can do something with her. She always liked you, since we lived there, over Joe's."

The door opened. These were larger rooms than the ones Ellen had left, a little cleaner, with a little more light and air seeping in. There were signs of vanished grandeur, comparatively speaking. Gladys was sitting on a straight chair, her hands folded in her lap. She was about nineteen, Ellen figured hastily. There was a bruise, a fresh bruise, on one side of her face. Her face was swollen, too, not with tears. The soft young mouth was set and sullen. Blue eyes, under smoky lashes, stared listlessly at Ellen. Her voice, husky, broken, said bitterly, "Who've you got there, someone from the welfare crowd? Ought to be a SPCA . . . "

Then she recognized Ellen.

"Gee," said Gladys, and something like a dim smile lightened her disfigured face. "Gee, I haven't seen you for ages."

Mrs. Markey was talking, talking, in incoherent rushes.

"A good job downtown . . . after I've worked my fingers to the bone—she pays me out like this . . . brings a bastard into my house . . . if her Pa, if Markey was alive, he'd kill her. . . . and her sitting there like a clam, saying she won't tell, she won't tell."

"Shut up, can't you?" asked Gladys, color like flame in her face, her eyes tormented, like an animal's.

"Stand up," said Mrs. Markey hysterically, "stand up and——"

Not necessary. Ellen knew. There was nothing to say. There was, as she saw it, only one thing to do.

She touched the girl's shoulder and the shoulder shook. She said: "If I can help, Gladys . . . ? If you'll come see me, some evening. You know the address. Or come to the sub-station . . . "

So many things she could do, teach the girl some care of herself, find a place for her to go when the time came. Practical things. No preaching. They didn't take kindly to preaching.

"Make her tell you who the man is," screamed Mrs. Markey. "She won't tell me. I says, 'He's got to marry you, see, I'll get the cops after him.' 'There ain't no law to compel him,' she comes back at me. I says, 'I'll compel him.' She says, 'He can't, he's

married. That's all there is to it.' Picked her up,
she tells me, in a cafeteria." She laughed, dangerously. "That's something for a mother to hear, ain't
it? Didn't I let her go to school when she could
have been working? Didn't I let her take that business course and go out scrubbing so she could? How
does she pay me for it?"

"Shut up, Ma," said Gladys again. She looked at
Ellen. "If I come to the station they'll ask questions," she said. Her mouth hardened. Her soft, weak
girl's mouth. "I won't answer them," she promised.

"You come to me instead, Gladys," said Ellen,
sickened, sorry.

Mrs. Markey had begun again. Ellen said, "Never
mind, Mrs. Markey, I'll——" But Gladys had had
enough. She looked at Ellen, a curious fleeting look,
despair and stubbornness, and flung herself across
the room and into the bedroom. The door slammed.

Mrs. Markey had not finished.

"Be quiet," said Ellen sharply. "What difference
does it make now? You've got to see her through.
Send her to me, when she'll come."

Mrs. Markey's sly eyes sharpened. She asked a
brutal question eagerly. Ellen looked at her a moment, in silence. The other woman's eyes fell.

Ellen thought, I'm tired. And it's hot. And it's
not the heat but the stupidity in this case. I mustn't
lose my temper. She said, aloud:

"You know better than that, Mrs. Markey; and I warn you against risking a life, two lives, and committing a crime into the bargain. Send Gladys to see me, if she'll come."

She turned and laid her hand on the door knob. Mrs. Markey pursued her into the dim hallway.

"Talk to Gladys," she said coaxingly, "get her to tell you—who the feller is. I—We got to get the money somehow, ain't we, to see her through? He ought to pay. I'll have the law on him if he don't," said Mrs. Markey.

Ellen reflected, going on out into the unbearably hot and sticky streets, that she couldn't "have the law" on a person or persons unknown. She felt sick about the whole business. No maternal love, no savage protective instinct there, in Mrs. Markey's case. Greed merely. In contrast, Gladys with her no doubt mistaken loyalty—or was it sheer fright?—actually shone.

She reached home to find Nancy dashing around in the kitchen and her mother talking to Mrs. Lenz, who had dropped in with a homemade coffee cake. The talk, snatches of which Ellen heard through the bedroom door as she changed her uniform for a house dress and washed the soil and heat from her face and hands, was mostly of Dot Brown. Where she went and what she did. "Can't tell me," said

Mrs. Lenz, "that she'll go on like this long. It ain't natural. Such a one don't stay decent."

Mrs. Adams, looking distressed, nodded, with, it seemed reluctance, and Nancy, drifting in and out, remarked briefly, "What's it to you, Mrs. Lenz, as long as she pays her rent and gives you no trouble?" In the bedroom Ellen smiled to herself. That was like Nancy, going to the heart of the matter, as far as Mrs. Lenz was concerned, with her usual terseness.

At dinner, the talk was desultory enough. Ellen pushed the heavy hair from her forehead. In season such as this she envied Nancy her cropped curls. There was a dragging weight at the back of her neck.

"What happened today?" her mother wanted to know.

"Nothing much." She thought of Gladys and frowned slightly. "Oh, yes, one thing." She began to laugh. She had a charming laugh, low, a little husky. "One thing. I wish you'd been there, Nancy, it was grand."

A pushcart peddler and an automobile racing through, just as Ellen was crossing the street. No, of course, he hadn't been hurt. But he'd been scared. Plenty. She'd helped McGuire, the cop, pick him and his scattered wares up and had listened to the colloquy between him and the car's driver, a taxi driver, of the pushcart owner's race. It had been glorious while it lasted, eyes and hands and shoulders flying. She and the great strapping Irish policeman had listened, helpless with laughter, while the two had called down the wrath of their gods upon each other's heads, ancestors and progenies. Traffic had been held up. She acted it out for her mother and sister, the words, and music, and Nancy, between shrieks of merriment, regarded her with admiration. "Talk about Fanny Brice," said Nancy. "You're wasted on your job, Ellen, you ought to be on the Big Time circuit."

"Speaking of circuits," said Ellen, taking a bow, "Jim's coming tonight, we're going out somewhere, I hope to a picture, as it will be the coolest place in town. Of course, you probably get pneumonia in these refrigerated houses, but what of it? It's not too high a price to pay for a couple of hours in an igloo—after all."

"You're not serious?" asked her mother anxiously.

"Well, rarely," Ellen responded, smiling. "Golly, Jim's due now any moment and we haven't cleared away."

"You haven't," her mother reproached her, "been very nice to Jim lately."

"Haven't I?" she asked noncommittally.

Nancy said:

"You go get dolled up, I'll do the dirty work. This is my evening for washing stockings and giving myself one of those eight-dollar facials for twenty-two cents and a little elbow grease. I'm going to set mother's hair, too. In fact, we're in for a large evening," she added, as she followed Ellen into the kitchen, "What's the word from Frank?"

"He had to stay over. He'll be coming home soon."

"Thought lawyers led the life of Reilly after courts closed," said Nancy.

"It doesn't look as if they did," said Ellen. Her eyes shone and her heart sang. Coming home—*soon.*

Something of her inner shining happiness was in her voice when she greeted Jim a little later. For the life of her, she couldn't keep it out. While she was getting ready for the street Jim talked to Nancy and Mrs. Adams. As rental agent he knew everybody in the district and knew everybody's business as well. Ellen heard him talking of a hundred people and a hundred things; comic stories, he told, and tragic, too. She said, standing at the doorway, polishing her nails on her narrow pink palms,

"I met Gilda Esposito again today. She's crazy about her new job, and she's getting prettier every day."

Jim looked up. His eyes were a little narrow.

"Esposito? The fruit stand people?"

"Yes. You know them, don't you, Jim? Remember Mike, the brother? A little wild, but a great youngster in lots of ways."

"I don't remember Gilda," Jim said definitely. Then he changed the subject. "Speaking of people we have met, remember the Markeys?"

Ellen was silent.

"She's a disgrace to any neighborhood," said Mrs. Adams. "I recall her perfectly. A born sloven."

"There was a girl, wasn't there? I seem to remember her, in school," Nancy said indifferently.

Jim shrugged.

"Yes, Gladys. It appears she's lost her job. I handle the rentals for the building where they live. They're 'way behind. The mother came around to see me yesterday. I have sent a man there two or three times; they wouldn't let him in."

"Everyone's losing their jobs nowadays," sighed Mrs. Adams.

"It isn't a case of depression," said Jim, "or repression, either, for that matter."

He lighted a cigarette and laughed. "The mother," said Jim, "talks too much for the girl's good."

He was good-humoredly amused. Such stories were old to him. He was, as he himself would say, plenty hard-boiled. Ellen, regarding him with exasperation, found herself unable to blame him, very much. Considering his environment, his work, the people he dealt with every day, you couldn't expect him to be an exponent of sweetness and light, could you?

"No daughter," said Mrs. Adams sententiously,

"of that woman could ever come to any good. I wouldn't be surprised at anything."

Ellen was sick of it suddenly. Sick of the gossip, sick of the casual bantering of names, the skating on the thin ice of rumor which hid such tragic and ugly depths, such fathoms of freezing black waters. She said furiously:

"I can't understand you, any of you. You don't seem to realize what these girls have to contend with. You don't seem to think that . . . that but for the grace of God it might be me—or Nancy—any of us. It might be——"

She stopped. They knew. It *might be Coral*. Her mother gave her one stricken look. Tears were imminent, reproaches. Nancy whistled under her breath.

"Let's get out of this," said Ellen to Jim.

He rose, awkwardly for a man as graceful as he. He said, low, "Sorry to stir you up, old girl."

Nancy waved them both away. She said brightly to her mother, "How about a manicure, now that we're starting a beauty salon?"

Leaving, Ellen was silent, kissing her mother's averted cheek, answering Nancy's flippant wave of the hand. "What's come over you?" Jim wanted to know, as they left the apartment. His car was outside. A new, shining car, of a very good make.

CHAPTER EIGHT

Bartlett had come home. "Dinner," he asked her over the telephone, "as early as you can. I'll get theater tickets. What have you seen?"

"Very little," she told him, laughing.

"I'll pick you up at the house," he said, "and won't take no for an answer."

"That's silly of you. I mean," she told him, "I haven't said no."

"But you might," he replied, not too mysteriously.

She found time to telephone Nancy, in the afternoon. "Frank's back," she said, "have you a date tonight?"

Nancy was yawning. She said, muffled:

"Sure, but it doesn't matter. Jim was in. Miss O'Connor is coming around to see Mother this evening. She'll stay till you get back."

"Nancy, take my new slippers over to Joe's, will you," asked Ellen, "if you have time? They hurt me, in the heel. I'd like to wear them tonight."

"Okay, baby," Nancy replied cheerfully. "I'll do it. You can pick 'em up on your way home. If anything ruins a tête-à-tête with the boy friend, it's a pair of aching shoes."

On her way home Ellen stopped for the slippers. Joe regarded them dourly. "Bargain?" he asked her. "Sure, I know."

"They were on a sales counter," she admitted, "but they are pretty, Joe, aren't they?"

He turned them over.

"Pretty; an' the soles, paper," was his verdict. "Not like what you wear. I t'ink. Stick to your last," Joe advised her, wrapping up the slippers.

In the end, she decided not to wear them. Tried on and discarded three dresses before settling on the cool, handkerchief linen dress, with its pert jacket, and a wide-brimmed hat. Her mother looked at her when she came out, ready to go. "You look very nice," said Mrs. Adams grudgingly.

She heard the car drive up, kissed her mother and flew out to meet Frank on the steps. "Lord, it's good to see you," he said, "and you look cool as an iceberg lettuce in that green outfit."

"What a comparison," she laughed. She got into the car and wondered why her knees shook. They had exchanged little or no greeting. She'd put her hand in his, of course, and murmured something. "Nice to see you again . . . " something banal.

Nice! There were not words, no, not in any language, to tell him how glad she was, how happy.

They went to a very quiet place to dinner. Good food, French food, waiters that gave you the proper service, but didn't hover. Lights, not too bright. No music.

"What will it be?" he demanded.

She shook her head, smiling.

"You order," she said.

He did so; and the order came. But she did not know what she was eating, if anything. She felt a little physically sick from excitement. Yet, before he had come for her she had been hungry. "I could eat the side of a house," she had told Nancy, and Nancy had commented, "Hard on the escort's pocketbook, but perfectly good form."

They talked of Frank's trip, of Bill, of Nancy's coming vacation, of her own, which would be in September. Bill was leaving for an upstate farm the following week. "Fix it up?" asked Bartlett, and when she nodded, he smiled, well satisfied. "All right with me," he said. "See that he stays as long as they will keep him."

They lingered over the dinner. Curious what a lot of time you could spend over something that didn't matter. It was cool in the dim, small restaurant. Bartlett looked at his watch. "We'll have to hurry," he warned, "if we're going to make the theater and find a place to park."

She said, yes, without much enthusiasm. She thought, I wonder why I care so much? He isn't, for instance, half as good-looking as Jim—but——

No, he wasn't as good-looking. And yet——

Presently Bartlett paid his check and they went out and got into the car. The night was breathless, still. They rode uptown, avoiding, as much as possible, the main arteries of traffic. He asked suddenly :

"Are you really so anxious to see this show? It's too darned hot to go to the theater anyway."

She laughed a little.

"I don't care anything about it," she said. "What made you think I did?"

He took the tickets from his pocket. She said, hastily, putting her hand on his as they waited for a light to change:

"Frank, how can you be so extravagant?"

But he had torn them across, and the little white bits of cardboard fluttered to the street, as he answered:

"But it's too late to turn 'em in, and even if it weren't, it's too much trouble."

They drove on, up the Drive, and on to the outskirts of the city. It was cool, the traffic was unusually light. Ellen took off her hat and leaned back against the upholstery, sighing for sheer pleasure. She had not realized she was so tired.

There was a parking place, high on the bluffs overlooking the river, and from it they could see the lights of the city and the opposite shore.

Bartlett said, after a moment, when the throb of the engine had ceased, and night seemed to close in about them with its many stars and its dark silence:

"When you had the letter Bill gave you, from me . . . did you wonder what I meant when I said I had something to ask you?" He waited a moment, and as she did not answer, went on: "I meant, perhaps, I had something to *tell* you, Ellen. It's just that I love you, so much. I've loved you from the moment I first saw you, out there in the street, worried over Bill and his funny little pup. You must have known," he said, low. "It isn't in reason that you haven't known."

Manlike, he hadn't asked anything—hadn't actually proposed. Took it perhaps for granted that she knew. Or, didn't he? She said, twisting her hands together:

"I—we haven't known one another very long, Frank."

"You don't mean that. Do you care for me, Ellen, at all?"

She wanted to tell him. Yes, I love you. As much as you love me. More, perhaps, who knows? But a thousand things crowded into her mind, halted her tongue. She said, faintly, as he leaned toward her, tried to tighten the clasp of the arm he had put about her shoulders:

"Frank, don't. Please. Let me think. I——" She looked up at him in the clear starlight.

"I care more for you than anyone I know," she said tremulously, and then at his low, broken laugh of triumph, she drew away. "But—I can't be bound," she said wildly, "there's so much to consider. I mean . . . my mother and——"

That sobered him.

"I know. She doesn't like me. Why?" he asked gravely.

"You don't understand her," Ellen said in defense. "She's had an unhappy time, and is, as you know, an invalid." She thought, if I explain I'll have to tell him about Coral. I can't. I haven't any right. Not now. Not yet . . . "She's distrustful of strangers," said Ellen, low, afraid.

"But—" he began, in honest bewilderment.

Ellen went on. "There's my work," she said. "I want to make you understand it, Frank. It means so much to me. I was born in the neighborhood. I grew up there; watched it change. Wanted, always, from the time I was a youngster, to help, to do something constructive for the people I had always known. I—I've just begun. I have to go on with it. I couldn't give it up, not now——"

She stopped. She felt her face flush, turn hot with the scarlet color that spread to her forehead and ears. Why had she said that? He hadn't asked her to. She heard him saying dimly:

"I wouldn't want you to give it up. Not now. I know how you feel. Sometimes I hate it for you, the things you have to do, the things you have to see, misery, wretchedness, dirt, despair. But I honor you for it, darling. Only, I couldn't wait any longer, I had to tell you, I had to tell you I love you."

She said piteously, "Can't we go on, as we were, for a little while?"

"You won't keep me waiting too long?" he begged. "You've given me something to go on with, that much I'm grateful for, you don't know how grateful. But you haven't told me that you love me."

She said, after a moment, under her breath, "Frank, *I don't know.*"

But she did.

Presently he straightened up and squared his shoulders.

"All right," he told her. "When you do know, I know you'll be honest enough to tell me. We won't plan anything. We'll just go on. But I'm a difficult person to discourage, Ellen, a little bit of hope goes a long way with me, you see."

She said:

"Thank you, Frank . . . please, will you take me home now?"

"It's early," he reminded her, disappointed.

"I know, but my head aches a little and . . . I'd like to think," she said frankly. "I mean . . . "

He nodded and presently they were driving back in an almost complete silence. She said, as they neared her corner:

"I'm not going to ask you in, mother has company with her, and——"

"That's all right," he told her. "I'll call you tomorrow if I may. I have to go out of town again soon. Promised some people I'd go to them for a week-end. Wish," he said, smiling, "wish you'd come, Ellen."

She shook her lovely head.

"I couldn't," she said, "I don't know your friends."

"But you will know them," he said eagerly. "I want you to. This particular couple, they're grand people, you'd like them a lot and they'd be crazy about you."

"I couldn't," she said again. "I couldn't leave mother. Nancy's vacation comes soon."

"Is she going away?"

"Not for more than a night or two at a time."

"What about your month's holiday?"

"I'll stay here," she said.

"Then I shall too," he declared, "and you'll dine with me every night—and——"

"No, Frank——"

It occurred to her how very little she knew about him. Where he went, what he did, who his friends might be. He led an entirely separate life of his own. She said, quickly:

"Please, you mustn't stay in town because of me. I know you must go places and do things summers, don't you?"

"Not this summer," he told her.

They had reached the house. They sat there a moment and then as he made no move to get out and open the door for her, she laid her slim hand on the handle. His own hand touched her shoulder, and drew her back.

"Wait, just a moment. Please . . . don't go," he begged, low, "not yet. I——"

Jim O'Connor was at the Lenz house. He was talking to Dot Brown. Dot was on the stoop, waiting for Dan. Dan was out, working. She was worried about him. Suppose something happened. Jim was saying: "I'm going next door to take my aunt home. You look lonesome, Dot."

A little laughter, a little wisecracking. A startled exclamation and Jim was leaving, going next door :

Dot, her hands to her mouth was crying, furiously, running into the house . . .

But the two in the car heard nothing, saw no one.

"Ellen, *please*——"

His face was very close to her own. His arms about her, strong, steady, unrelenting. She gave a half sob and closed her eyes and lifted her mouth to his own, generously, sweetly. He kissed her, long; hard. He said, "You're so terribly sweet . . . "

Jim, on the steps, saw.

He waited for no second look. He slipped into the entry like a shadow, pressing the button marked Adams with a strong thumb. His dark face was ashen, twisted, his mouth set in a straight line.

When Ellen reached the apartment, Jim was there ahead of her. He greeted her casually enough. His aunt, fat, placid, kissed her. "How grand you look," said Miss O'Connor, "Sure, you're not working so hard as Jim was saying you are, to have that fine color."

Her cheeks were flushed, her eyes shone. She thought that her mouth must betray her, sealed, with the crimson seal of Frank's kiss. She stammered something, fled to the bedroom.

A moment or two later Jim and his aunt left. Mrs. Adams was tired. Ellen helped her to bed immediately and her mother asked, drowsily, "Did you enjoy the play?"

"The play?" She was half in dreams. Her mother said fretfully: "What's the matter with you, Ellen? Tell me about it. Did you like it?"

"We didn't go," she answered, after a moment. "It was too hot. We want riding instead."

"Well, I never!" Mrs. Adams stared. She said, after a moment, "I see." It seemed to Ellen that she must see. That everyone must see. Mrs. Adams said, "I don't approve of you driving all over town alone at night with that young man, Ellen. But I suppose there's no use my saying so."

"No use," admitted Ellen, laughing. But her mother knew that beneath the laughter there ran the undercurrent of absolute determination. She turned her face to the wall, wounded; and afraid.

Ellen, back in the living room, was picking up, tidying, opening windows in order to postpone the moment when she would have to go to bed and think. There was a little knock on the door. A double knock. Low, almost like a scratch.

She opened it, wondering. And stood back. Jim! He said hoarsely, "I had to see you."

"Jim, it's so late."

"Not very."

"Mother's in bed. You can't come in here," she said.

"If she hears, tell her I came back for something my aunt left. A purse—anything. Ellen?" His hand shot out, seized her wrist. "Come into the hall a moment."

She said bewildered, "You didn't ring the buzzer."

"The front door's open on the latch. I left it that way." He was drawing her into the hall. With a little gasp of resignation she permitted herself to be led. The hallway was dim. They were alone. He began at once furiously:

"I saw you . . . in the car . . . in that . . . in *his* arms . . . "

She asked quietly enough:

"What business is it of yours?"

"It's my business, all right. I'll make it my business. You belong to me, do you hear?"

His dark tortured young face was thrust close to hers. He said bitterly:

"I'm not good enough for you, am I? Always putting me off, laughing at me. Giving me a kiss now and then as you'd give a kid a stick of candy to shut him up. But tonight——I *saw* you, I tell you. I'll kill that bastard!" said Jim.

She cried out furiously, trying to keep her voice down, twisting her hands that shook from anger one within the other, "You've no right, no *right* . . . "

"I have a right," he said sullen, "to look after my own."

"I'm not yours!" she said.

"No? Some day you'll come to your senses," he

told her; "meantime if you don't tell Bartlett to lay
off, I will."

She said:

"You'll do nothing of the kind. If you dare . . .
I'll never speak to you again."

She meant it. He knew it. He turned from anger
to pleading, his dark eyes soft, his hands eloquent,
his voice gentler.

"Ellen, please . . . forgive me. I'm out of my head
with jealousy. I know I'm a fool. But . . . all these
years . . . and then, the first man who comes along.
You know I'm crazy about you . . . there's no one
else . . . never will be. Ellen, listen. Forget me, forget my feelings. Think of this. You know me, you've
always known me; since we were kids. This fellow,
what do you know about him. You never laid eyes on
him until a few months ago. What do you know
about him?" he asked again. "Nothing. That he's a
lawyer! That he has an office and a car! How do you
know he isn't married? How do you know he isn't
playing you for a fool, laughing to think how easy
you are . . . "

"Ellen . . . "

It was her mother calling, restless, perhaps
aware although she had no visual proof that Ellen
was not in her room next door.

Ellen said:

"I must go. Please, please let me go, Jim. I——"

He turned and went down the hall, his shoulders stooped, weariness and despair in every line of his figure. That's torn it, I guess, he told himself. Would he ever forget? he wondered. Ellen, close in Bartlett's arms, kissing . . .

Ellen was back in her mother's room. Her mother said: "I must have dozed off. I didn't hear you when I woke up. Where were you?"

"I went out into the hall for a moment," Ellen told her, trying to control her voice. "Go back to sleep, darling. I'm going right to bed."

In her room she sat down and regarded herself blindly in the mirror. Here were her eyes, her gray eyes, that wavered and fell before her own regard. Here was the red, shaken mouth which Frank had made his own . . .

Jim. Jim had no right. She hated him suddenly, bitterly, and it seemed implacably.

And yet——?

What *did* she know of Frank Bartlett? A few dull facts, but half verified.

Yet she knew him. By heart.

He hadn't asked her to marry him. Still, if she had said she loved him? She hadn't said it. He'd said about her work, "I wouldn't want you to give it up . . . "

If he had wanted to marry her, would he have said that?

She put her suddenly cold hands to her face. Cool against the heat of cheeks. Bewilderment, doubt . . . eating at her. She said aloud, after a long moment, "I won't believe . . . *anything*."

Jim, ranging the street, stopping to speak to the officer on the beat, coming back to stare at the windows of Ellen's home. No light. She'd gone to bed then.

He sunk his hands in his pockets, curled into fists. She was in love with Bartlett then . . .

Someone spoke his name. A stocky man, coming home late. Jim whirled about on his heel. It was Dan Brown.

"What you hanging around here for?" asked Dan grimly. "Knew I was going to be out, didn't you? Scram, see," said Dan. "Dot's not interested."

"How," asked Jim dangerously, all his emotions of the past hour crystallizing into an insane dislike of this intruder, "how do you get that way exactly?"

"Dot's told me," said Dan, "how you pass by now and then . . . and stop for a *friendly* word. Leave her alone, do you hear me?" said Dan. "And take this to remember me by."

He was shorter than Jim. But he packed a wallop. "Damn you," said Jim, staggering a little under the blow, his hand flung up to his face.

The cop on the beat strolled toward them. Jim turned and went the other way. What if he had a word to say to Dot now and then? He hadn't meant to upset her tonight. She used to be pretty free with her own speech, after all. What harm was there in a little kidding? And Dan hadn't known about tonight. Not yet.

Reaching his own house a tall young figure slouched out of the darkness.

"Jim!" said someone in a low, heavy voice, much accented, "I been lookin' for you. I'm quitting, see?"

Jim's eyes were swelling. He said abruptly.

"No, you're not. Come to the office tomorrow, Fontana. No, meet me at Tuccio's—at noon."

"But I tella you, I'm quit——"

"Oh, go to hell," said Jim, and turned on his heel and went into his own door.

CHAPTER NINE

You couldn't, Ellen discovered, go on "as you were."
The situation between herself and Bartlett had
changed, subtly. He was considerate; sometimes she
found herself thinking, with a little scorn of her own
inconsistency, *too considerate*. They met, frequently;
and when he left town for a week-end, a brief holiday, flowers came in his stead, notes. Now and then
there were moments brimmed, as a cup is brimmed
with wine, with a dark, beautiful danger. Moments
when they were alone, in the car, in the secrecy of
her dim, empty hallway. The moments passed, hastened by her small plea for pity . . . "Can't you
see we mustn't, it isn't fair, not to either of
us," and by his surrender. Sometimes, leaving
him, she wished, almost savagely, that he would
sweep all her hesitation and doubt aside, close his

ears to her "sensible" arguments, take her into his arms . . .

But he didn't.

Add to this Jim's growing insistence, his impatience, his sullen suspicions, and her mother's increasing dislike of Bartlett, her discomfort, perfectly apparent, when he came to the house, and you have Ellen's history. She was nervous, a little sharp-tongued, she lost weight.

Nancy's vacation came and went. During it, as had been planned, she and her mother went for a few days to Cousin Laura's little seaside cottage. During those days Ellen made every known excuse not to see Frank Bartlett. He had been complaining for some time that he never saw her save in comparative public, in restaurants, and theaters, in the midst of traffic. He was not, therefore, to be put off when the small family left town. The least Ellen could do was to give him her free Sunday.

They drove out into the country where the hills were very green and a little lost blue lake was dropped like a jewel into the valley. Frank had brought a picnic basket, complete, and they ate their luncheon by the narrow sandy lake beach, and afterwards he leaned back against a great boulder and smoked a pipe and looked at Ellen, the sun turning her hair to splendid gold, and smiled, and was, for the moment, happy.

They had agreed, or rather Ellen had decreed and he had been forced to agree, that this one day would pass without any discussion of their personal problems. They talked of a hundred things. Of himself, for instance. Ellen asked him something about his little boyhood and later life and he told her readily enough. "Nothing," he said ruefully, "very exicting. I'm a very average man, my dear."

But he went on to talk of his work, and some of his more sensational cases, and she listened, enchanted, sifting the sand through her slender fingers. "Sometime," he told her, "we must come out here in the fall when the trees have turned. I'll bring a steak and a coffee pot and we'll make a fire, and you'll do the cooking. Or don't you like camping?"

She would love it, she said; not that she had had much opportunity.

He knew a place in the mountains, he told her, very wild and very secret, with a lake like this one, only less "domestic," and great sentinel-seeming trees against a blazing blue sky. In the autumn they were clear torches burning up to heaven. There was a camp there, he said, a shack built of logs, with the bark still on. There was a fireplace, big enough to walk into, and plenty of logs. And the nights in the fall were cold and very clear and there were a million stars, more or less. It was, he said, a place for lovers. "For you," he said, "and for me . . . "

She was silent then, turning to repack the basket. For—lovers.

They had dinner somewhere along the road and danced. And then drove home. He took her up to her door. "You'll let me come in for a moment?" he begged.

"No—" She smiled at him to soften the sting of the refusal. "No," she said again; and then, "I'm awfully sleepy, Frank."

She was, her lids were drowsy with summer sun and summer winds and the long day in the open. Her hair was a tumbled mass of pale gold, warm silver and her gray eyes were dreaming. But her heart was wakeful enough, hammering against her side.

Now, he caught her to him for a brief, breathless, mindless moment. He said the thing that Jim had said, but it made a different pattern in her brain. "You belong to me," he said. "When will you realize it and tell me so . . . Ellen, will you—will you——?"

But she reached up her free hand and laid it across his lips, and as he kissed the palm, twisted out of his hold and slipped inside the door. She leaned against it, panting a little. What had been the end of that unfinished sentence had she permitted it to come to its conclusion? She knew. "Will you marry me . . . will you risk an estrangement with your mother, will you give up your work . . . ?"

But she had not permitted it, afraid perhaps lest she surrender, seduced by sun and wind and the shining of blue water and the sense of his nearness, all day long.

But she slept, smiling. It would come out all right, somehow. Her mother would recover from this baseless terror and dislike, as one recovers from a fever, and perhaps, for a little, he might let her go on working, if not in this job, then in some voluntary work.

The next morning as she was leaving the house she was astonished to see Gilda Esposito hurrying toward her, her slim arms burdened with a package. "I hoped to catch you before you left," she said, smiling, pretty as paint. "Mother sent this. It's homemade wine. She told me to tell you it was good for you, it would make you strong."

Ellen took the package, laughing a little, and Gilda waited while she went back and put it in the house. When she returned, "That was good of her, Gilda," she said, "I'll stop in and tell her so. How is she?"

"She's all right," said Gilda.

"Like your new job?"

"I'm crazy about it. I'm going to get somewhere, some day," promised Gilda, black eyes glowing.

"I'm sure you will. Father all right, too, and Mike?"

"They're fine. Mike's been going to school all year, nights. He drives a taxi daytimes, you know. Father wishes he wouldn't, but what is there to do? There isn't enough money in the business for them both," explained Gilda. "Not that either Father or Mother care about money. But Mike does, of course. You can't blame him. He wants to go ahead."

They parted and Ellen went her way. It was a terribly hot day. Leaving the sub-station a little while afterwards she saw the ambulance of the City Hospital clang toward her. A heat prostration, possibly, or another case of polio. The continued heat, she reflected, wouldn't help matters any. The epidemic would never get under control until the summer passed and cold weather set in.

On the ambulance, a white figure, leaning out, waving. That would be Pete, she thought. She wondered vaguely why he never came to see them any more. Perhaps it hurt too much. Yet, probably by now, he'd forgotten—Coral.

The last advertisement she had had inserted in the theatrical papers had brought no answers. She was always looking though, always wondering. Surely if Coral knew how dearly she would be welcomed, she would come home to them. If she could. If she were not long past her earthly homecoming.

Not the first time Ellen had admitted this possibility nor yet the hundredth, yet it never failed to sicken her, to turn her heart cold, and her palms damp with the little icy prickles of sweat.

She cut short her free time at noon to stop in at the Espositos. They lived over the fruit and vegetable store. A cluttered apartment, but clean. Mrs. Esposito was a mountain of flesh, a smiling mountain. She helped in the store part of the day, but when Ellen reached there Esposito, a tall lean man, darkly handsome, his black hair feathered with white, told her that his wife was upstairs, cooking. He had a helper in the store, a half-grown boy, a nephew, he told Ellen.

The Espositos had always interested her. "Mike," his Americanization apparent in his name, and Gilda; and the father, who was, she had often thought, considerably above his neighborhood, the fat and smiling wife, hysterical, as Ellen knew, quick-tempered, sentimental, speaking very little English, just enough to get along with, although her husband's English was fluent and almost as unaccented as the children's.

She spent a few moments with Mrs. Esposito in the spotless kitchen, with its odor of oil and garlic, thanking her for remembering her. "It maka da good red blood," Mrs. Esposito said, "gooda for healt'."

Esposito came up to eat his dinner. "You stay," begged Mrs. Esposito of Ellen. She added something in rapid Italian to her husband and he laughed and translated. "She says you are too thin, all Americans are too thin," he told her, white teeth gleaming. "She wants you to take dinner with us. She's always complaining about Gilda, you know, trying to make her fat."

Ellen stayed. She liked the Espositos. And it was a good opportunity to find out about the little Vitar boy next door. She had been called in there a week or two previously to look at the child. There was a suspicion that the stepmother ill-treated him. If so, something had to be done, and quickly. But all her questioning of the other neighbors had brought forth no fruit. They were afraid, she thought, of Vitar himself and his dark, thin, dynamic second wife. . . .

During dinner—soup and ravioli, spaghetti and melon—the hospitable Mrs. Esposito talked continuously about Gilda and about Mike. Her husband, smiling, translated. They were both intensely proud of the two children. "So American," said Esposito, with, it seemed to Ellen, a certain wistfulness.

She managed to speak of the Vitar boy. Esposito shook his head and held up his hand to stem his wife's eager flow of conversation. Mrs. Esposito understood English far better than she spoke it, as is often the case. Yes, Esposito told Ellen, frowning, the child was ill-treated, the woman beat him with a leather strap. You could hear him screaming.

Ellen nodded, somberly, and said nothing. "Sometimes we beat our children, because we are hasty and because we love them. Not this woman. She hates— the other woman's child. And Vitar is afraid of her. Sicilians. She is quick with the knife. They have been in the courts already, one, two times."

Ellen presently took her departure. Standing a moment at the doorway, Esposito having left and gone down to the shop, she was saying good-bye to his wife, when she saw a tall dark young man coming up the stairs. He carried a small package in his hand. He hesitated, seeing Ellen; and Mrs. Esposito's face darkened. She screamed at him, in Italian. He said something, thrust the package into her hands. *Gilda*, Ellen caught that much and left again. Mrs. Esposito held the package gingerly, opened it. A little box fell out. She picked it up, stooping and grunting. A string of imitation pearls. She tossed them from her. "*Madonna!*" said Mrs. Esposito to Ellen, "that Fontana. Always after mia Gilda. She not like heem."

Ellen left, smiling a little. So Gilda had a beau, whom she didn't like, whom, presumably, her mother and father didn't like, who brought strings of pearl beads to lay at her feet. Literally. For when Ellen had last seen them, the string was, contemptuously, upon the floor.

She went on to the sub-station to make her reports and to see what could be done about the Vitar boy, to get in touch with SPCC and other authorities. The boy should be taken away from those dreadful people.

So much cruelty in the world.

So much kindness, too. She thought of the Espositos, a happy, united family for all their bickerings, which were, she judged, merely the usual disagreements between two generations: one, exemplified by the mother at least, clinging to old customs, to a lost country . . .

And now Nancy and her mother had returned, a little color in Mrs. Adams' face, a little weight on her small bones while Nancy had managed to tan beautifully during her short stay. "I'm glad," stated Mrs. Adams, "to get back. Much as I like the country, I hate visiting." She was, it was evident, more at ease among her own things, in her own place.

"It was swell," said Nancy. "All I did was eat and sleep and bake in the sun. Chick," added Nancy, grinning without self-consciousness, "came down Sunday though."

"What have you been doing?" Mrs. Adams wanted to know of Ellen.

Ellen told her.

Mrs. Adams was silent. She then remarked, "I hope you had good sense enough not to bring Mr. Bartlett to the apartment while I was away."

"Only," said Ellen, "as far as the door. You *do* stay conventional, don't you, Mother?"

"It pays," said Mrs. Adams, and her eyes darkened.

A few days later, just before the start of her own vacation, Ellen, coming out of a house on the outskirts of her district, was walking down the street, when from a tall, narrow, dingy looking lodging house a woman rushed out, wringing her hands and screaming. "Police!" she was shrieking, at the desperate top of a high-pitched voice. An elderly woman, slatternly, her gray hair uncombed, carpet slippers on her feet, a soiled blue wrapper caught about her meager bones.

People started to hurry toward her but she had seen Ellen the instant after the scream had left her lips. She ran to her. "Nurse," she said, "Nurse!" Her loose lips were white, they shook. "A woman— my house—suicide—you can smell the gas——"

The officer on the beat hurried up. Ellen knew him, of old. He nodded to her briefly. "What's this? Stand back, you!" he ordered the little gathering crowd.

He jerked a thumb at Ellen. Together they raced into the house and up the rickety stairs, the woman at their heels, her slippers tapping loosely on the uncovered boards. "Top floor, back," she gasped.

A knot of people, possibly other lodgers, were gathered on each landing.

The sweet smell, faint and insidious, reached them. There was no need of a guide.

They reached the door. It was locked. The cop said to Ellen tersely, "Hold everything!"

A shove of his strong shoulder, another, another, and the flimsy lock had broken.

The woman stayed outside, wringing her hands, crying weakly. There was a permanent odor as of gin and unwashed flesh about her.

The room was small, dark, narrow. There was one dirty window. There was a bureau which had seen better days. A straight-backed chair with a coat flung over it. There was a washstand. There was also a narrow bed.

Ellen, choking, got to the window and opened it. The officer was bending over the bed. The pipe line to the gas jet had been wrenched away, by what desperate and despairing hands, and was pouring its deadly invisible freight into the room. The cop said, "We'll have to get her out of this."

He carried the woman who lay on the bed out of the room and down to a lower landing. He said: "Will you take charge, nurse? I'll ring headquarters and get an ambulance and the gas company. She's not dead," finished the cop, without brutality but with the indifference engendered by a hundred such scenes in a workaday world.

She was not dead. She lay there fully dressed. She had in her poor cheeks the false glow of color which gas poisoning brings. Ellen knelt down beside her. The lodging house keeper came closer. "She only come here last night," she said. "Said she'd pay me today for a week in advance."

Ellen was staring down at the unconscious woman. There was a window on the landing which a moment before she had raised, high. A little wind stirred through. A little sun. Ellen thought, I mustn't faint, I *mustn't faint* . . .

She was working, while she fought against the sickness, the blackness which crept over her. Working. Nothing much she could do until the emergency crew came with its inhalators, its trained men.

The cop was back.

"Not very far gone, is she?" he wanted to know.

Ellen said faintly:

"Get the people away, will you? She needs all the space and air we can give her."

Dark hair, with red lights in it; faint color in thin cheeks, eyes that were closed but that would be blue, Ellen knew, if ever they opened again.

"There's the emergency wagon," reported the cop, after what seemed years.

The men were coming up the stairs. The police-man had left, was scattering the people crowded on the landings, at the door. He came back, as the gas company's crew came in and started to work in their matter-of-fact way. One or two of the men knew Ellen, nodded to her. "Tough break, Sister," said one, to Ellen.

Sister——

She spoke to the policeman, standing a little apart, her hand on his blue sleeve, her eyes never leaving the slim form stretched out on the dirty boards, wrapped in the blankets Ellen had managed to pull off the bed and put about her. The cop gulped and swore, under his breath.

She thought of the police blotter, the report that must go in, and so she said, merely, "I'll attend to things when the ambulance comes. I know her, you see."

The ambulance clanged down the street. Ellen's heart was choking her. Pete would be on it. Oh, God, why hadn't she thought of that!

"Coral, Coral, why did you do it? Didn't you know how much we love you, didn't you know that we wanted you to come home?"

CHAPTER TEN

Down the street swung the dark ambulance, leaving a trail of sound, sinister sound, the backwash of an insistent clangor. Hurry, hurry, hurry, screamed the ambulance. It stopped before the undistinguished front door of a brownstone house. People were standing clustered closely about there. A second policeman had come up. Traffic was more or less halted. People were whispering, exclaiming. "Wisht," said a gaunt individual, "wisht *I* had the noive . . ."

People, morbid, curious, making the most of the mordant moment which brought into the drab pattern of discouraged lives a thread of scarlet, a symbol of danger, a vicarious excitement.

This was life; it was death. Indivisible.

Pete McGregor swung himself off the ambulance

and spoke briefly to his driver. He ran up the steps of the house, carelessly shoving aside the people who, despite the law's edict, had gathered on the peeling stoop. "Suicide, doc? Is she dead?" asked someone. "How the hell do I know?" inquired the interne.

He spoke to the policeman who was on the stairs. "Gas," explained the cop briefly.

"What! Another?" asked Pete. "Can't they do something different for a change? This gets monotonous."

Hard-boiled, you see. Because he had to be. Because his own years had been so strange and difficult. The boyhood of the neighborhood, this neighborhood. More to eat, warmer clothes than a lot of fellows. Baseball, spring evenings; football; a second-hand bike. School and a girl with dark thick braids, roughened into curls at the ends. A darkness shot through with ruddy lights. Blue eyes, very deep. *His* girl. Growing up, growing out of the adolescent braggart attitude toward girls, growing into manhood, very young manhood, loving, planning to work, to *be* something. For her. Then, disaster, and the drifting downward. Too young, too hurt to pull himself up by the boot-straps and tell himself there were other girls . . . a pool-room brawl, a young man rescued from the quick flash of a knife, out of sheer perversity, perhaps, because Pete didn't happen to like the knife's possessor. Then, inter-

The stretcher had been shoved into the waiting car. The cop swung himself aboard. Pete said to Ellen, "It can't be Coral."

He knew it was.

She said dully, "I ought to go with her. Nancy will come right away. Pete, be gentle with her, won't you?"

He laughed. He had to laugh. He couldn't help it. She said, her eyes blazing:

"If you dare to——" She said, and her eyes were tragic and accusing: "How do you know—anything —about her? And what right have you to judge her? Or any other man?"

He lifted his hand in a signal to his driver. The lodging-house keeper pushed her way through the stammering circle of people and cried urgently, "Where's my money— She said she'd pay—to-day." The woman stared at her.

Ellen said, curiously, "She has paid, hasn't she?" Pete's hand flashed toward his pocket. And Ellen said, strongly, "No . . ."

It had all taken only a moment or so. The ambulance, clanging, drove off. Ellen stood on the curb. The woman plucked at her sleeve; she said, whining, "She won't give me no money now."

"I'll pay," said Ellen.

She paid. And went away slowly. The crowd, some

of them, followed, asking their interminable questions. She shook them off.

Presently she went into a phone booth and called her home. Nancy, if only Nancy would answer. Waiting, she looked at her wrist watch. No, she'd be asleep. Nancy, please answer, *please*.

"Ring them again, operator," she said sharply, "I know someone's at home."

Nancy's voice came to her, thick and petulant with drowsiness. Ellen asked, "Nancy, where's Mother?"

"For crying out loud!" said Nancy. "What's happened? She went out for a walk I guess, with Mrs. Lenz. I heard 'em go. What's up?"

The drowsiness was clearing from her voice and eyes. She listened while Ellen talked, briefly, rapidly. No time to break things gently. Just keep it from her mother, that was all.

Nancy said, in a dull voice, a voice that was flat and oddly bruised sounding:

"I'll get dressed and go right over. I'll say—oh, anything. Leave a note. Mrs. Lenz will stay with Mother, or Mrs. Meader. Get home as soon as you can."

"No, I'll go to the hospital," Ellen told her, "at the noon hour. Meet me there, if you can."

She hung up and went about her work. Efficient, unsentimental, sympathetic, capable. She couldn't think, but her hands thought for her. She gave a strong finger 'on the pulse beating in the too thin wrist. A good pulse, rapid perhaps, but good in tone and quality. Presently Coral opened her eyes. Such very blue eyes. The lashes, broken short with mascara, were heavy. She said, "Nancy?" She said, "It isn't Nancy . . . it's Ellen." She tried to sit up. Ellen eased her back on the pillow. "Take it easy, Coral," she said, her tone perfectly matter-of-fact.

"Does Mother know . . .?" whispered Coral.

"No . . . You'll come home tomorrow. We'll say you've been ill, in the hospital. I'll tell her. You're not to worry."

"Tell Pete, please—stay away——" said Coral.

Nothing astonished her. She was going home. She was too weak and sickened to ask questions. She'd leave it to Ellen—to Ellen . . . Once, before she slept again, she raised the incredible eyes—she said, and tried to smile, "What you made up for, Ellen?" and indicated the uniform.

Then she slept.

Nancy came back and Ellen went out, to get her calls, to do the rest of her work. The afternoon was light enough. She was able to be back at the hospital quite early. "What about Mother?" she asked Nancy.

"I phoned Mrs. Meader to tell her that one of the girls was sick and had no one and I'd gone to the

YW to see what I could do." She was drooping with weariness.

"Go home and go to bed, until time to get to work," Ellen ordered her. "I'll see to all this."

They were talking in the corridor. Then Ellen went back to the ward.

"All right, Coral?"

"So much better, I——"

"Don't try to talk. Rest. You'll be taken care of here, tonight. Tomorrow, we'll bring you home."

Tomorrow, she thought, my vacation starts. A lucky break. It all fits in.

"Sleep, Coral . . ."

She could sleep. She could eat a little, a very little. Pete, his young face set and old under his sandy hair, spoke with the charge nurse. "Go easy," said Pete. "Half starved. A malnutrition case, if ever I saw one."

It had all been fixed up. The paragraph in the papers wouldn't amount to a hill of beans. People wouldn't even notice it. So many suicides anyway. Suicides, attempted or otherwise, weren't news, unless they concerned well-known people, brokers jumping out of windows, or men who took the leap from bridges and made their going a sensational one. A girl who took a room for the night and turned on the gas——that wasn't news, was it? Just a commonplace, an everyday commonplace.

He said to Ellen, "She won't talk to me."

"Later," said Ellen. "We'll take her home to-morrow. You'll sign her out, Pete?"

"Sure——"

Hands in pockets, very hard-boiled.

He'd given Coral's name. The stage name. Cora Carmen. The name he had hated. It had been bitter on his tongue . . .

Tomorrow, they'd sign Cora Carmen out.

Ellen said:

"You'll see she's looked after tonight? Oh, if only she hadn't had to come here——"

"What's wrong with the hospital?" he demanded.

"Nothing. But—a ward, a charity ward!"

"We don't have private rooms," he told her, and tried to grin.

"No . . . but . . ."

"Run along," he said. "I'll look after her."

Afterwards he wondered if it hadn't been a vow.

She said:

"Tomorrow I start my vacation. I'll come get her. She—she hasn't talked much, but I think she's glad."

She went back alone to the bed and slipped into the tiny space. The curtains were still drawn. Mannering had seen to that. There were other women in the ward. Many of them. Some, indescribable. There was a woman fighting her way out of ether. There was a woman, an alcoholic. There was one who lay quietly and plucked at the counterpane.

"You're going . . .?"

Coral clutched at her, with her hot thin hands. She said: "I—Oh, Ellen, I never meant you to find me. I came back, the way a dog crawls back, I suppose. I thought maybe I'd see you—and Mother—and Father—and Nancy. From a distance. I didn't mean you to know. There was nothing on me, you see, I couldn't have been identified." She gasped a little for breath, she said, "I've always been a flop, I couldn't even kill myself—properly."

The bright tears ran down Ellen's uncontrolled face. Her eyes remained open—wide. She kept her voice steady. It was as if someone else wept. She said, "You're not to think about anything. You're coming *home*."

"I couldn't try it again. I haven't," said Coral bitterly, "the guts. I was afraid, Ellen, when I lay down on the bed. Afraid, I tell you. No, I couldn't do it again. Will they take me in at home?" she asked. And she added, "I haven't any fight left."

No. No fight left. Nothing left with which to fight.

Ellen said, "Go to sleep, Coral. I'll come for you tomorrow."

Then she went home.

Coral didn't know that their father had died. She'd have to know, "I'll have to tell her," thought

Ellen. Her mother must be told something. Yes, what she had agreed with Nancy was as good as anything else. Coral had come home. On the way home she had been taken ill. Of some disease. What? Flu. Flu was as good as anything. High temperature, delirium. She'd been taken to the hospital, unable to tell them who she was. That was the story. It had to be.

She reached the apartment. Walking up the short flight of the stoop she had thought she couldn't, possibly, go a step further. Her mother met her at the door.

"Nancy," said her mother indignantly, "has been gone most of the day. Someone sick, she said, a girl she knew. As if she didn't need her sleep. She'll be sick next. Mrs. Meader," she went on, "was kind enough to stay until Nancy came home. I declare I've been so worried!"

Ellen sat down, tossing her hat on the table. She put her fingers through her hair. Her scalp hurt. She ached all over. "I hope I haven't picked up something," she told herself dully, trying to think.

No, it was fatigue, it was shock, and she'd had nothing to eat since morning. Her mother said, "Nancy's sleeping . . ."

"I'll get supper," said Ellen. She rose and dragged herself into the kitchen. Before she had gone to bed, Nancy had made gestures toward getting things together. She'd let Nancy sleep. however, and give her something before she went to work.

"That Mr. Bartlett called a few minutes ago," said Mrs. Adams. "I answered."

She sniffed audibly. Ellen came back from her puzzled and aching thoughts with a start. Frank! A different world. A person she hardly knew. Yet someone she loved. A warmth came over her, she moved about more lightly, she was freer, she could think more easily. For hours, she'd not thought of Frank. Now, thinking of him was, somehow, comfort. "He said," Mrs. Adams told her, "that he'd call again . . ."

He did so, when supper was on the table. Ellen spoke to him, briefly. No, impossible to see him tonight. She'd talk to him, say, tomorrow. She hung up on his exclamation of disappointment, cutting him short. "I have to run," she said. "Call me tomorrow then?. . . 'Bye . . ."

Supper was over. The most difficult twenty minutes she had ever endured. She carried the dishes to the kitchen. She came back and sat down on the hassock at her mother's feet. She covered both small hands with her own. She was afraid. Yet joy, joy wouldn't kill. Joy would do almost anything, it would drive you temporarily insane, but it wouldn't kill.

She said, "Mother?" very softly and as Mrs.

Adams looked at her startled, apprehensive, she spoke her name again. She said, "Mother, I've news. Such good news. You must be strong enough to hear it. I've found Coral, Mother," she said simply. "She's coming home, tomorrow."

CHAPTER ELEVEN

No, joy does not kill. Ellen put out her hand for
the little glass with the spirits of ammonia that she
had set on the table back of her mother. The amyl
nitrite was in the black bag there. But nothing was
necessary, no restorative. The little pinched-looking
face was scarlet with the rush of startled blood, then
it was white again. "Drink this, Mother," said Ellen.

The small hands pushed the glass away.

"No . . . where is she? . . . take me to her . . ."
demanded Mrs. Adams. "I—oh, Ellen, Ellen, are you
sure?"

She was crying but it was not the sort of weeping
which would hurt, which would bring on an attack.
Ellen said, steadily:

"Quite sure. I've seen her. She's been very sick.
You see, she was coming home from, from out
156

the kitchen to put on coffee and cut bread and butter and make sandwiches. Then she went into the bedroom and told Nancy all she had said. "That's the story," she told her; "you'll remember it?"

There were tears when Nancy came out of the bedroom, the weak tears of happiness. "To keep it from me all day," her mother said, reproachfully.

"Blame it on Ellen," Nancy told her, "she wanted to tell you herself. She was afraid you'd be too upset."

"Upset?" said Mrs. Adams. "I've never felt as well, no, not in years. Pete found her, you say?" She paled. "Then she was in——"

She halted.

"Yes. But, you see, no one knew who she was. Naturally she was taken to the hospital," said Ellen hastily, "to that hospital. And it was some days before Pete happened to see her."

Well, that was gotten by. Her heart, which had tightened, was released again.

"Pete," murmured her mother, remembering.

Nancy finished her supper. Ellen said, "You must be tired, Mother, you must get right into bed. And sleep. For tomorrow's another day and I'll have Coral home before you know it. You—you must try to be courageous," she told her mother gently; "remember, she's been very ill, we must be careful of her."

Nancy was going after her mother was in bed. Before she went she drew Ellen to the door with her and held her in a quick hard unusual embrace. "You're pretty darned marvelous," said Nancy.

Left alone, Ellen sat down at the little desk in the living room to write to Frank. He would, he'd said, call her tomorrow. She'd better write. Tomorrow, everything would be different.

She wrote quite simply.

"My sister," she said, "has come home after so many years. Everything's pretty much in a whirl, I'm writing to explain. I'm bringing her from the hospital tomorrow, she's been very ill. I'd rather you didn't phone for a day or two. I know you'll understand." She slipped out to mail it, special delivery, at the corner box.

She thought, returning to her own room, the room which would be made fresh for Coral the next day, "How will we arrange things? . . . oh, this place is so dreadfully small now!" She planned, standing in the middle of the room, a finger at her lips. Daytimes, Coral could be in the living room or in her mother's bedroom. Nights, in the other bedroom. And Ellen could sleep on the davenport. It was comfortable enough. When Coral was better, stronger, things would work out more easily.

She thought she would never sleep. Yet she slept as soon as her head touched the pillow. And suddenly it was morning. Nancy came in showing no signs of the lack of sleep of the day before. Mrs. Adams was up early. "When are you going for her?" she demanded.

"Soon, but not too soon. They'd throw me out," said Ellen, laughing.

She herself went out early, and uptown to the shops. A plain little silk dress, a thin coat, a smart quilled tam. Powder and rouge and lipstick. Underwear, nightgowns, slippers. A tailored robe, a robe of silk. Stockings. Shoes. She guessed at Coral's size, vaguely, but as it happened, correctly. Enough to go on with. A suitcase, new. She unwrapped the things in the women's rest room and packed them in the case. Coral must come home equipped.

Nothing that she had worn would come home with her.

She took a taxi to the hospital and telephoned from there for a private, comfortable car. Her vacation money, not much would be left. But she had certain savings, she could carry on and keep up her share of the apartment. Only Coral must come home head high, eyes steady, not creep home with the broken suitcase, the poor clothes——

She took the new things up to the ward with her and displayed them. "There," she said smiling to see the faint color in Coral's face and lips, and her rested eyes, "there, that's enough to go with, isn't it?"

Coral said: "You're so good. Why are you so good, Ellen?" She caught her sister's hands. "Little Ellen . . ." she said.

She tried to laugh as Ellen drew the stockings up over her lovely, too slender legs. "Ellen, you didn't tell me what you were made up for, yesterday."

"Oh, the uniform?" Ellen explained briefly, "I'm a district nurse," she said. "You know what that is, don't you?"

"Sweetness and light?" inquired Coral. She'd always been pert. She still was.

"Not exactly," Ellen told her, smiling.

"And Nancy——?"

"Works nights." Ellen elucidated fully. Coral's blue eyes widened.

"Dad . . . doesn't he kick? Ellen, will he take me back?"

Ellen looked around. They were alone, the curtains drawn. She said swiftly, steadily:

"You've got to know, darling. He's—been gone— six years . . ."

The faint color faded. Coral said after a moment: "Funny. I can't cry. I've cried so much, I suppose. Ellen, it wasn't worrying over me, was it?"

Her eyes pleaded and implored.

"It was pneumonia," said Ellen.

"He—did he forgive me?" asked Coral quietly.

"Of course," Ellen answered. She lied. She had to lie. "Of course, he forgave you. And asked for you, wanted you home."

"And me not there. Ellen, if I'd known, if I'd *known*. But I was afraid, afraid to write, afraid to come back."

"Let's not talk about that now," said Ellen.

Pete was not in evidence as they went down the corridor. Ellen carried the new suitcase, supported Coral, helped her into the elevator. When they were in the car Coral said:

"Mother? I mean, I would have thought that after Dad went she couldn't go on."

"She has gone on. She's not awfully well. It's not serious," added Ellen hastily, "but——" She explained as best she could. Coral nodded. "I'll be careful of her, too," she said. "Ellen, what have you told her?"

"That you were coming home to us. That you were taken sick on the train." She went on coaching Coral in the poor little story. "It's only," said Coral afterwards, "a half lie, isn't it?"

She spoke of Pete. "He was awfully good to me. But I couldn't bear the sight of him. I knew he hated me."

"He doesn't hate you," said Ellen.

"He knows?" asked Coral in a whisper.

"He had to know, dear; when you were brought in." She thought, we mustn't ever tell her that he was on that ambulance. Never.

"Pete, a doctor. That's funny somehow. It's not funny you're being a nurse. You always liked that sort of thing, I remember when you were very little," said Coral from her two years' seniority. "Ellen, you haven't changed much, have you? You haven't cut your hair?"

"No."

"I'm glad. I used to think of your hair. When I saw a gorgeous blonde somewhere I'd think—'pooh, not a patch on Ellen,' " said Coral.

Now her eyes widened. The car had turned a corner and was entering a familiar street. "The same house?" she asked. "I thought perhaps it would be the same. I—I wanted to look in the phone book. I didn't dare . . ."

"Mother sold it," said Ellen. "We've an apartment there. We'll be comfortable enough."

"The neighborhood's changed," Coral commented sadly. "So changed. Is Joe still cobbling shoes? He is? And is Jim still your heavy suitor? No, things haven't changed so much. And yet—nothing stands still, does it?"

The car stopped. She clung to Ellen a minute. She said, low: "I'm frightened. I can't face her.

What shall I tell her, Ellen? What shall I tell her?"

"Tell her nothing," answered Ellen clearly, "that would hurt you or her."

And now they were going up the steps, the driver carrying the bag. Now the apartment door had opened . . .

"Home . . ." said Coral, very low, and stumbled across the threshold ignoring Ellen's swift out-stretched hand, going straight into the frail arms, suddenly strong, that were held out to her.

Home . . .

And so time passed and the nine-day wonder of her homecoming faded. She was gradually becoming herself again under Ellen's watchful care. It was Ellen that saw she had nourishing food and drinks, Ellen who took her walking in the sunlight, Ellen who defended her from the neighborhood. "But I hear dot Coral Adams come home," said Mrs. Lippinsky to the neighbors. "Vonder vhere she's been all dese years. Oi, her momma must be out of her head vit joy to hev her but she don't look any too good," said Mrs. Lippinsky. "I vonder."

As a whole, however, the neighbors were kind.

Jim came, hearing the news by that underground circuit of his. Coral stared at him, laughter on his lips. "All grown up," she mocked him, "big business man now, Jimmy . . ."

And presently Frank came too. Frank, whose flowers had arrived the very day Coral had come home. "For Ellen's sister," the card read.

Coral liked him at once. She told Ellen so. "I like the new beau," she said. "He's regular. I can tell. Ellen, what's come over Jim? He's different from what he used to be."

"No, he's the same," said Ellen, laughing, "he hasn't changed a bit."

Coral's eyes were puzzled.

"Yes, he has. Ellen, are you going to marry him, or the new applicant?"

"I'm not going to marry anybody for a long time." Ellen evaded the question gaily.

"Sez you," said Coral in her old slangy way.

She wanted to work, she said. When she was strong she'd find some work. No, not the stage. Never that. She told Ellen, alone with her one day, "I never made good. Ellen, you don't know, you don't *know* . . ."

She was silent, somber. Remembering. Cheap third string road companies . . . heat and cold, odors, quarrels, dingy costumes, stale tunes . . . No, she had never made good.

The man had repudiated her. *That* man. Then the drifting away, the one-night stands, the company that had gone to Australia, the company that

CHAPTER TWELVE

But he did come.

Ellen saw him first. Her vacation was over and she had started back to work. "Not much of a vacation—for me," Frank told her ruefully, on that last evening, taking her out to dinner. "The things I had planned! But I've hardly seen you."

"You exaggerate," she contradicted, laughing. "You've seen me a lot."

"Twice, perhaps, for dinner. Other times, dropping in to call, only to find you completely surrounded by family," he reminded her.

"I had to get Coral back on her feet." She looked at him levelly. "She's had a pretty hard time, you see."

His pleasant, attractive face was grave with an unspoken sympathy.

"So I fancied. I didn't even know you had another sister," he said.

"She's been away from us for a long while," Ellen murmured. She said something vague about a family estrangement. Frank nodded.

"I imagined that," he admitted. "Once or twice she's said little things, to me. Nothing very much. But I gathered she had been on her own for some time and not in communication with you. She's a pretty fine person, isn't she?"

Ellen looked at him, radiant. She said:

"I'm glad you feel that. She's—flippant, now and then. She might give you the wrong impression. But that's not the real Coral. Underneath, she's so loyal and . . . and . . ." Her voice broke, and her shining eyes filled. She said, after a moment during which his hand reached out and covered hers, "Well, that's all over now. The loneliness, I mean; and the wandering. She's anxious to get work, and I think she'd be happier if she could find something she liked to do. But mother won't let her out of her sight."

"Your mother's changed," he remarked shrewdly.

"I know. You've noticed, too?" asked Ellen. "I suppose that was all she needed. Someone to fuss over. We never thought of that. We fussed over *her*. She hasn't been as well or as active in years. And she's so grateful."

"Grateful . . .?"

"To Providence, to Fate, to God, she'd say, for bringing Coral home again. She *believes*," said Ellen, "so she's prayed, every day, every night . . ."

"And you don't believe?" asked Bartlett seriously.

Ellen regarded him soberly. After a moment she replied, thoughtfully: "I hear; I have to doubt. I mean, there seems so much sheer, cold injustice . . . I put it badly—but some things simply don't make *sense*. Unless it's because we can't understand the pattern, can't see it as a whole, just in isolated bits. But you can't force yourself to believe by telling yourself you do. It's something you can't explain, I suppose, something that's part of you, as close as hands and feet, as little regarded, as natural. Other times when I see instances of sheer wonder, and see momentarily into a human heart, I think I do believe. I want to, anyway. The people who can, the people who do, they're the happiest, aren't they, the most useful?"

He answered awkwardly, manlike, a little embarrassed at speaking of things hitherto held in the intimate silence of his own soul.

"I was brought up in a religious household. Not a bigoted one. There's a difference, you understand. Adolescence brought the usual fevers and frets of doubting and an acquired cynicism, and years at a university the normal amount of puzzling and arguing and trying to settle all temporal and spiritual questions to one's own intellectual satisfaction. But —well, in the end one swings back. Although lawyers are commonly supposed to believe in nothing and to argue themselves out of heaven."

He paused and regarded a crumbled bit of roll.

"Forgive me. I don't usually do this. But when it comes to arguing oneself out of heaven—or being argued"—he looked at her and smiled the very engaging smile which always twisted her heart as if that organ were soft, pliable clay—"that's different. Sometimes I believe that's what you're trying to do to me, always. Argue me out of a heaven which is perfectly terrestrial and which has nothing to do with what happens to us after we die."

She asked, flushed, evading the implication:

"And what *does* happen to us after we die? Do we go on? Or is our immortality a matter of grass and trees?"

"If we *don't* go on," he said, "there isn't very much logic in the entire scheme, is there?"

It was on the following day, the first day of returning to work, that she saw Pete. He telephoned her, surprisingly, at the office.

"My night off, tonight," he told her. "I want to talk to you, Ellen."

Her heart leaped against her side, in happiness for Coral or in fear for her; she did not know which.

"Come to the house, will you?"

He said, "No, I'd rather not. Not till I've seen you, if you don't mind. Will you have dinner with me somewhere? I'll get you home early. I've got to go see the folks."

Now that Coral was at home and comparatively well, Ellen and Nancy were freer, less bound to consult each other about their evening plans. Ellen said, instantly, "All right. Where?"

He set the time and the place; a funny little Italian restaurant, in the neighborhood, or still of it, although uptowners came there for the marvelous veal in marsala, the matchess *antipasto*, and the *minestrone* that was nourishing enough for an army. Ellen had been there once or twice only in the last few years but knew it well enough.

At home she said she was going out; and made no further explanations. Her mother sighed. "Two evenings, hand running?" she murmured. Coral smiled. Her unhappy, pretty mouth was pink with health once more and touched to a brighter shade with the lipstick Ellen had brought her. "Somehow," she had said, regarding the lipstick and rouge, "these gadgets restore my self-respect. A cockeyed way to figure, isn't it? But mine."

"Ellen," she told her mother, "knows what she's doing. That's more than can be said for most of us."

Nancy lifted a dark eyebrow. Ellen spoke to her briefly, alone.

"It's Pete. I'm not saying anything to Mother and Coral. He has—something on his mind."

"Coral?"

"Perhaps."

She met him, his sandy hair ruffled into a crest, at the basement restaurant, and they went into the back room which was decorated with violent murals representing the Bay of Naples and Como, and Vesuvius in, it appeared, eruption. The ceiling was latticed and in summer paper roses were twined about it. Now, in the beginning of autumn, golden and glorious and unseasonably warm, there were synthetic autumn leaves.

The proprietor hurried up. He knew Pete. He took the order, put a fat, straw-protected bottle of red wine on the table, in bland defiance of any laws that might be existent, murmured, *"Che bella!"* when Ellen, conscious of a dull pressure at the base of her skull, took off her hat; smiled, *"Bueno appetito,"* and scurried away.

"Decent of you," said Peter to Ellen, "to come. But I had to see you. Look here, I haven't been able to sleep, or eat——"

She suggested, "Then eat, at least. Now. Later, we'll talk. You *do* look thin, Pete."

"I feel thin," he said glumly, "and I'm liable at any moment to diagnose a clear case of measles as phlebitis. That's how shot I am."

She laughed at him.

"Nonsense. Eat your antipasto and pass me the funny stuff which looks like celery and tastes like paregoric. And tell me about the hospital."

It was clear to him that she had no intention of ruining a meal with serious conversation; not that the hospital wasn't serious. But it wasn't, at least, emotional.

"Doc Travers wants me to go in with him," he said, after a while, when they had almost finished and the coffee had been brought. "I'm keen about it. They tell me I'm crazy, that I'll never make any money. Well, what of it? I have a chance to go in with Mallory, too—that's the gastric man, you know, on the Avenue, carriage trade, and all that. But somehow—I told Doc Travers I'd take him up. I wonder," said Pete, "if I'm making a mistake."

"I don't think so," Ellen answered. "What you can do down here—oh, the other isn't comparable! Besides, Pete, you know perfectly well that it would go hard with you to acquire the proper uptown bed-side manner. You'd have to practice calling on patients in your soup and fish, with a gardenia in the buttonhole."

"Good God!" exclaimed Pete, genuinely horrified.

They laughed together.

"Mallory's the man who gave me my chance, you see. Somehow I feel I owe it to him to—do as he wishes. Yet, I wouldn't fit in. I mean, I'm more at home down here, I understand these people better. I have, perhaps, more patience with them. Mallory's decent. He understands. He wouldn't hold me back, he says."

"Whatever happened to that boy of his, the one you got out of the jam?" Ellen asked curiously.

"Nothing. That's literal. He sort of drifts about. Not very bad, not very good. In a broker's office, nowadays. It just about cracked the Big Doc's heart when he wouldn't take up medicine. He married, some gal with money. They had me up to dinner once. She didn't approve of me. Said, I believe, that I smelled like a dispensary or such. Not that she'd ever been in one. Bert—that's young Mallory, was apologetic. He sort of regards me as a rescuing angel, a little soiled as to wings. He also consulted me deeply about shooting pains in the left knee or something. What he needs is a horse doctor, and a little common sense."

Dinner was over. They drank their coffee. Pete lighted a cigarette, apologizing, "I always do things backward," and offered his case to Ellen. She shook her head, smiling, "No, thanks. I don't like them, really. Now and then, if I have to. But if given my own preference, no. I leave hiding butts to Nancy." And then before she had thought, she went on. "You'll be astonished, but we've actually accustomed

Mother to Coral's smoking now and then. I would never have believed it possible. But it was too hard on Coral, she'd smoked so long, she was so nervous. I've cut her down, for her health's sake, but she actually has Mother broken in to seeing her take a cigarette, after meals. It's marvelous. I——"

She stopped. Pete's fair skin was scarlet, he was red to the roots of the untamable sandy hair. His steel-gray eyes shifted nervously, came back to hers and held them.

"You guessed it was Coral I wanted to talk to you about?"

"Of course, Pete." Her tone was quiet, steadying. Gradually the hot color receded, leaving him a little whiter than normal.

"She hates me," he muttered.

"Don't be childish, Pete. She says that about you."

"About me?" His eyes were astonished. "About me—what have I done?" he inquired, with marked bitterness.

"Nothing. Everything. Oh, she said you were good to her, in the hospital."

"Good to her . . .?" He laughed abruptly. "She hates me, I tell you. She turned her face to the wall and cried, every time she saw me."

"That doesn't sound like hate," Ellen told him.

"Perhaps it was—fear. Perhaps it was remember-ing."

"Remembering? How much has she remembered all these years? Do you think I've ever forgotten?" he asked savagely. "I've tried. No one knows—by every possible means. Some of them weren't so pretty. You know, you've heard. No good. I kept thinking of her, always, wondering . . . till my mind was sore, as if it had been beaten, as if my thoughts tore their way through. I used to walk through the wards and look at the women, the dopes, the alcoholics, the women from the street——"

"Pete—*Pete* . . ."

"Sorry. But it got me. Not knowing. What did I know . . . afterwards? Just what the newspapers had. Just what your father said. Sometimes I dream of that night I went around to your place and he was there . . . and talked to me . . . You see it had always been Coral for me since we were kids. I sound like a—radio crooner," he ended abruptly, disgusted.

Ellen reflected fleetingly that life was, after all, sentimental and melodramatic, banal and tragic, and comic, too, with the sudden senseless comedy of the custard pie. Life was like that, no matter how much we talked of hokum, no matter how trite the ancient verities seemed. . . .

She said, quietly:

"Why don't you come to see Coral, Pete? Or don't you want to? Now—that you've seen her—are you trying to tell me you're—cured?"

He said violently: "No, it's worse than ever. When I saw her there—when I brushed by you, on that filthy landing . . ." He stopped, and his face worked terribly. Ellen said:

"Please don't. We have to forget that, if we can, all of us."

"You know we can't, Ellen." He clenched his strong, nervous hand on the table. Words broke from him, isolated, ugly. She listened, unflinching.

"Why do you bother to curse—*him*, Pete? That's over. Over and done with, years and years ago."

"I know." He had the grace to flush. "I—I kept track. I looked things up, I knew men who worked on newspapers. She went back to him, didn't she, his wife? But after all . . . all these years? Why didn't she come home? Coral? What happened, in between? God knows——"

"Yes. Coral knows, too," Ellen said. She felt as if she were fighting for something dearer to her than life, fighting with words, fragile words, which broke, which turned blunt, which could not shine and dart, attack and defend as one would have them; which were rusty with the blood of things unspoken, things unspeakable; which cut two ways . . .

After a moment, during which he stared at her, she said, bravely:

"I see no reason why I should defend her to you. She's had a rotten time. A damnable time. Lonely. Lost. Hungry often. Cold." She saw him wince at that; was glad. "Earning her living, somehow, in ways she may have hated but which were clean ways, Pete. Laughing through it, hard-boiled—like you——"

"Like me?" He stared at her. "*Clean ways* . . . You're trying to tell me . . . She—she got along without love, all these years. Coral!" He was silent, remembering her dear response to his young, shy boy's passion. "Trying to tell me that there wouldn't be a hundred men mad about her, that having once——" He stopped. Ellen's eyes were blazing.

"I believe *her*," she said. "Listen, can't you see this straight? She was nothing but a youngster, dazzled by promises, thinking of the stage, of the man who offered her opportunity, in the most extravagant terms. She was a little crazy . . . you get like that when you're young and want life and good times. She was brought up in a pretty strict household. Rules and routine. And Father was alive then. He and Mother—you know, you've been with us enough. So wrapped up in one another there wasn't at that time much left over for us, except discipline and a sort of unexpressed affection. Father

was absolutely puritanical in his ideas about us, you
know that. And Mother didn't fight for us, for the
little freedom that might have contented Coral, who
was older than Nancy or me. His word was law to
her; she was dependent upon him, for everything,
even her opinions. So Coral ran away, not thinking,
not, I suppose, even caring. But it didn't mean she
couldn't come back."

"She didn't come back," he said stubbornly.

"She wanted to, she was afraid. Afraid because
she hadn't been successful, afraid because she
couldn't say, no matter what happened long ago,
I've put that all in back of me, I've made good.
Can't you understand that? Even as a very little
girl she had so much pride . . ."

"I'm sorry. I—if I went to her, if I told her I
love her . . .?"

"Do you, really, Pete?" she asked him earnestly.

"What else?" He stared at her, in authentic astonishment. "What else, all these years?"

"It could be—so much else," she murmured.

He ignored that.

"I do love her. I've never stopped, not for a moment, even when the thought of her was like dying.
If I go to her and tell her I believe her . . . and
trust her . . . and forgive her . . ."

"Forgive her?" Her eyes were clear scorn. "What
have you to forgive, exactly?"

He flung a man's name at her, defiantly. He said, "You can't deny that, can you?"

"No," said Ellen, white. "I can't . . . We'll take that for granted. Very well. Shall we say that you forgive, then, her—her unchastity although *you've* been perfectly chaste?"

"That's different," he said flushing, "that's not fair of you, Ellen, A man——"

"A man," said Ellen, "can regard his chastity as something to be disposed of as quickly and as lightly as possible. A man can, of course, do as he pleases— deny himself nothing. Not, I suppose, a woman. A woman can—you call it sin in a woman, don't you? —sin once, because she is foolish, because she is young, because she thinks herself passionately in love, because promises are made her—and that's her finish, I suppose. It's a swell world," said Ellen grimly.

After a long minute he said, very humbly:

"There's no need for us to quarrel over standards, over—anything. Ellen, if I go to her and ask her to forgive *me* . . .?"

Her eyes were gentle now. But she said again: "For what? Oh, can't you understand, Pete, that there isn't such a word if you really love? Forgiveness . . . pardon—pretty cold terms. Love doesn't bother with them. Just *is.*"

She believed that. Later she was to remember it.

After a long time he said, "If she'll have me, I'll be so good to her."

"You'll have to be more than good," said Ellen, "you'll have to be strong enough—to forget. Strong enough to get through the times when you're tired, when you're irritated, when reproaches come easily. If I thought for one moment that you couldn't be strong enough, I'd do everything in my power to keep you from ever seeing her again."

"You would, you know, Ellen," he said, regarding her. "I believe you would. But—I've been a fool," he told her quite simply, "but somehow the hurt stayed raw, septic, wouldn't heal. Now, it's different. You've done a lot for me. Made me, perhaps, grow up. It was all, I suppose, jealousy. Damnable," he said, "you don't know——"

She didn't know—yet.

He leaned across the table, lean young face intent. "I may come then? You'll ask her . . ."

"Just come," she said, smiling.

Later, on their way out, she saw in the front room two people. One was Gilda Esposito, another a young man whose face was vaguely familiar to her. She remembered, suddenly. Fontana, the man with the imitation pearl offerings whom "Gilda no like." She hesitated, wondering if she should go over and speak to them, while Pete was getting his hat. No. They were quarreling, very openly. Gilda's face was flushed and her eyes—Ellen could see her eyes. No, she would not stop.

Someone else was approaching their table, some-one who had come in from a side door. It was Jim O'Connor. He pulled out a chair and sat down. Ellen went on out quickly with Pete. Her eyes were puzzled. Jim had said he didn't know Gilda. Perhaps he knew Fontana, rented to him, something of that sort. Then, she forgot them all, thinking of Coral and of Pete, confident that they were going to be happy.

CHAPTER THIRTEEN

So Pete came to the house, but Coral was not, after all, unprepared. A letter reached her first, a thick letter, blotted, hastily written in the slightly insane scrawl which seems to be the lot of the medical profession. It came by special delivery. Nancy, who was there when it arrived, reported to Ellen, afterwards.

"When she got it, she looked so darned funny. Mother said, of course, 'Who's it from, dear?' And she said, 'Oh, Pete,' in that way she has, sort of tossing it off, as if it didn't matter. She knew, although I suppose it's years since— Well, she didn't read it, for minutes. Mother asked, 'What does he say?' After a while she opened it. I saw her hands shake. She read it for a page or two. Then she said something, I didn't hear what, and went into Mother's bedroom with it. Shut the door. She came out after a while. She'd been crying, I guess. But she didn't say anything. I mean, she just came out, trying to look unconcerned. And when Mother said, '*Well?*' sort of dragging it out the way she has, you know, Coral said, 'He just wants to know if he can come over some evening.' So that's that. She's called him up and asked him for supper, his next night off."

"Did she talk long?"

"No, just—'Hello, Pete, when do you get off, we'd like to have you for supper.' Something like that, anyway."

"All very well," said Ellen, "but I'll take Mother to a movie—Oh, I can't, but you can. In the late afternoon. Pete will get here early. I—they ought to have a little time alone, Nancy. You manage, will you? Now that Mother's gone out once or twice she thinks it's quite all right. Movies, I mean. Look here, we've *got* to manage."

They managed.

Ellen's calls kept her rather late that day. After that she made an errand or two an excuse to be even later. A special trip to the grocer's, for one; to the bakery. It was half past six before she got home, Nancy and Mrs. Adams hadn't as yet returned. "Pete," they had told the elder lady mendaciously, "will be awfully late. We can't possibly have supper till, oh, 'way past seven. And you know you're dying to see Marie Dressler!"

Pete, as it happened, had managed to be early. Ellen had phoned him. "If you could . . .?" she said.

He could.

They were sitting rather close together when Ellen opened the door. Pete rose, self-consciously. Ellen dumped the packages into his arms. "Kitchen," she ordered briefly, "and make it snappy." She looked at Coral. Coral curled up in a corner of the davenport, looked back. She was ten years younger, and ten years softer. Her eyes were happy eyes, the corners of her mouth curled upward.

"Is it all right?" asked Ellen.

Coral said,

"It's all right. He—he wants me to marry him . . . as soon as he goes with Dr. Travers. We can live in the apartment above the office, you know, the third floor, which Dr. Travers fixed up for Mel. Ellen," she said, "should I . . . dare I?"

"Goose!" said Ellen, and kissed her.

Pete came back. He was whistling. He said: "She's told you, I see. I wanted to. Women can never keep anything to themselves. Like me for a brother?" he inquired.

"She'd make you a better wife," said Coral, "nurse and all. Why didn't you fall in love with her—in-stead—instead—" A sudden unusual shyness overcame her. Pete laughed and put his big fine hand roughly on her short pretty hair. "She's going to let her hair grow," he announced importantly; then, "Why didn't I fall in love with Ellen? I don't know. It would have been suitable, wouldn't it? But she wouldn't have looked at me."

"If you'd wanted suitability," suggested Ellen, "there are always lots of nurses at the hospital."

"And how!" said Pete, grinning cheerfully.

"Mother," Coral reminded them, "Mother—I wonder how she'll take it. I mean, leaving her, and all."

"But you won't be. You'll be right around the corner, more or less. And Mother will adore a married daughter. She's despaired of Nancy and me, you know. She's bound we are to be severe spinsters and cheat her out of a lot of housewifely advice and such."

Ellen went to change her uniform and to start supper. Coral and Pete helped, in a desultory fashion. Nancy and Mrs. Adams came in presently, Mrs. Adams considerably fluttered. "You did get here, after all, didn't you, Pete? And Ellen, is she home?"

"Can you hear the kitchen clatter and not deduct my arrival?" Ellen called. "We're having—all sorts of things. It's a celebration."

"A celebration?" asked Mrs. Adams.

Nancy without another word went over and hugged both Coral and Pete impartially. Mrs. Adams looked from one to the other. Pete said, gently, "It's all right with you, isn't it, Mrs. Adams? Coral and I, I mean."

Laughter and tears and embraces. If it had been Ellen perhaps, or Nancy, things might have been different. But Coral, thank God it was Coral. Coral would be secure now forever, and contented, Coral would be doubly her own.

"Remember," said Ellen, when the first excitement had passed and Pete had mopped his future mother-in-law's eyes with his own large handkerchief, "remember, Coral, it won't be roses all the way. What a young doctor's wife has to endure, waiting meals, being pleasant to his patients and making out his bills, is just nobody's business."

"I'll hound 'em," said Coral placidly. "I'll say, 'See here, here's your doctor's bill and here's my butcher's bill and let's call it square!'"

So they had talked everything over, thought Ellen as Pete said, instantly:

"I put it up to her, Ellen. Mallory's offer, I mean. She says she'd rather stay here, with me."

"He'll be happier," said Coral.

Oh, everything was clear between them now. That you could see. If only it would stay so. Ellen's thoughts went briefly to the girl next door. But that was different, she said to herself. They weren't happy. Dot and her young trouble shooter. Or so Mrs. Lippinsky said. "She cried, by night," Mrs. Lippinsky reported to the customers. Whose fault was it? Not Dot's. Not, perhaps, his. Other people's. If they would move away, perhaps?

But Coral and Pete needn't move away. People would have a different attitude toward Pete. He was of their number, of course, but he had chosen a profession which the majority of them held in a respect amounting to worship. He would be able to take care of his own. Whatever the newspapers had once said of Cora Carmen, she was dead; and buried. Many people had never known that she had once been Coral Adams. Those who had known had forgotten, or found it best to forget. It wasn't like Dot, at all, it couldn't be.

Looking at the two of them, Ellen was content, and no longer afraid. She felt as her mother did, that Coral was harbored. Coral felt so too and crept into the living room long after Pete had gone and Nancy had gone, after Mrs. Adams slept and Ellen was tucked in on the davenport.

"You know I'm happy, Ellen?"

"Crawl in here, little idiot. There's room enough if I lie close to the wall. You're shivering."

"I'm not cold, Ellen. Pete said he saw you, talked with you."

"He took me to dinner," said Ellen.

"I know—but, Ellen, you do understand? You do believe me, all I said. You and Nancy and, of course, Mother, although we've not talked much. And Pete. That's all that matters. I—I will be a good wife," said Coral. "I will. I love him, so much. I never stopped, really, down deep. I thought he despised me. But——"

She was crying now. She said, once, "*so happy.*" And again "*safe.*"

Ellen let her cry herself to sleep. It would, she thought, do her good. She was cramped lying there, and the arm under Coral's shoulder prickled intolerably and then grew numb. But she didn't move. She lay awake, thinking. And after a long time Coral stirred, and laughed, a little sleepily and confessed . . . "I went to sleep—" and mourned, "Oh, Ellen, you must be half dead," and crept out from under the blanket and back to the bedroom, with Ellen following to tuck her up and lean over her and kiss her goodnight and then go back to the davenport again. This time to sleep.

She saw Jim, a few days later, and told him about Coral and Pete. "Gee, that's great," said Jim with enthusiasm. "I haven't seen much of Pete in years but he's a good guy. So Coral's the first to be married," he reminded her slowly, and asked, "Who's next?"

"Nancy," she said firmly.

They were in his new, his shining car, coming home from dancing somewhere. He guided it deftly through the traffic, flashing his white teeth at a sedate traffic officer who saluted him, grinning, but who afterward looked after the car, its newness, and its expensive lines with a frown of speculation on his Irish brow.

"Is that so?" asked Jim after a while. Ellen, dreaming to herself, regarded him, startled.

"Is what so?" she demanded.

"Nancy. I suppose you mean that chief whatever it is of hers."

"Chick? No, I don't think so. I don't think she's in love with him," said Ellen. "I don't think she's in love with anyone. She's just having a good time, playing around."

"Like you?"

"Like me? I don't," said Ellen, smiling faintly, "play around much, after all. By the way," she went on, changing the subject, "I saw you the other night. In the Napoli. We were going out of the door, Pete and I—and you were coming in a side door, and sitting down with Gilda Esposito, and some man." She wrinkled her brow. "Fontana, isn't he? An Italian, I saw him at the Esposito's once."

"Who, me?" asked Jim astonished. "I haven't been in the Napoli for months."

She thought, he's lying. She said stubbornly:
"As if I wouldn't know you! Don't be silly!"

"But it wasn't me," he protested, "I tell you I
haven't been near the place. I can't stand Italian
cooking for one thing although I was brought up on
it—*and* Irish stew," he added, grinning.

Well, perhaps she'd been mistaken. She hadn't
seen, very clearly, the face of the man who had
gone up to Gilda's table. She had, she supposed,
recognized Jim by his walk, the set and swing of
his shoulders. It didn't matter anyway. She'd probably been wrong, because, if not, why on earth
should he lie about it? It didn't make sense, she
told herself. She was always telling herself things
didn't make sense.

"Well, it doesn't matter," she said lightly, "there
must be more than one good-looking man frequent-
ing the Napoli."

"Thanks. I wish you meant it," said Jim.

It was some nights later that she saw Gilda. It
was late afternoon really, a rainy, gray dusk, night
closing in more swiftly as the season drew on toward
winter. Ellen had made her last call for the day and
had returned by subway. Coming up the stairs
crowded with people, she thought she saw Gilda
just ahead of her and hurried to catch up with her
but lost her in the crowd. Arriving at the street level,
she looked for her but did not see her again. Then,

she did see her, walking swiftly, gracefully ahead
of her, on the way home. Ellen increased her pace,
but was halted, crossing a side street, by lights,
and Gilda had slipped across as they were changing. On the opposite side of the street, a car was
drawn to the curb, its engine running, waiting for
someone, possibly someone who would come by subway, and cross over there where parking was permitted. A blue car, a sedan, Ellen noted mechanically. There was a stationer's shop at the corner, the
outside paper stand crowded with people who picked
up papers, threw down pennies and dispersed. There
were two half-grown boys about, cutting up monkey-
shines with a grocery barrow.

"Gilda," called Ellen.

Gilda didn't hear. Now she was passing the car.
Someone must have spoken to her from within it,
for she stopped a moment and turned inquiringly.
The door opened. Someone reached out.

The door shut. Gilda was gone. The car pulled
out, suddenly, swiftly . . .

Friends of Gilda, giving her a lift home? But
she lived only a block, two blocks away. Ellen reached
a corner. The boy who had been holding the metal
barrow had dropped it—and the other boy in it—
with a clamorous sound of crashing metal. "Jees',"
said the boy to the other, "didye see dat?"

"See what?" asked Ellen.

They had not seen her come up to them. They knew her, well enough. One was the stationer's son. He grinned at Ellen.

"I mean," he explained, "it looked funny, what I mean. That was the Esposito dame wasn't it, coming home? The car's been there, half an hour. We didn't pay no attention, see, cars wait here to pick up people from the subway, see? But she goes along, easy like and someone shouts something from the car and she stops and then first thing we know they yank her in and drive off."

"Probably friends," said Ellen, but she was frowning.

"She hollered," said the other, younger boy, suddenly.

"Gwan! I didn't heard no holler," said the stationer's son.

"Wash your ears," advised his comrade. "I heard her holler. Not loud. Sort of surprised. Then, she quit."

"You didn't, I suppose, look at the number of the car while it was standing here?" asked Ellen.

"Naw," said both boys, amiably, but then one remembered. It hadn't borne the state license plate but that of a bordering state, he said. He didn't notice the number.

Ellen went on home. Somehow, she couldn't dismiss the incident from her mind. On the surface it was absurd to think—anything. Out of town friends of Gilda, her common sense argued, who'd gone to her house and found she wasn't home, as yet; and who'd driven to the subway, to wait for her. And surprised her. That was why she had screamed, if she *had* screamed. The youngster's testimony was probably not very reliable, that was all.

But in the morning she still remembered. The little gnawing at her brain was not to be quieted. She went to the Esposito shop, at the noon hour, wondering what she would say. She'd say nothing. A friendly call, "I happened to be in the neighborhood," something like that.

Esposito was not inside the shop; nor his wife. The helper jerked a thumb upstairs. Outside, as she had entered, she had seen Mike's taxi standing, waiting. . . .

She went upstairs, thoughtfully. Mike didn't, as a rule, get home for dinner. But today he might have managed. Why should the sight of the taxi have filled her with such an unreasoning anxiety?

She knocked at the door. No answer. She knocked again. She thought, "they're like everyone else, half the time they don't bother to answer knocks, they're not interested or else they're suspicious." She knew people were beyond that closed door. She could hear voices. She pressed herself against the panels. Now she could hear weeping. She knocked again. "It's

Ellen Adams," she called; and then, the sesame that had opened so many closed doors " . . . the visiting nurse."

The door opened. Mike looked out at her, stocky, short Mike with the heavy shoulders and the friendly smile. He wasn't smiling now. And his eyes were bloodshot.

He said, "Come in," and looked beyond her as if he expected to see something, he didn't know exactly what—or whom.

Mrs. Esposito was crying, there in the corner. She had a shawl dragged over her head and eyes. She was crying noisily, she was rocking to and fro. The air was blue with cigarette smoke. Esposito explained, coming forward, trying to smile. "You must excuse my wife, she is upset . . . "

Ellen asked, "Gilda?"

Mike came closer so suddenly, so almost tigerishly, that she drew back. Esposito touched her shoulder. He jerked his head at Mike. The door closed. Was locked. Ellen said, steadily, as the shawl fell from Mrs. Esposito's hands and exposed her distorted, her entirely terrible face, "It *is* Gilda, isn't it? Did she come home last night?"

There was a dreadful silence. Esposito then said, "No," heavily. "No," he repeated after a minute. "She didn't come home."

"I saw her," said Ellen, "that's why I came. I—"

"Where—*where?*" They were crowding around her. Mrs. Esposito, understanding, was clutching at her with frantic hands, "*mia figlia, mia figlia . . .*"

Ellen reconstructed, briefly, tersely, the entire swift scene as she had seen it.

To her astonishment, after Mike's rapid translation to his mother, there were no exclamations. Nothing. There was simply silence. Then Esposito said, "It is as we thought."

"What did you think?" Ellen asked. "You mean, you thought she had been—been kidnapped? But no, in this day and age, a grown girl . . . That's too absurd." She knew it wasn't absurd. One read of such things every day, one heard of them.

There was still no answer. Mrs. Esposito was crying again. Ellen heard a name repeated over and over "*Fontana . . . Fontana . . .* "

There were other words . . . which Ellen heard and understood and tried to piece together . . . the word *disgrazia* . . . too soft in sound for its bitter meaning; the somber word *morte* . . .

"*Brutto!*" raved Mrs. Esposito, "*e cavitto e sporcissimo . . . !*"

Mike turned on his mother. What he said must have shocked her into silence. She sat there rocking, the shawl over her face.

This was a mad household; mad in their curious, secretive way. Ellen spoke decisively.

She addressed Esposito.

"You think she has been kidnapped by someone? Why didn't you go to the police, last night?"

He said, and shrugged, "What good would that do? They wouldn't believe us. They'd say she was —bad—that she went, of her own accord—I know."

"Then I'll go," Ellen cried at him, "as soon as I can. And take those boys with me, who saw the car. One says he heard her scream. Oh, why didn't I come here, last night?" she said. "Think of the hours we have wasted."

Mike said, "What's the use? This is our job, we'll see it through." His dark strong hands were curled into fists. Esposito laid a hand on his arm.

"Wait—if—if she can do anything?"

Ellen cried, "Of course I can, Mike, be sensible. This isn't Italy, Sicily, this is America. You don't have to bother with vendettas and things while meantime—meantime—Gilda . . . Let me go to the police . . . and see what I can do. I'll go alone. And . . ."

Suddenly she put her arms about Mrs. Esposito, kneeling beside her, there on the floor, while the two men stood back, silent, unhappy . . .

"*Mia figlia . . . mia figlia . . .*"

"I know. We'll bring her back," said Ellen, "but first you must help, you must tell me what you know, and what you suspect."

CHAPTER FOURTEEN

There was no immediate reply to her question. After a long time, during which she alternately pleaded and commanded, bringing her every natural resource of eloquence and tact and understanding to bear on the situation, Mike spoke, with the sullenness of shame.

"It was Fontana . . . " he said . . . "if she wouldn't marry him——"

He left the sentence unfinished, and relapsed into his painful brooding silence. Ellen looked from one to the other. Esposito's dark face was rigid, his features carved from some swarthy metal in which only his eyes lived. His wife's face was, by now, almost unrecognizable.

"That," argued Ellen sharply, "is absurd . . .

but——" she turned to Mike, "have you tried to
see Fontana, do you know where he lives?"

"I know. He ain't there," answered Mike heavily.
"No one knows where he is."

He added, after a moment, "If they did, they
wouldn't tell. He's up to his thick neck in some
racket or other." He clamped his lips; and said no
more. Esposito added:

"Gilda never liked him. I forbade him to come here.
He is not for Gilda."

"*Mia figlia,*" wailed Mrs. Esposito, monotonously
. . . and then clutching at an English word, childish,
tragic, she said, "spoiled" . . . and was silent, rocking.

A quiver passed over Esposito's iron face. Mike
cursed, under his breath. Ellen rose.

"I'll report to my office," she said, "and get leave
to go to the police station. After school, when I can
round up those two boys."

Someone, possibly Esposito, said heavily, "Too
late . . . "

She whirled on her heel at that, gray eyes enormous.

"No," she denied, "you are not to think it. No
matter what has happened."

She turned to Mike. "You come with me," she
said, "or your father," and then, "no, meet me
there,"—she looked at her watch—"say, at four

o'clock." She frowned and bit her lip. So much precious time wasted. "Go on before," she said, changing her mind. "I'll come as soon as I see the boys. Meantime, tell your story."

She made her way back to the office swiftly, spoke briefly to Miss Renwick. Miss Renwick nodded. The Espositos belonged, in a manner of speaking, to her, to all of them. Ellen must, and would, do what she thought best.

Ellen picked up a telephone and called the police station. She spoke to the sergeant, at length, trying to explain. He knew her, he knew her organization. She hung up. "He'll put a detective right on the case," she reported, "Scarpia, an Italian."

She got her calls, and went out, stopping for a malted milk at a drug store. When school let out she was waiting in the stationer's shop. She had explained to the bent, agile man who ran it. When the boy came in unkempt, whistling, his father spoke to him sharply. "You go with the lady, see, and tell what you know. The other boy, that was Jake, wasn't it? Find him too."

Something of a triumph. "I don't want we should be mixed up in this," the stationer told Ellen, "it's not good to be mixed up with the police."

"The boys have no responsibility," Ellen had assured him, "beyond telling what they saw. That's all they'll be needed for." She had argued half despairing, but finally he had given in.

With the two boys, important and excited, in tow, she went to the precinct station. It was not the first time she had appeared there. The genial sergeant at the desk greeted her. There were people milling about the room, people were waiting. It was close, it smelled of smoke. The floor was stained. The Espositos were not there. She looked around. No, they had not come, said the sergeant, answering her inquiry. Scarpia had been to the house. He hadn't come back. He listened, frowning, to her story.

Now Scarpia came in, a good-looking Italian, a plainclothesman. He took Ellen and the boys into the rear office. Two desks, telephones, cuspidors, walls covered with handbills, photographs of wanted men.

For the second time Ellen told her tale. The boys, theirs; as plainly and tersely as possible, disagreeing on one point . . . "She *hollered*," insisted the younger boy, Jake, firmly. "I didn't hear no holler," said the stationer's boy, as firmly.

Scarpia leaned back in his chair. "There's nothing," he said, "to be gotten out of the family. I tried. It seems they have changed their minds. They weren't coming around. She'd come back, they said. I couldn't do a thing with them. These wops are all alike," he said, in easy scorn of his own, "scared to death to come to the police, they'd rather shoot it out, among themselves—stab it out, if you like that better."

Ellen said, distressed:

"Something has to be done, don't you understand that? The girl must be brought back, the man found." She repeated what Mike had said to her. Scarpia shook his sleek black head, "We've nothing on him, this Fontana. He hasn't a record."

Another plainclothesman, at the other desk, an older man, looked across to bark suddenly,

"Suppose you got this wrong, sister? Suppose the girl went of her own accord? Most of 'em do."

"Not Gilda," denied Ellen angrily. "She loathed the man. She—she had a good job, she's happy in it, this man had been bothering her, I believe, for months." She spoke of the little scene in the restaurant, which she had witnessed. Scarpia pricked up his ears, "It doesn't look as if she hated him," he said shrewdly, "going out with him, that way."

Ellen said sharply: "What does that prove? Perhaps he threatened her. I tell you she's been taken away by force."

"Hundreds of girls," said the older detective, "disappear, every day. Vanish. Napoo. Thin air. They come back sometimes, married. The family meantime races around, comes to us. We put our men to work. What do we find? An elopement . . . or a voluntary runaway. These girls weren't born yesterday . . . "

She asked, furiously, "Have you any daughters?"

"Sure, two." He was Irish, he had the Irishman's slow, amused grin. "Why?"

"It's incredible," said Ellen, "that you can take that attitude about another man's daughter."

He reddened a little, and busied himself with the papers on his untidy desk. Scarpia said, soothingly,

"We'll do all we can, see. But if the family won't talk . . . I tell you, I yelled my head off at them."

That was hardly the way to go about it, Ellen reminded him tartly.

Scarpia shrugged. "I know these people," he said. "All for their 'honor.' But they don't want anyone else crashing in, see. The old lady, she doesn't even speak English . . . "

"Yes, a little. She understands."

"I asked her, *Capisce Inglese?* She shook her head. As far as that went, she didn't speak Italian either. Not a word! Wouldn't talk. The father—a different kettle of fish, yet he and the boy wouldn't talk much either, just said it was a mistake that we were sent for, they'd handle it. If the family won't lodge a complaint, let alone give us any information, our hands are tied, see?"

Ellen rose. The two boys got out of their chairs, their eyes wide, their jaws moving in rhythm, savoring the sticky sweetness of gum. She said, dispiritedly:

"I'll try and make them see reason."

"Good. Find out where the girl is, we'll do the rest," said Scarpia. "Meantime I'll have 'em all looked up. But, you understand, our hands are tied?"

"I understand," said Ellen, not too pleasantly. The Irishman grinned at her again, his rancor forgotten. "You're barkin' up the wrong tree, sister," he murmured. "She'll come home. With a wedding ring. Or, without . . . After all, she ain't a minor, you know. Age of consent, and all that."

Ellen went back to the Espositos, leaving the boys on their corner with strict injunctions to talk to no one, and stopping a moment to tell the stationer that he must keep his son quiet. The stationer was only too happy to oblige. "If he shoots off his face," he said darkly, "I'll whale hell out of him."

The Espositos were not at home. Mike's taxi was not there. The helper, alone in the store, was ignorant, shrugged; he didn't know, he said. "The boss, he go out. Come back, bimeby."

She went on home presently, discouraged. Delay, and obstinacy on every side and meantime—Gilda?

Very early next morning her telephone rang? She went to it, her heart beating quickly. She had given Esposito her number. Mike's voice reached her, low, guarded.

"Someone phoned," Mike said, without preliminary. "She's all right . . . if the folks say she can marry him, he'll bring her back."

"Did you notify the detective . . . ?"

"Nope. It ain't his business, now," said Mike. Nor yours, said his tone; his tone definitely dismissed her, lay off, it told her, in effect. He hung up. She dressed rapidly, after putting on the coffee and made no lengthy explanations to Coral and her mother. Nancy was not yet in. "I have to go out," she said, "on a special case."

She walked quickly through the crisp autumnal morning, reached the Espositos'. This time they opened to her knock and she went in and sat down, marshaling her arguments.

After a long time.

"What else is there to do?" said Esposito. "She will marry him, of course. Someone will phone again today. That's all there is to it," the father said.

"But she *hates* him," said Ellen wildly. "Why on earth should she marry him? Marriage, by force, it isn't legal, it isn't——"

But he only lifted hands and shoulders, fatalistically. Mrs. Esposito sobbed. Mike turned from the window, his hands sunk in his pockets. "He'll marry her, all right," said Mike, somberly.

"When she comes back," begged Ellen, fighting the tears of futility and despair, realizing that she was up against a blank wall of absolute incomprehension, "you must let me talk to her."

She added: "But if—oh, if only you would see it my way! If only you would see it my way! If you feel the police are out of place here, I know a lawyer, I will get private detectives, I can do *something* . . . "

A look passed between Esposito and his son, a look almost of hope. Ellen realized, it was the police they feared, the publicity. Esposito nodded. "Perhaps," he said slowly, "perhaps that would be good."

She would, she thought, get in touch with Frank, he could help her.

Later she called his office. He was in court. There was no way to reach him, all day long.

She found him finally, at his apartment. He would, he promised, come around at once, that evening. Arriving, he took her out in the car. It was, he agreed, listening, damnable. But, was she sure? He asked the question the detective had asked. Was she sure the girl hadn't gone of her own accord? Men were all alike, she told him angrily, wasn't there the telephone call to *prove* that she hadn't gone of her own accord?

He tried to quiet her. He said, "You know I'll help. I know a private investigator. He's under some obligation to me, I'll try to reach him. I'll find him surely, tomorrow, or next day. But meantime, I wish you'd keep out of this, Ellen, it's dangerous business."

"It's my job," she said wretchedly, "can't you understand that?"

He couldn't. There was something of a coolness between them when they parted. He was, she saw plainly, more interested in her and her possible situation than in Gilda.

The next day the phone rang again early. It was Mike, once more. "She has come home," he said cautiously. "She will marry him. There isn't any use your getting the detective."

Impasse.

She phoned Frank, and explained briefly. "Good," he said heartily. "So, that's all over."

It wasn't.

She went, as soon as she had a free moment, to the rooms over the fruit store. Gilda was there. She looked amazing, her face almost green-white, her eyes shadowed, and her mouth twitching. She was sitting in a corner of the sofa, her hands folded in her lap. Fontana was not there. Nor Mike.

Gilda cried when she saw Ellen, slow tears, running unheeded down her cheeks. Had they, Ellen wondered, been unkind to her?

It did not seem so. Esposito walked restlessly about the room. Ellen asked her, "Where is he?" and Esposito shrugged. "He's gone out," said Esposito, "to buy himself a suit. Mike went along." He was silent. He did not tell her that he had locked the future bridegroom in, all last night, after their arrival, locked him in an unused storage room.

"Please let me talk to Gilda alone," Ellen demanded.

Esposito went out, heavily, downstairs to the store. Mrs. Esposito, curiously recovered and plainly resigned with the strange heavy resignation of Latin women, went into the kitchen. Ellen took Gilda's cold hands in her own.

"I can't tell you—" said Gilda shaking.

Ellen said, "You needn't. And you needn't marry him, Gilda. See, this is today, not yesterday. Nothing that happened was your fault. You need not marry him. No one need ever know. I'll see that he doesn't annoy you any more."

Gilda said, "You don't understand." She said . . . "I—I fought him—hours—days——"

"Hush," said Ellen, "yes, I do understand. But that doesn't mean you must marry him."

Gilda shrugged. In that moment she looked like her mother. She hadn't a feature of her mother's save her eyes. Yet she looked like her, patient, resigned.

"Gilda, wait, please, give it a day's thought, two days, a week, before you take this step," Ellen urged her.

Gilda rose. She made no reply. "I must help Mother," she dismissed Ellen, "in the kitchen." She, moved toward the door with Ellen, the elasticity gone from her step. At the door she caught Ellen's hands in hers, a tight, frantic grip. "I—I'm grateful," she whispered, "but you can't do anything . . . "

Ellen was alone, on the other side of the closed door.

That was final. The case, such as it was, would be dropped. Gilda would marry him. She mustn't. She must be brought to see reason.

On an impulse Ellen turned her steps toward Jim O'Connor's office. She found him in, barking through a telephone. His face lighted when he saw her. He drew her into the back room, closed the door.

"It's an honor," he assured her.

She tried to smile at him. "Not a social call, not a friendly one even. I need your help."

"Shoot," he said.

She could tell Jim. He would understand. Better than Frank. He knew these people, their hates, their tragedies, their blood ran in his veins. She told him briefly. At the back of her brain there was a little sore spot. The restaurant, that night, the man who had looked like Jim, at Gilda's table. But it hadn't been Jim.

He listened gravely, fingering a pencil. He said: "It's a damned shame. Of course, I agree with you entirely. She shouldn't marry him. But—you know these people, Ellen, there is nothing you can do."

She said anxiously: "You know everyone in the neighborhood. You know people, perhaps you know this Fontana. If the police can do nothing, perhaps you can. Find out about him. Get something on him, get him out of town."

He said, "I'll do my best, Ellen. But perhaps you are making a mistake. Shouldn't you let them run it? It's their show after all."

It was, she realized dully, leaving. It wasn't hers. Her job was looking after the sick bodies of people. She couldn't, she supposed, interfere in their lives . . .

And yet—was her job only sick bodies? Wasn't it sick minds as well, sick hearts and souls?

When she got home, the letter was there, with the scrawled address, that read simply . . . "Nurse" —and the number and street. It had, of course, reached her. The postman had been much amused. "That's fame for you," the postman had said to Coral.

The paper told nothing, nor the unformed hand but the printed letters carried a definite threat . . . "keep out of this."

What was it? Coral wanted to know; and Nancy was curious.

"Just one of my kids," Ellen told them, lightly, and crumpled it up in her hand.

Bartlett came again. Driving uptown, he urged her once more to clear her skirts. "Keep out of it, what good will it do you? You can't tell about these people—hot-blooded, impulsive, quick to quarrel, to kill, even."

She admitted, under his literal cross-examination, that she had had a letter. "Where is it?" he demanded. "You must take it to the police, they must give you protection."

Nonsense, she said, she could take care of herself. She had, of course, destroyed the letter. She wouldn't give up. She'd go, once more, talk to Gilda.

"Ellen, you're crazy," he said, "you can't meddle like this." He said angrily, because he was afraid for her, "You women are all alike, trying to play God——"

She resented that, very much; and told him so, in no uncertain terms. Suddenly they were quarreling bitterly; he, because he loved her, because she seemed no nearer to surrender than months before, and because he was in terror for her, and she, because of the emotional strain she had been under, and because, where she had looked for sympathy and understanding, she had received instead a scolding which might have been directed at a careless and stupid child.

"Oh, this doesn't get us anywhere," she said wearily, after a while. "Please, Frank, take me home."

They drove home, almost in silence. There was

no embrace, in the car, in the hallway. She went into the apartment wearily, alone.

The next day was Sunday. She slept later than usual, worn out, and toward noon went once more, determined if not hopeful, to the Espositos'. Gilda let her in. The parents were not in evidence.

"I've come," Ellen began, and then stopped. Fontana was there, resplendent in a checked suit, happiness writ plain all over his face. It was the first good look she had had at him. Not a weak face, not a very noticeable one. Yet good-humored, even gay. She couldn't somehow reconcile him with——everything. She felt a little dizzy, wondering.

Gilda made the introduction with an almost absurd punctiliousness. Fontana regarded Ellen closely. His small dark eyes were quite gentle, intent on her own. But she had a feeling that if she made a false move, a false step——

Under some strange compulsion she asked him, clearly,

"You wrote me, did you not, Mr. Fontana?"

CHAPTER FIFTEEN

" '*Scusi?*" asked Fontana apologetically.

He had been turning Ellen's name on his unaccustomed tongue; had asked Gilda, "*Commo se chiama?*" And at the repetition of the name, "Adams" had uttered, naïvely, "*Má . . . e curioso!*"

"Ask him," said Ellen to Gilda, "if he wrote me . . . a letter."

Gilda's eyes widened. She shot a look at Fontana, black, despising. She asked him, rapidly. He spread his hands, with deprecation, and chattered for a moment. Gilda turned. "Yes, he had someone write it for him; he says he was afraid you would make me change my mind."

A ready admission. Ellen looked at the young man, the great strength of his physique, heavy in the shoulders and chest, narrow in waist and hips, a taller man than most of the Italians she knew. She thought—a dreadful man, unspeakable . . . nothing, he stopped at nothing . . . kidnapping—rape——

But there was something childlike about him, something disarming. That was the key to him: he was a child, who took what he wanted; he knew no laws, he disregarded everything but his desires. She hardened her heart, she spoke to him directly, without anger in her tone, with a sort of curiosity, as one would question a visitor from Mars.

"Why did you do it?"

He understood that. He broke into torrential Italian. Ellen looked at Gilda. Slow color came into Gilda's face. She turned, shrugging her slim shoulders, unwilling to interpret. So Fontana himself tried, carefully, with his shattered English, his unaccustomed speech stripped to essentials . . .

"I lov' her so mooch. *Si.* Crazy for her. You know? I see her, long time ago. I can't eat, I can't sleep. I say, that girl, *my wife*. She won' leesen. I gotta have her. I—gooda man for her."

He broke off, crimson under the swarthy skin tone. He went, quick and soundless as a cat, into the kitchen. He came back, with small brimming glasses, one, two. Gilda jumped up. "*Stupido*," cried Gilda. She went out, came back with a tray. Ellen's throat constricted. That was tragic, somehow.

"You drink?" asked Fontana coaxingly, child-like, "to me . . . to Gilda . . . wine good for you. Lika da *medicina*."

Gilda's lips were shaking. Ellen reached out and took a glass and touched her lips to it. Out of all reason that she should drink their health. She said, "Gilda?" once, appealing, and finally rose to go. Fontana took her hand in a tremendous grip.

"Goodabye," said Fontana, beaming. He turned to Gilda, he said something . . . *simpatica*, Ellen heard that much. "Evert'ing okay?" asked Fontana, proud of his good English. He was sorry he had sent the letter, he told her so brokenly. When he and Gilda were married she must come see them, he added, in his own tongue, Gilda, stony-faced, translating.

She tried to draw Gilda out into the hall with her. Fontana, his big hand lightly on the girl's shoulder, was watchful, smiling, and did not permit it. Gilda said, quickly, "Never mind me. It's all right. I'll— I'll make the best of it," Gilda promised.

Ellen went back home. Gilda would make the best of it. Somehow that was heartening. And yet . . .

Wrong, terribly wrong. She shuddered, thinking. And yet, that young ignorant creature, snatching at his desires . . . "I lov' her so mooch———"

"*A rivederci*," he had called out as she left.

There was nothing she could do now; she had

probably done more harm than good. Frank, if he knew, would tell her so. He didn't, couldn't understand. There was, in certain respects, a gulf between them. Even Jim, who understood better, had regarded her with tolerant eyes and advised her not to "meddle."

She had meddled. Much good it had done her— or Gilda.

Astonishing of Gilda, Gilda whom she knew as vivacious, clever even, entirely Americanized, ambitious . . . Gilda had, as it were, reverted. Could not, somehow, break the old tabus.

Could anyone, safely?

Jim came, that afternoon. He had been inquiring about Fontana. Fontana was well enough off. A small trucking business. Nothing on him. "Nothing to be done." His eyes were anxious, regarding Ellen. "You look tired, you've let this get on your nerves."

"Perhaps I have. It's all right, Jim, don't bother any more. Gilda has consented to marry him, they'll be married as soon as possible. I've nothing more to do with it. I've phoned the precinct to drop the case."

Jim was obviously relieved. "Let's go to the movies and forget it."

They went. The drama, the emotional drama unfolded itself on the screen. Life, thought Ellen, regarding the fleeting pictures, listening to the voices raised in anger, in terror, in pleading, is so much more melodramatic, so much cruder, and so much more inexplicable. There aren't any solutions to life, and happy endings don't stay that way—if there are happy endings. The play doesn't stop, the screen doesn't darken, the audience doesn't file out. It goes on . . .

Gilda would go on, making the best of it. She would marry Fontana, she would keep his house and bear his children, she would forget her ambitions, her Americanization. Perhaps, in a way, she would be content. Would he ever revenge himself for her long refusal? Ellen thought not. He was avenged. He would be gentler with her perhaps, remembering that she had been impossible to win, remembering his guilt. Gilda might, as the years went on, have entirely the upper hand.

She wondered if Gilda would grow fat, like Mrs. Esposito, fat and emotional and contented, easily moved to laughter, easily moved to tears. Or would she grow sharp-faced and shrewish, ruling the giant's physique and the child's brain she had married with an iron hand?

This marriage was wrong; more than wrong. Yet Gilda, relinquishing her bright dreams, would "make the best of it." There was a ray of hope there. Perhaps, after all, she would not so much alter but would transfer her ambitions to her husband, and to the house she must keep; perhaps what Ellen vaguely termed her "reversion" was something of the blood and spirit, something traditional and bone-bred and had nothing whatever to do with those traits of character which were released in action and which, for all their surface importance, were, in the last analysis, non-essentials.

She tried to say something of this to Jim, endeavoring to put into clumsy mold of words something of her fluid thoughts. He listened, a little puzzled, not, she saw quickly, understanding.

"Oh, sure, she'll be all right," he agreed. "Fontana's a good sort, even if he isn't quite up to the Esposito standards . . . the old man thinks he's somebody, you know; he comes, they say, from good stock back in the old country," he added carelessly.

She was, in her turn, puzzled.

"I thought you didn't know——" she began. Jim looked down on her, as they were walking toward a place where they might have tea.

"Oh, I asked questions, around, after you told me," he explained.

He might, she reflected, have given her that information earlier. Even a general estimate of Fontana by the neighborhood would have quieted, a little, her anxiety; and the casual statement about the elder Esposito was, in a sense, the key to him.

When they reached her home they found something of an assembly. Pete was there, he had come to take Coral around to view the apartment Dr. Travers had renovated for them over his own. Pete was saying seriously that as soon as he could afford it they'd put in an elevator. For there were flights and flights to climb. Office floor, and the doctor's bachelor quarters next and then theirs. And to Ellen's astonishment Frank Bartlett was there also, with Bill. He had, he solemnly explained, a date with that young man, and Bill had expressed a desire to come calling.

Bill was arrayed like the lilies of the field. Bartlett had taken him shopping on the previous day and had outfitted him from sturdy square-toed shoes to the cap which rode rakishly the red crest of his unruly hair. Bill had a suit with knickerbockers and a vest although Bartlett had a little protested against this final glory. He had a shirt, in fact, several shirts, although to his sorrow he could not wear more than one at once; the same held true of ties and socks. He also had sweaters, and a leather, wool-lined coat. And warm underwear. And wool-lined gloves. He was absolutely radiant and every freckle shone as if it had been polished against the tan, now paling, which he had acquired on the farm.

High tea was in progress, presided over by Nancy. The little group appeared to be in accord. Even Mrs. Adams unbent toward Mr. Bartlett, the outsider, under Bill's benign influence. Bill was now attending school with an astonishing regularity.

Bartlett had somehow persuaded him and Bill, set upon following in his idol's footsteps, was reluctantly confessing that once you got the hang of it, studying wasn't so "turrible" hard, after all.

On Ellen's entrance with Jim a slight awkwardness pervaded the little group.

Jim, to make an understatement, was not markedly cordial to Bill's hero. But Pete was there to carry things off with his high hand, and Coral, and Nancy. They were soon laughing, all of them, and Ellen was drinking her second cup of tea. "But," commented Mrs. Adams mildly, "the tea is never strong enough in those places." Mrs. Adams had, in common with many women of her type, a distaste for and a scorn of all public eating places. Food was better prepared at home, she stated. And much more safely. One heard of such dreadful things . . .

Frank and Bill took their departure presently. But Bartlett had a word with Ellen at the door, Bill standing beside them, small and sturdy, regarding with almost hypnotic fascination the toes of his shining shoes.

"That was grand of you," Ellen said, "I had no idea that you——"

"Oh, it was our secret. We wanted to surprise you. We carried all the bundles home, yesterday. Bill wouldn't hear of having them sent; you see, he

was afraid something would happen to them en
route. Weren't you, old timer?"

Bill nodded, partially comprehending. Some instinct of chivalry, of astonishing tact, caused him to
move off down the hallway, hands thrust into new
deep pockets, whistling shrilly through his teeth.
Bartlett said, "I phoned and Nancy told me you were
out. But I decided to come and wait, anyway. Will
you go out with me soon, Ellen?"

She said she would and laid her hand in his for
the brief but close and hurting grip. She smote
Bill lightly on the shoulder, desiring to flutter a
kiss on the tip end of his snub nose but refraining
sacrificially, knowing Bill's prejudices. Presently she
turned back, smiling, and went into the living room.

Supper would be late, they informed her. And
Mrs. Adams had decided to go around to the Travers' with Coral and Pete. "Oh, no, all those stairs!"
argued Ellen distressed. Pete flexed his muscles. "I'll
carry her up," he promised. But Mrs. Adams looked
wounded. "I'm perfectly all right," she said briskly,
"I'll take them slowly."

She added, "Jim will stay to supper, of course."

Jim would, accepting with a delightful flash of
his very white teeth. Nancy effaced herself in the
kitchen, leaving Jim and Ellen alone. They could
hear her singing, stacking and washing the tea

things and looking over the constituents of the supper menu.

"Plays up to you a lot," said Jim, smoking furiously, "Bartlett, I mean."

"What *do* you mean, exactly?" she asked.

"Oh, with that kid. Gentleman Bountiful or something. As if it meant anything?"

"He's very fond of the boy," Ellen told him quietly, "and intends to give him every opportunity to make the most of himself."

A sententious sentence. But there still was between them that awkwardness which had its origin in the two men's meeting. Jim burst out so loudly that Nancy, overhearing, dropped a pan to acquit her, a fleet second too late, of unintentionally eavesdropping.

"Are you going to marry him, Ellen?"

She replied, flushing, "I have no intention of marrying anybody."

"And that goes for me too, I suppose?" His hurt dark eyes turned to her own. He said desperately, "Why I hang around here and keep on hoping, God only knows. I don't get anywhere with you."

He made a gesture as if he repudiated her and everything about her. She did not answer, having no true words to console or reassure him. He said presently, rising, "Guess I'll go on . . . "

"I thought you were staying?"

"I don't feel like it," he said bluntly.

"Very well."

She watched him gather up overcoat and hat. He was sulky as a child is sulky, a child who has been reproved and disciplined. She smiled a little, inwardly. Jim had really never grown up and never, she supposed, would grow up.

But there was nothing she could do. With each day that passed she realized her, as yet but half-confessed, allegiance to Bartlett. Coming into the familiar room, seeing him there unexpectedly, this afternoon, had made the room seem strange to her for a moment, the other people in it, beloved as they were, as aliens, shadows. She had come in talking to Jim, laughing; and there he had been rising to greet her, Bill scampering about like a puppy at his feet, shouting at her—"see my new suit, Miss Ellen" (Bartlett had weaned him away from that absurd "Mis' Nois") . . .

Lamplight in the room and dusk outside, winter dusk. But for a split second in Ellen's heart it was spring.

This was pure love which she carried hidden with her, which walked with her by day and dreamed with her by night. There was to be no permanent denial of it. That he waited, she knew. That he imposed upon himself a close restraint, she knew also. Had she not heard him say so, in as many words?

"I've got to let you go now; if I don't, I'll keep you here in my arms. I can't, I mustn't, it makes it too difficult for me."

He did not want, any more than she wanted, that semi-relationship analogous to the dusk beyond the windows somehow; that relationship of kiss and clasp, blunting the senses, eventually, interminable, unhappy; a relationship that had no daylight in it, that was a drifting which ended—how? In a lessening of desire or a desire too strong to be denied.

That he relied on her to come to him earnestly and tell him that everything was clear before them, she knew. And thought, some day, she must. Things were altered, somehow. There was Coral, returned, and all the changes her coming had brought. Their mother would not now perhaps be so stubbornly set against the intrusion of Frank Bartlett in the family circle. Ellen realized suddenly and blindly that perhaps she would never have been set against it at all had she realized the possibility. It was merely that she had thought him casual, not serious, and therefore, dangerous. Once regarded in the light of a sedate suitor, a genuine claimant, her attitude would surely change. Ellen had not thought of this before. Now it pierced her with its certainty.

And meantime, while she thought all this, while the swift thoughts and images passed through her mind, she was looking at Jim, watching him shrug

his broad shoulders into an overcoat, take his hat
in his strong dark hand. She was tender toward
him momentarily as all gentle girls are toward men
who love them and whom they do not love. She said,
"I wish you'd change your mind and stay."

"You don't mean that." But his face was eager,
the look of the reprimanded child vanished. He
dropped the hat somewhere and came over to where
she was standing and took her hands in his own,
"Ellen, don't be kind to me, I can't bear it. You
don't mean it. All these months, ever since last spring
I've been losing you. To *him* . . . " he added savagely.
"You've been going further and further away from
me . . . "

"Please," she said, "don't be foolish . . . "

But he had taken her into his arms. She tried to
laugh, to free herself, twisting, turning her flushed
cheek aside. "Jim, let me go, Nancy's coming in
any minute."

For they could hear her banging oven doors, taking down plates, still whistling.

"Oh, damn Nancy——"

They did not hear the light knock on the door
which was not, after all, quite closed. Bill's red head
came in, cautiously. Bill said, "Say, Miss Ellen——"
Bill stopped, appalled. "Jees'," said Bill out of his
old habit.

Jim's arms had loosened. "Why, Bill," said Ellen between laughter and embarrassment.

"I forgot me new gloves," explained Bill. "I run all the way from home."

She found them for him.

He departed, thoughtful. Should he tell? You shouldn't never tell on a lady. But, if she was two-timin' his pal? . . . That was different. Bill's loyalty went out to his own sex. Bill's allegiance was as fixed as a star. If she was double-crossin' the best guy God ever made . . . ?

He set his square stubborn chin but it trembled. Gee, he liked Miss Ellen. She was pretty. She could laugh with him, she was a swell dame. But Bartlett came first. Somehow, he'd have to let Bartlett know.

He didn't like O'Connor. He'd heard things about O'Connor. If Miss Ellen didn't have sense enough to see the difference between the two men . . .

Frank, as Bill was permitted to call him, was crazy about her. Bill realized dimly that perhaps his own relationship with his idol was dictated, in part at least, by his hero's desire to "stand in good" with Ellen. Gee, this love stuff was the bunk. It did things to you. It would, he feared, "do things" to Frank. Gee, he hoped he'd never fall in love. Dames was all alike. Two-faced. Not for him the soft deceptions of the gentle passion.

He swore, feeling that this was the appropriate

occasion although Frank had pointed out to him that language could be expressively employed without the embellishments of picturesque profanity.

Bill spat, with accuracy, into the gutter. The warmth had departed from the new suit, the radiance from the shirts, the glamour from the ties. The shoes didn't shine as they should. He stubbed a toe deliberately against the curbing. The thought of horsehide coat, of sweaters, of wool socks with gay turned-down tops, of actually the faintly effeminate touch of pyjamas and handkerchiefs and gloves failed to move him for the first time in twenty-four hours. Frank was a good guy. He oughter be put wise.

CHAPTER SIXTEEN

This was the late autumn when certain wiseacres decided that the abortive launching of the Eugénie silhouette had been a base, secret scheme of the United Taxi Drivers because of the inability of Eugénie-clad women to travel in subways or cross crowded streets with any degree of safety or suitability. Eugénie, a wistful ghost, departed by degrees. Ellen, looking over a newspaper and regarding the advertisements, asked Carolyn Mathews in the sub-station office:

"Are you a mind reader or an astrologer?"

Carolyn, her brow wrinkled over her reports, glanced up from her desk.

"Neither," she replied briefly. "If I had been born with a caul or something I probably wouldn't have to struggle through my State Boards in order to become a ministering angel."

But an unimportant memory teased at Ellen's mind.

"Just the same, last spring when the talk was all Eugénie you predicted Flórentine tams or something. Here they are ... Borgia bonnets for lady poisoners. How come you're so far in advance of the styles?"

"You may notice I never take advantage of my knowledge," Carolyn said laughing, "but if the truth were known, I've two sisters. One's a stylist, and one's a buyer. Gowns, millinery. They have their ears to the ground. Emily—that's the stylist, says by spring we'll be going back to padded shoulders and tailored suits. Not that that means anything to me."

Ellen returned to her own work, smiling and reflective. She worked with Carolyn every day yet, though she had known vaguely that she had several sisters and brothers, she knew nothing whatever about them. How little she knew about any of her associates although she saw them, now and then, outside of work. Funny to be with people day after day and not to know, she thought.

It was the people who were in a sense complete strangers to you from whom you learned the most intimate and secret details of their curious lives, she reflected.

The telephone rang presently. It was, it happened, for her. She rose to answer as Miss Renwick nodded to her. A girl's voice came faintly over the wire. "It's Gladys—Gladys Markey. Could you come see me? I gotter talk to someone. Quick."

Ellen promised, and hung up, frowning, thoughtful. She looked over at Miss Renwick, the gray hair brushed back smoothly, the sagacious unastonished eyes behind the horn-rimmed glasses, the capable clever hands. Gladys hadn't asked for her advice professionally. Or had she? In any case there might be something they could do. She went over and sat down beside Miss Renwick's desk and spoke to her, briefly, frankly. Miss Renwick nodded. They'd get together on it, she said, if the girl was willing to put her case in their hands. Meantime Ellen had a free hand to do what she could.

Ellen managed to see Gladys during the morning. She found herself going dispiritedly up the stairs wondering if, before Gladys was willing to follow up her impulse toward confidence, the mother would interefere. She knocked and Gladys' voice said, "Come in."

She was alone, huddled near the window in a chair. The mother was not in evidence. She saw Ellen's quick glance around and tried to smile . . . "She's not home, she went out, she won't be back till night," Gladys reassured her.

She looked wretched, the pretty common little face drawn and a dreadful color. Ellen sat down beside her and asked her a few entirely practical questions. No, she hadn't been to a doctor. She must see a doctor, Ellen told her; she would arrange with Dr. Travers, she could go to his office.

Gladys further effaced herself in the chair. She hadn't, she admitted, gone out on the streets till after dark, if at all, for weeks. Everyone was talking; her mother loudest and longest of them all, she added bitterly.

"What are you going to do, Gladys?"

"I want to get away somewhere, anywhere, until the—until it's all over," Gladys told her hysterically. "I tell you I can't stand it any more. She nags at me all day; she won't give me a decent word. I've gotta get away . . . "

Ellen said quietly:

"It can be arranged, I think. There is a very good place; it is, of course, institutional. You'll have to expect that, rules and regulations. I think I can get you in any time; but you will have to stay six months afterwards, and work out your time. The girls who can't pay have to work. The baby will then be sent out for proper adoption, if you wish."

Gladys made a gesture of despair.

"What else can I do?" she muttered. She looked up; her eyes were enormous . . . "It isn't like a jail, they'll send me to, is it?" she whispered.

"No, of course not. You'll have good care, good treatment," Ellen told her.

Gladys said sullenly:

"She keeps telling me what a fool I was to go through with it. Sometimes I think she's right."

"No," said Ellen.

"I need money," Gladys told her wildly. "If I had money I wouldn't have to stay in that place, I could get the things I need too and everything. I *gotta* have money. But . . . " She looked down at her hands. "I haven't worked since, since last summer," she said, "someone said something . . . I was fired."

"Have you seen the man again?" Ellen asked her.

Gladys shook her head, and her disordered hair masked for a moment her expression; then she pushed it back from her forehead with both hands.

"I telephoned," she admitted after a while. "I used to sneak out and walk and walk until I got somewhere where people wouldn't be likely to know me and go into a booth." She stopped a moment and Ellen could somehow see her, standing in the booth, the close hot cubicle, sweat running down her forehead, her hands wet with it, speaking into the indifferent black mouth of the transmitter . . . "I called his office. There was always a girl answered on a switchboard. I'd ask to speak to him. 'What name shall I say?' or 'Who is calling?' she asked me. I wouldn't tell. 'He'll know, all right, let me speak to him,' I came back at her. And twice I got some-

one else after that. A secretary, I suppose. The
second time I told her straight, 'Tell him it's Gladys
—Gladys Markey,' I said, 'and he'll talk. He's
gotta.' But he didn't. He was there, though. I heard
her ask him ... 'It's someone called Gladys Markey,
she says you know her.' And she comes back to the
phone, 'Mr. Bartlett says he does not know you.
Can you give me the message?' "

She was silent.

The blood rushed up to Ellen's face, receded. She
felt definitely faint. She thought, how silly, as if
there weren't a hundred— She asked, pulling herself together:

"Where did you meet him, Gladys?"

"In the cafeteria near where I worked. He come
in one day and sat at my table. We got talking.
Pass the salt, or something. You know how it is ... "
She laughed without mirth. "He said he hadn't never
been there before. He said he was glad he come." She
was slipping back into her mother's way of talking
as she leaned forward, more animated, as if it helped
her to tell, as if in a way she were *proud* of telling.
"He was a wisecracker," said Gladys, reminiscently,
"he kept me laughing, he certainly could clown."
She paused, remembering; and then went on, "I
kidded him back, see? He said, 'You eat here often?'
and I said, 'Sure, Big Boy, every day except when
my car calls to take me to the Ritz.' And he laughed

and said, 'You're a wisecracker, aren't you?' And then he said—I was getting ready to go—'I'll be seeing you.'"

"And then?" Ellen prompted.

"He came back, not the next day, but the next. He told me then who he was." Ellen made a little gesture and then sat back, waiting. But Gladys went on. "Then he started meeting me for lunch. Other places. You know, funny places downtown, where there's sand on the floor and little booths, like. He said, 'We can be quiet here.' Then he got me to go out to dinner . . ."

"He never came to your house?"

"Who, him? Not likely," said Gladys in sincere astonishment, "he — he's a big man. He's a lawyer . . ."

Ellen said faintly:

"What was his name?"

Gladys said after a minute: "I said I'd never tell. But I sort of gave myself away a while back, didn't I?" She added, after a moment, matter-of-factly, "Bartlett, Frank Bartlett."

Ellen thought, It isn't possible. I'm not sitting here, in this room, listening . . . It was a nightmare, it was madness. She looked at Gladys, dimly trying to see, trying to understand that the ravaged features were not what he had seen; trying to remember that Gladys had been pretty and pert; a wise-cracker . . .

She thought she cried out, No—*NO*. But she hadn't moved or spoken. Gladys said curiously:

"Gee, you look funny. Do you know him?" Her eyes were wistful, eager, and still curiously proud.

Ellen said slowly: "Perhaps. Are you sure? Sure of the name and——"

She couldn't go on. Gladys said impatiently:

"Of course, I'm sure. You can look him up in the book. I seen his card once. The name, the address . . . "

"Have you written him?" Ellen asked. She thought, "I've got to get away from here, got to go somewhere and think, I must——"

"No," said Gladys, "that secretary—do you think I want everyone knowing my business? I been down a couple of times, hanging around there, waiting. But I never seen him."

Ellen said, perfectly aware that she was not asking merely professional questions, aware that she had to ask, had to drag out of this girl every last little detail, had to know, had to kill herself knowing:

"He—said he was in love with you? . . . Promised to marry you?"

"Who, him?" Gladys was amazed again. "No . . . I mean, he said he loved me . . . and that some day . . . " She was silent. She went on while Ellen's

throat grew more and more constricted with the
tension she put on herself, the suicidal restraint.
"He was married, see? I mean, not living with his
wife or anything. They didn't get along. He hated
her, he said. They were separated . . . She wouldn't
divorce him, she was a Catholic."

Not Frank, it couldn't be Frank. And yet . . .
what proof has she that Frank wasn't married—
and separated from his wife? Or, had he lied to
Gladys? Or was it to her he had lied?

"Look here," said Gladys desperately, "I don't
want to get him in no trouble, see. I went into it with
my eyes open. I wasn't born yesterday. I—if he'd
help me, if he'd give me the money to get away,
that's all I ask, all I want. But I'm afraid of Ma.
She knows something, or pretends she does. I haven't
no letters, or anything. But—I'm afraid she's got
some way of finding out. If she does, she'll go to
him; or to the cops; or something. Blackmail," said
Gladys darkly, "I know her game. All she thinks of
is the money."

"And he's a gentleman," said Gladys . . .

Ellen rose and touched the girl's shoulder. She
loathed doing it, she forced herself, her hand was
leaden. She said, after a moment:

"I'll do what I can. I'll go with you to him if that
seems necessary. Give me a little while to think this

over. Then I'll let you know and we'll see. What time does your mother get in from work?"

Gladys told her.

Ellen said, "I'll get in touch with you, Gladys, and we'll do what we can."

The girl stammered, there were tears in her eyes. She had been strong enough to bear what she had had to bear all these months, from her mother, from unfriendly people with mean eyes and careless tongues. But now she was weak, frightened. Ellen had strength. Ellen would, somehow, see her through.

Ellen went out and down the stairs. She found herself fighting for breath, clinging to the dirty railing, unheeding. She thought, "I've got to go through with it." She thought, "It can't be true, it isn't."

It couldn't be, the name alone would prove nothing, or even the profession. There must be other men by the same name—But the address?

It wasn't, it couldn't be.

But what, after all, did she know of him?

Her mother had been right, Jim had been right, everyone had been right, but herself. Still, she thought, her brain bruised, it didn't all fit in . . . not with Bill, even. But why not? Why couldn't he play up to Bill, to her . . . if he saw fit. Why couldn't he even like Bill, want to help him? Because a man was rotten in one respect didn't mean he wasn't devoid of decent, of generous impulses. She knew enough about life, about people, to know that. Men who murdered, raised gardens; men who robbed women, were kind to animals . . . She laughed hysterically and people passing looked at her curiously . . .

After a long time, during which her work managed to get itself done, she made up her mind. She went into a telephone booth and called Bartlett's office.

The booth was close and smelled of rank smoke. The breath of a thousand other people had left a mark on the transmitter. She stood there waiting, listening to the faint ringing along the wires, waiting and thinking of Gladys, in a booth like this booth, also waiting.

The girl at the switchboard answered. Ellen gave her name. It was, she said, important. The secretary, coming on the wire, was pleasant. Mr. Bartlett had stepped across the hall. He would be right back. Would Miss Adams hold the wire or would he call her back . . . what was the number?

"I'll wait, I'm in a booth, Miss Marlowe."

Three minutes, five. Interminable, a hundred years, an eternity. Then he spoke.

"Ellen, hello—what's on your mind . . . ?"

She said steadily, brushing the greetings aside, the thread of laughter which like a visible smile ran through the words, "I have to see you, Frank, it's terribly important."

"Where are you, I'll come down?"

She thought. No. If she took him to Gladys, the mother might return, there might be a thousand contretemps.

She said, "No, I have to finish my work, I——"

"I'll come over tonight, then?"

"No, please." Then she spoke, making up her mind, "This is something that can't be discussed at home. Could I—if I came to your apartment . . . tonight . . . early?"

She could feel the blank astonishment at the other end of the wire. Suddenly, she was crying. She hated herself, she despised herself, she was clinging there for support, leaning against the greasy pencil-scrawled wall, crying bitterly. He could hear her, the forlorn catch of her voice. He said:

"Good God, darling, what is it? Is it your mother, or Coral? Not Nancy? What's happened?"

She said, brokenly:

"No . . . If I come at eight o'clock, then?"

"Of course. But I can't understand . . . I mean, why can't I take you out or—I mean . . . Ellen, *Ellen* . . . " He jiggled the receiver frantically, there was no sound. "Operator," he shouted, "you cut us off." "Sorry, the party disconnected," reported the operator blandly. "Get them back," demanded Bartlett. "Sorry," said the operator, "what was the number?" "I don't know," Frank said blankly, "they called me."

His secretary, a tactful woman, had been out of the room. She returned to find him scarlet with rage. He said, "Miss Adams . . . I can't get her back, it was so important . . . "

Miss Marlowe said soothingly, "She told me she was phoning from a booth."

"Oh . . . " He set the telephone aside and ran his hands through his hair. His blue eyes were anxious and bewildered. What had happened . . . what could have happened? He thought, I must go to her now, immediately. But he couldn't, he didn't know where she was, even. No use calling the sub-station, asking her to get in touch with him when she made her reports, nothing to do but fret through the rest of the day, somehow. And wait.

A little after four that afternoon, Miss Marlowe came in to him smiling.

"It's Bill, Mr. Bartlett; he came to see you, to bring his report card."

Bartlett grinned. Bill was always a tonic. He dismissed for a moment all the things which had been puzzling and worrying him for hours and sat back in his chair. Bill marched in, very well dressed, very conscious of it. Yes, he had his report card. That was now a routine matter between the two of them, the report card, marked with the shining A for attenda ce.

"I brung it along," said Bill casually.

Bartlett offered him a chair gravely. Took the card in his hand, smiled over an item or two, shook his head over another. Then returned the report card with a brand-new dollar bill, also a routine.

Bill volunteered:

"I seen Mis' Ellen when I was making for the subway. She didn't see me. I hollered at her, though."

Bartlett's brief respite from anxiety was over. He said, "How is she?" mechanically enough, without much reason. Bill answered literally.

"I don't know. She looked sumpin' fierce. Maybe," said Bill, thinking himself rather brilliant, "it's the boy friend."

"Boy friend?" asked Bartlett, astonished.

"Sure, you know Jim O'Connor. They're going together," said Bill with importance, but afraid; and sorry, somehow. He looked at his hero anxiously.

"Oh, they're old friends," Bartlett said, smiling easily.

Bill snorted a little.

"Sunday—you know, when you took me around, I went back, after, I'd left my gloves," explained Bill, blushing at the mere thought of the effeminate admission, "and they was there, him and her . . . doing a regular Garbo . . . "

"Never mind, Bill," said Bartlett shortly, angrily. Bill shuffled the feet in the new shoes.

"Gee, I'm sorry. I didn't mean to spill nothing, Frank, only I thought . . . "

"Never mind what you thought. Gentlemen don't talk about ladies," said Bartlett.

Bill rose to go, to scamper home, riding the great swift beast of the subway, tumbling in, hungry for supper. He looked up at Bartlett, at his preoccupied face, his estranged eyes and burst out, not able to restrain himself another moment.

"I suppose you're sore, but I had to tell you, Frank. Gee," said Bill, sighing with utter adoration, "you're such a *square* guy, Frank, and wimmin," said Bill, "are funny as hell!"

"I—that's all right, I understand. Run along, Old Timer." He gave Bill an abstracted pat on the shoulder. "I'm not sore."

Bill departed, wondering if he had been clever or dumb. Perhaps they don't *want* to know if their janes is double-crossing them after all, he reflected as many an adult has reflected before him. Bartlett, left alone, had returned to his desk. Legs straight out before him, hands in pockets, he thought things over . . .

Doing a regular Garbo . . .

That could mean . . . No, it could mean only what Bill had meant it to convey.

Was this the explanation . . . ?

CHAPTER SEVENTEEN

Ellen had notified Gladys. She'd gone back to the house after work. She told her what to do and where to go. Gladys demurred, hung back, was suddenly desperately frightened. Ellen was abrupt with her, insistent. "It's the only thing to do," she said, thinking that after all it was, in a way, pretty comic, the sort of comedy you shrieked at wondering at its insanity. "After all, you won't be alone. I'll be with you."

Then she went home and listened to Nancy and Coral comment on her appearance.

"Heavens, you look dreadful," said Nancy, "like something the cat would scorn to bring in." She exchanged a glance with Coral. The glance said . . . what's up? . . . she's been crying . . .

Ellen, who never cried . . .

"I've a headache," said Ellen briefly. "Look here, I've got to go out tonight. On a case."

"Good lord, don't they give you time to sleep?" asked Coral, disgusted. "You're almost as bad as Pete."

"This is special," Ellen told her.

Nancy looked at her sister sharply. Something was wrong. Terribly wrong. She had an instinct to protect her, and as she put it to herself, to call them off the trail. She said, suddenly:

"Dot's husband has left her, next door."

Mrs. Adams said, "I'm not surprised"; but Coral's face clouded. "Poor devil," said Coral slowly.

That was the wrong lead, thought Nancy, annoyed with herself, and Ellen hadn't even heard. She hadn't taken off her uniform. Wasn't going to, perhaps. Yes, she was. She rose and went slowly into the bedroom. Nancy looked after her, frowning. Presently she came out again in a dark dress and put her coat and hat and bag on a chair. "I got out of your way," she told Nancy. "You're going out with Chick, aren't you?" She looked over at her mother, "What about you?" she began.

"Pete's night off," said Coral, "we'll stay in. Mother dotes to hear him talk about operations." She laughed, the momentary cloud gone.

"I don't," said Mrs. Adams indignantly.

But she did, in a way. And she was proud of Pete. "My daughter's fiancé," she would say importantly. "Dr. McGregor." She would mention his hospital . . .

Pete, on his rotating service, always had something to tell. If he had wanted to stay at the hospital another year as some of the luckier men could, he never said. He couldn't, really; he owed it to Mallory to get out and go to work, especially after disappointing him. Some day he'd pay back Mallory every cent. He'd told him so. "But I don't want you to, son. I've been trying to pay *you*," Mallory said. "But if I paid it double, the money I mean," Pete told him earnestly, "I wouldn't be repaying you really . . . for all you've done for me," Pete reminded him stubbornly.

Now he had Coral to look after, to guard, to love. The color was back in her cheeks, there was flesh on her bones, she was the girl he'd always loved, he'd be so careful of her, she'd never regret it. And neither would he. He knew that now. Ellen had set him straight, had helped him to fight it out himself, to set and keep himself straight.

At supper Mrs. Adams was engrossed with the subject of Dot Brown and her misfortune despite Nancy's warning interruptions. "I said it would happen," she said. "I told you so, didn't I, Ellen?"

Ellen, coming back from her dark thoughts, looked

up from her untouched plate. She had been staring down at it for five minutes.

"I'm sorry, Mother," she murmured, "I wasn't listening."

They had to tell her about Dot, all over again. A quiver of something like distaste, of a faint bitter sorrow passed over her set, very pale face. She made no comment. Nancy said briskly, fighting a sensation of pure and it seemed baseless fear: "Look here, let's talk about something cheerful. Christmas, for instance."

Christmas was, as a matter of fact, just around the corner. Mrs. Adams, forgetting Dot, began to plan. She'd have them all home with her this year, Nancy, Ellen—Coral. Pete would come when he could get off, if at all. Pete's getting off was a joke. Coral remembered out loud *the* last theater date they had a week or so ago. Remembered how, as he had after reported it, when he was through and under the shower, a message had come. Two new cases on his floor, the man taking his calls busy with emergencies and would he hurry, please——

He had hurried, and they had made the theater; but he hadn't had any dinner and was, Coral said laughing, when she saw him, half dressed, and literally, one side of his face shaved.

Yes, all there for Christmas. And Jim and his aunt would look in in the evening; they always did. Mrs.

Adams thought of Christmas and her heart that was narrow, but very deep, expanded a little. She said gaily to Ellen, "And perhaps Mr. Bartlett would come?"

That was a real concession. But Coral had been at her; and Pete and Nancy. All of them, arguing, pleading. "What's wrong with him, Mother? You only make Ellen unhappy by your attitude." This would show Ellen, maybe, that she hadn't meant to be unkind and suspicious. She had been afraid, that was all. She'd been so afraid ever since Coral . . . But that was all over now.

Ellen was ghastly. Her mother repeated the question. She added, "Of course we don't know if he has other plans."

"It's quite likely," said Ellen briefly.

Nancy said quickly, "He hasn't a relative in the world except those people, you know, West somewhere."

Ellen said nothing and her mother, forgetting her own astonishment, said, "You haven't eaten a thing."

"It's my head," she said and tried to smile, and rose and left the table. "Asperin in the bathroom as you very well know," Nancy called after her. She went in, they heard her running the water. Coral and Nancy looked at one another again. "It isn't like Ellen to have headaches," remarked Mrs. Adams, worried, "I hope she isn't coming down with something."

By half past seven Ellen had gone. She met Gladys where she had said she would meet her, on the corner. Gladys, bulky yet pathetically small somehow in a shabby big coat, was waiting impatiently. It was cold and cloudy, a few flakes of snow drifted down, melted when they reached the pavement. Gladys said, gasping: "I was early . . . I was afraid you wouldn't . . . Gee, I started to go back twice . . . I told Ma I had to go to the drug store, not that she believed me, or cared. She didn't follow me, I looked . . . I came the long way around."

Ellen asked, not listening, "Are you warm enough? Here," she hailed a cruising taxi and put Gladys in. She gave the address to the driver, steadily.

They drove uptown almost in silence. Once Gladys said, "Gee, I'm cold." Her teeth were chattering. Ellen forced herself to take the girl's icy hands in her own. She said, "You're not dressed warmly enough." Looking down at Gladys' feet, "Those ridiculous heels and flimsy stockings! Gladys, you should know better, especially now." She was talking to her as if she were a patient, any patient, forcing herself, trying not to think what waited for them both at the end of the long ride. She thought, "When he sees her . . . and me. I'm glad, I'm glad he'll have to see me . . . with her . . ."

But she wasn't glad. She was afraid. She was more than afraid. There were no words for her fear and her unhappiness and her resentment.

Other women.

She hadn't thought about other women and Frank. That he must know many, that he must have cared for one, for several perhaps, before they met, was obvious enough. That she had always taken for granted, without thinking very much about it. And as far as his having been faithful to her went, these last few months, she had never thought of that. She might even, had she thought, have understood, if reluctantly and with bitterness, his *not* having been faithful. Men don't live on hope, she thought. But Gladys and a cafeteria—and a man who "clowned." No, she couldn't understand it, she never would.

She was trying not to think of the wife from whom, so Gladys had said, so he had said to Gladys, he was separated. Whether it was true or not, whether he had lied to Gladys or to her, didn't much matter now. Nothing mattered now. That was a non-essential, absolutely. It couldn't mean anything to her whether there was a wife in the background, whether, for that matter, there were two wives . . . now.

That was all just part of this senseless fabric.

They had reached the apartment house, standing back in the usual heavy, rather handsome massive architectural design, built around a great open court. A good neighborhood, a respectable neighborhood.

Gladys' teeth were chattering again. She whimpered, "I can't. I'm scared. He'll be sore, he'll be wild at me. He'll have me thrown out, maybe. Let's go back, I'll go to that place and stay there as long as they keep me, I'll manage Ma somehow, let's go back."

"No, we're not going back," said Ellen. She helped her from the taxi and paid the driver, and took the girl's arm. "He won't throw you out," said Ellen, and her little jaw set and her lips were drained of color. Her eyes were almost black, the stormy gray eyes, startling against the pallor of her face.

They went into the apartment house. Warmth was there and subdued coloring and good furniture. She gave her name, the fact that she had an appointment. She was expected, they told her, looking curiously, not at her, but at Gladys.

The small cage of the elevator shot upward. They were alone in it save for the indifferent attendant.

At the eighth floor they got out; and Ellen, half dragging the shivering girl with her, rang the indicated bell.

A manservant opened to them. He said: "Miss Adams? Mr. Bartlett will be with you in a moment. He's on the phone."

A square foyer. Ellen shook her head as the man

made a gesture toward her coat. Gladys huddled herself more closely in her own. There was a living room, a fire burning on a hearth. Deep chairs, low, smoking tables, books lining the walls. A pleasant room. A man's room. Old hunting prints against the beige background of the wall space left untouched by shelves.

A door was shut somewhere, through it faintly they could hear a man's voice speaking urgently.

A door opened. There were steps, down a hall. Frank came in. He said, quickly, his eyes going to Ellen at once, in his impatience not seeing Gladys who stood over in a darker corner back of a great wing chair, "Ellen, I've been out of my mind with worry all day . . . I'm sorry I kept you waiting a moment, I had a long distance call . . . "

He was coming closer to her. She thought, "I'll never see him again, I must remember what he looks like; no, I never want to think of his face again, I must forget it." But she kept her eyes on his. She said clearly, "Gladys——"

But Gladys was clutching the chair, swaying, making curious sounds in her throat.

Ellen ran to her immediately, ignoring Bartlett who stared at her and now came forward, ignoring his exclamation . . .

"Gladys," she said and put her arm around the girl and faced him, "this is Frank Bartlett—you—"

But Gladys had screamed, Gladys was screaming . . .

"No, it isn't . . . I never seen him before," Gladys was screaming, the hysterics she had so far restrained having their way with her. "*I never seen him before . . .*"

"She's fainted," said Ellen sharply, as the girl's entire weight slithered toward her, leaned against her.

Bartlett sprang forward, together they carried Gladys to a divan and laid her down. "Flatter," said Ellen. She was working over her. "Get water, have you spirits of ammonia?" she was asking. She had no time for anything, not even for this overwhelming relief, this utter shame, while she worked . . .

Bartlett went out and came back without a word with the things that were needed; Gladys opened her eyes and shuddered, pushing Ellen's hand away.

"I feel so sick," she said. She was gray.

"Can I take her into a bedroom?" Ellen asked.

Bartlett nodded. They helped the girl to her feet and between them they got her down the hall and into a bedroom. His. A frankly masculine bedroom, well, rather sparely, furnished. They stretched her out flat on the bed and Ellen said, "If you'd leave us . . . is that the bathroom there . . . ?"

He said . . . angrily, "If you'd tell me what the——"

"In a moment," said Ellen frantically—"*please.*"

He went out and left them.

About ten minutes later Ellen came out to him in the living room. He was walking up and down, chewing savagely on an unlit pipe. "What in God's name is it all about?" he began, "this girl . . . Ellen, for heaven's sake . . . "

"She's half asleep," said Ellen. "I thought you'd let her rest a minute before I took her home." She said, "I know I owe you an explanation, Frank, I'm so ashamed . . . "

He was gentler with her now, made her sit down, sat down beside her on the couch. But he was angry with bewilderment.

She said, "I don't know how to begin . . . "

But she knew. There was only one way. She told him, straightforwardly, the whole story.

He said, first of all, blankly:

"*And you believed all this——?*"

"I didn't want to." She had taken off her hat and coat there in the bedroom and now, in the dark dress, her face blossoming up, purely as a flower, very white. Her hair loose about her temples, the heavy knot of gold close to the nape of her slender neck, she had never looked as tired, as defeated . . . nor as lovely, somehow . . . "I didn't want to. I *couldn't* at first. But the name, the address. Everything. He—had shown her his card," she said, "and she'd called your office, and been told you didn't know her."

"So that is the woman who called. Naturally, I didn't know her."

He rose; he looked down at her.

"I'll have him jailed, whoever he is," he said furiously, "but—all that doesn't matter. It's you, I tell you. *You,* to believe!"

"Frank," she said piteously, "what was I to think? It all fitted in, it was such clear evidence." He would understand that, she was speaking his own language now, she thought. She said, as no sign of pardon, no line of softening or understanding altered the hard young face, the almost unknown face at which she looked, "I knew nothing about you, really, *nothing*——"

"Nothing? I'd told you everything," he said.

She said, "He—the man told her—he was married . . . separated from his wife——"

"And you believed that, too?"

He began to laugh. "Really, Ellen, it *is* funny. You believed that, too——"

She pushed her hands through her hair, held them to her aching, throbbing temples.

"Frank, I didn't know . . . I didn't know. You— he—could have lied to Gladys . . . as an excuse— or you could have lied to me." She was becoming more and more confused. "I mean, that's what I thought . . . then . . ."

"Lie to you? When I've been asking you to marry me, ever since practically—we first met."

"No——"

"Couldn't you guess, that much? If I didn't make speeches about it," he said angrily, "it was because you held me off. I know why. I know why now. It was, of course, O'Connor." He added, "I wish you joy of him."

She was on her feet now. "Jim——?"

What right had he . . .? It was like him, she thought, like a lawyer to twist things, turn them, put you in the wrong. She had been ready to ask his pardon, on her knees, beg for it, weep out her relief against his breast. But he didn't want it, the apology, or the other. He was looking at her as if he hated her——

"Yes, Jim. . . . It—it may please you to know I've something of a line on Jim, I——"

Gladys was calling her from the bedroom. She said, "I don't want to hear. It isn't important——"

"Of course you don't. Get that girl in here and let me talk to her," he ordered.

"Not in that tone. She—it wasn't her fault she came here," said Ellen bravely, "and it's not necessary to put her on the witness stand. She's been through enough."

"Why not? Don't you think I'd have some interest in knowing who's been using my name?" he demanded.

Ellen went without a word into the bedroom. Gladys was, she assured her, all right. Presently they came back together, Gladys with the utmost reluctance.

But he was gentle enough with *her*, brief, too, businesslike; settled her in a chair; ignored Ellen, asked his patient questions. But Gladys could tell him only what Ellen knew; where she had met the man calling himself Frank Bartlett; the places they had gone together; obscure speakeasies; places where there were rooms to rent by the hour. He'd always had money, or seemed to have. He'd given her presents, oh, stockings, perfume, nothing valuable. Yes, she could describe him, "Older than you, Mr. Bartlett, short and thick-set. His hair's growing gray, a little. He has blue eyes."

No, there was nothing more to tell. Gladys stammered, "I'm so sorry . . . I thought . . . She thought——"

"I know," said Bartlett. His glance at Ellen said, *I know what you thought.* It was an ugly glance, on the surface. Too ugly for her to see the wound, the pain. Innocence wears a less convincing face than guilt, even acknowledged innocence.

Gladys said, "We'll go now." She added quaintly,

"I'm sorry we give you this trouble, Mr. Bartlett. Me passing out and all. Only, I was so sure, see? And then you came in. And I'd never laid eyes on you before . . ."

Ellen said, "I'll get our things and we'll go." She left them together for a moment. When she came back carrying the things, Gladys was saying, "No, please, I can't take it, she—she'll help me, I've got a place to go."

Bartlett pushed the bills back into his pocket. He took them to the door. There was not time, no moment alone, no speech between them, except for Ellen's faint, "Frank, I'm sorry——"

But he did not answer.

Going back in the taxi she held Gladys close; the girl was shaking with sobs. She was saying, pitifully:

"What I mind most—lying like that—saying he was a gentleman—a big shot, somewhere . . . and *not* being . . . Not like him, he's the real thing——"

Suddenly something broke in upon her bewildered mind. She controlled herself, sat upright.

"You did know him, then, Mr. Bartlett? Well, I mean . . . I mean—you thought . . ." She looked at Ellen, astonished beyond adequate speech—"and you went to him, with me . . ."

Ellen said nothing. There was nothing to say.

"I didn't mean," said Gladys, "to get you into no trouble. I mean, if you and him——"

"There's nothing between me and him," said Ellen steadily. She knew she spoke the truth. Nothing. It was finished. Over and done with. He would never forgive her.

Listening, unhearing, to Gladys' talk, the rest of the way home, talk and speculate, resigned, she said: "Never mind. I'll find the other man for you. Don't worry. I'll find him. There must be a way."

There would be a way. It wouldn't, she thought, help her now, even if it helped Gladys. Nothing would help her now.

But a wave of pure anger shook her, shattered her. Why had he been so—implacable? Couldn't he see that she had had no other choice than to believe what she had believed? Men believed evidence, even circumstantial evidence. She remembered now all they had said of Dot Brown around the supper table that night. She had fancied herself deaf to their voices. Now it came back to her. Dan had left her because of something that had been evidence to him, because of something he had heard and had believed. Men were quick enough to believe. Must they feel themselves so superior that they demanded that women disregard evidence, to trust them and sustain them in the face of everything . . .?

CHAPTER EIGHTEEN

But if a dream were over and a hope extinguished, life went on, resistlessly; and there was Gladys to think of and her immediate necessity.

Ellen took the girl home; and went in with her. Mrs. Markey was waiting in the cluttered room . . . "And where have *you* been?" she began shrilly as Gladys, weariness dragging at her, opened the door. Then she saw Ellen.

Ellen was brief with the hostile woman. She explained only as much as was necessary. Gladys had come to her, together they had ascertained that the man responsible for the disaster had given, not his own name, but another's. There was nothing to do now but to look after Gladys. Ellen would do that— if Mrs. Markey would promise not to make any trouble. She put it to her practically and brusquely.

She had no sympathy whatever with this sharp-eyed
woman whose soiled palms so obviously itched; and
she had a very shrewd suspicion that Mrs. Markey
had not been deaf, dumb, and blind in the beginning
of the affair but had, by stimulating these qualities,
encouraged it. At least she had made no effort to
interfere. Easy Street was Easy Street to her, and
it apparently didn't matter to her how Gladys came
to it, by what devious and heartbreaking, hidden
paths or by what open highway.

Gladys said suddenly, "Never mind Ma." She shot
a vindictive look at her mother; she added, "She
isn't, anyway——"

Mrs. Markey went an unattractive scarlet.
"Haven't I tried to do my best by you?" she demanded. "Haven't I slaved and worked and done
for you as if you was my own?"

Gladys shrugged. Ellen looked from one to the
other. Gladys was outspoken in her subsequent recital. Mrs. Markey was Markey's second wife, a
cousin of Gladys' mother. He had married the
woman shortly after his wife's death in childbirth,
in order to maintain his home and keep his child
with him. Ellen thought, so that's it . . . I'm
glad . . .

It made things a little easier, for everyone concerned. Gladys had, of course, no other mother. Mrs.
Markey had never told, had sworn her husband not

to tell, for, she had put it to him, the child's sake. At his death there had been a matter of some insurance, and a few possessions. Naturally, the mother would take it all, provide for "their" daughter. It had only been during the last few months that Gladys, during a bitter quarrel, had been informed.

Ellen left presently and went home. Pete said, getting up from the table where he and Coral and Mrs. Adams were playing three-handed bridge: "Lord, you look all in . . . I was just going, Ellen, we won't keep you up any longer." He took her aside and asked anxiously, "What's up, anything I can do?" There was nothing, she told him, trying to smile.

Then he left, and after a while she got into the bed davenport and tried to think: of what she must do for Gladys; of . . . of . . . Frank.

There wasn't much sleep for her that night, too tired to sleep, she told herself; too unhappy, she knew.

Early the next morning she tried to write to Frank; made several attempts and tore them up. If he really cared, she told herself, he would understand . . . would forgive her . . . would realize that in the face of evidence so overwhelming any woman would have doubted . . .

If he really cared, she would hear from him.

She did not hear.

Meantime, there was Gladys to consider. Miss Renwick was making the arrangements, and during the time which elapsed until the formalities were complied with, Ellen was following up a forlorn hope.

This was to go to the cafeteria and see if the man ever returned there. Gladys, when questioned, shook her head. She didn't think so. Long ago, last summer, for instance, she had gone downtown every day and gone in and waited. "Until I grew ashamed," she said, "of not being able to buy a square meal."

Three days running, during Ellen's lunch hour, she went downtown on the subway and met Gladys in the crowded noisy shining white place. The cashier remarked, that first day when, after eating something for appearance's and hunger's sake, they made their way out and Ellen paid the check. "You don't come here any more." She was looking at Gladys with open curiosity. Gladys told her pitiful lie, "I'm not working," she said, "I'm married." She dropped her ungloved left hand to her side quickly but not quickly enough. The cashier raised a plucked eyebrow and a tart retort was imminent. But she looked into Ellen's quiet eyes and was silent. Gladys asked hesitantly, "Do you ever see him any more—I mean, my boy friend, the one I uster eat here with sometimes?"

The cashier shook her head, indifferent. Gladys

said, "I heard he moved away." The cashier decided to remember. "You mean the short feller with the spats and who was always wisecracking? I seen him—leave me see—last week, I guess. He stopped coming for a while."

Gladys said, hastily, "If you see him again you needn't mind saying I was asking for him. We split up, see."

The cashier was warned. Ellen had taken no part in the conversation, but there was an authority about her which the girl behind the high desk respected. She nodded, "Okay by me," she agreed carelessly.

"He started coming back maybe," said Gladys eagerly when they were out in the narrow, crowded street, "because he thought it was safe and I wouldn't be showing up any more. I coulda jumped in the river for all he cared," commented Gladys bitterly.

On the second day Ellen spoke to the cashier herself, after sending Gladys outside to wait for her. Her uniform allowed her latitude as well as authority. She said, frankly, "I am anxious to find this man, the one you spoke of to us yesterday, to learn where he works. If he comes in again, can you find out discreetly? It would be more than kind of you . . ."

The cashier was "on." She said so. She had been

on all along. She observed, "Gee, things is fierce for
girls, ain't they?" She was grave as she said it.
Nothing would ever happen to her, she knew, she
was too wise. But even the hard-berled ones got
theirs some day . . . She remembered Gladys, and
the man. You couldn't forget him, such a wise-
cracker. Once he had asked her, the cashier, for a
date and she had said, "Run along, Big Boy, and
don't do no two-timing, I'm a married woman with
six children all under five."

She nodded at Ellen; being taken even partially
into confidence was exciting, it made her feel important. She asked one thing only. "It won't get in the
papers, will it? The Boss is perticuler. He has cat
fits if there's a scandal. Once they tried to put a guy
on the spot here. And there's strict rules about picking girls up."

Ellen reassured her and went out to join Gladys.

On the next, the third day, they saw him. They
had been there perhaps ten minutes, in the back of
the room, when the cashier manufactured an errand
and slithered past their table. "He just come in,"
she whispered, "he's over there, to the right, see?"

Gladys was sick-white. Ellen wrote something on
a slip of paper and passed it to the cashier. The
girl nodded and slithered away, touching her hair
with elaborate casualness, returning to her desk.

Ellen said, "If you'll just point him out to me, Gladys, and be sure of your identification!"

Gladys did so, presently. Ellen looked over, after a moment. She fixed in her mind the amiable, unimportant features of the man Gladys had indicated. Gladys was beginning to breathe quickly. Ellen said, "We'll get out of here . . ."

Their order had come, it was untouched. Ellen rose and maneuvered Gladys quickly toward the door. She stopped to pay the check and the cashier merely nodded. Ellen said, once they were outside, "I'll hear from her, I think, in a day or two."

She heard the next day, at noon, for she had written the office telephone number on the slip of paper she had given the cashier. When she went in the following day at the noon hour, Miss Renwick had the message. It was merely the name and address of a business house.

Frank's address: the same building, the same floor.

The rest was comparatively easy. Ellen went to the building and looked at the name board—Smith, Lambert, Mason & Company, and made an inquiry of the elevator man. Yes, he knew a man of that description in the office she spoke of. A bookkeeper, Nelson.

A telephone call ascertained the rest. He lived far uptown on the outskirts of the city. Gladys said . . . "I'll go to his house . . . I'll . . ." But

Ellen shook her head. "I'll go, if necessary," she said, "and do what I can. Meantime, *you* have nothing to do but get ready and next week I'll take you over to the Home."

She had been to the Home and made the arrangements. Everything was settled. There remained only the faint hope that Nelson would shoulder something of the financial responsibility. Ellen thought, "If he offers to marry her . . .?" That, of course, was the solution, the one way out. And yet, two wrongs couldn't make a right. What sort of a marriage would that be—a marriage of coercion on one side, of expedience on the other?

She went, first of all, to the office and asked to see their bookkeeper.

He came out to her in the reception hall, a stocky man, going gray, with very blue eyes. He turned white when he saw her. "It isn't one of the kids, is it, Nurse?" he asked.

That told her much. She answered "No," quickly, and motioned him to sit down. There was no one with them in the little anteroom. She said bluntly, "No, Mr. Nelson, I've come here because of Gladys Markey."

There was one moment when she thought that from reaction he would strike at her. His face altered, a hand rose. Then he looked down at the floor.

"What about her?" he asked sullenly. "What's she been blabbing about? I—I don't even know her."

"That won't get you anywhere," Ellen warned him.

"She's of age, isn't she?" he demanded. "You haven't anything on me, I wasn't the only one."

"That's not true; besides, it's neither here nor there." She sketched the situation, briefly. His face hardened but there was terror in his eyes. "You can't pin it on *me*," he said.

"Perhaps not. But things can be made unpleasant for you. If Gladys were to go to your employer——"

He swore, at that. She listened, waiting. When he was through she said, "You're married, of course."

He nodded. "What's it to you?"

"Nothing. But you can help Gladys, with money."

He hadn't any money, he said. On a bookkeeper's salary? He laughed outright. With a wife and three kids to support!

Nothing to be gained there. She rose and looked down at him. He stayed there, seated, sullen. She stated abruptly, "If Gladys can't prosecute you, Mr. Bartlett can."

"What do you mean?" he stammered.

She said quietly: "You used his name. That's a punishable offense. His name, his business address."

After a moment Nelson said:

"I didn't mean to. I—I gave her the first name that popped into my head, see? I see it every day. On his door, across the way there. When the door of the room I work in is open, I see it. I've seen it for months. *I didn't even know I remembered it.*"

"You had Mr. Bartlett's card."

"He—he's my boss's personal lawyer. Lambert's. One day, he was in here, he left a card on the desk. I came in, I picked it up and put it in my pocket. I forgot it, and then, well, I showed it to her, that's all."

So simple, so easy an explanation.

"You told her you were separated from your wife," she said.

"I support her," he said sullenly, "we don't get on, that's all. She nags at you to drive a man crazy."

"Would she divorce you?" asked Ellen.

"Who? Her? Don't make me laugh. Not while she has her good bed and three meals a day."

He added. "She found out something. She held it over me, a long time. Till she began thinking that if she did divorce me I'd be a lot better off. Then she quit crabbing at me about it."

No, nothing to be done, here. Now he said: "You—you wouldn't go to the boss? I tell you, I treated that girl white, took her out, gave her things, spent money——"

He broke off and was silent. Presently Ellen left. She would, she decided, go see the wife. She wouldn't, she knew, hurt or astonish her; and the wife might be persuaded to influence Nelson.

It was a long trip uptown. The Nelson house was a two-family affair. There was a little back yard, with wash hanging out in it. The small porch was littered with scattered toys and scattered belongings of children. There had been a snowfall the night before and all the neighborhood children were out in the street, dragging their old sleds, their boxes on runners, over the scant white of what snow remained. Dirty children, and rosy children. Ellen went up the steps and regarded the spotty windows, the lank, discouraged ivy in a cement pot.

She rang. Mrs. Nelson opened. Tall, very thin, she looked older than her husband. She was not clean, she was unkempt. She brushed at the hair straggling from under a soiled boudoir cap. She said, on the defensive, "You needn't come round here, snoopin'. What I do with my garbage can is my own affair!"

From which Ellen judged that the nurses in the sub-station recently opened to care for this new, raw, rapidly growing district had been having their own troubles with Mrs. Nelson. "And Tommy's all right, too," added Mrs. Nelson, about to shut the door.

"Stummick, that's all. I said to the other nurse it was his stummick."

"I'm not from this district," Ellen told her, "and I've come to you on a personal matter."

"If it's money," warned Mrs. Nelson sourly, "I haven't got it. I haven't a cent. We paid what we could the time Gloria was sick and they sent the nurse around."

"It isn't money," said Ellen patiently.

Eventually she was ushered in. The house was dark, it smelled of cabbage, of wet clothes, of human emanations. Ellen sat down in the small parlor, cluttered up with massive "suite" furniture and one of the most enormous radios she had ever seen in her life. "Well?" said Mrs. Nelson, not at all friendly.

Ellen told her.

"I wouldn't have come," she finished, "if your husband had not told me that you—knew about this, originally. And I'm coming only to ask you to influence him, and to help this girl. A hundred dollars would see her through, Mrs. Nelson; and I pledge you my word that she will never worry you again."

Throughout the entire recital the woman had sat there, with a face like stone. The youngest baby, Tommy, in an indescribable state, crawled in and under her feet. She pushed him away and shouted for Gloria. Gloria, all eyes and legs, appeared and took the baby away. "Why isn't she in school?" Ellen demanded, while the child was in the room.

"Her throat isn't good. They want her to have her tonsils out. The school nurse sent me a message. I'm to take her to a clinic." She added something bitter about interference.

Gloria had gone, poor misnamed child, dragging the baby with her. "Well?" asked Ellen.

Mrs. Nelson rose, definitely.

"You can go back to that——" she used an ugly word—"and tell her she'll get no hundred dollars of mine. It isn't my fault. As far as he goes, I don't care what he does. As long as he brings home the pay envelope, and leaves me alone," she said, "I don't care. It's all right with me what he does, as long as he gives me my money and I don't have any more kids. Understand that. He's married to me, he'll stay married. He's gotta support me and the children. Tell his sweetie that, for me."

And that was all there was to it.

Where, thought Ellen, on the long trip home, where had he obtained the money with which he had entertained Gladys so royally? And how? She knew his salary. He had told her. It was sufficient to feed and clothe his wife and children, to keep a roof over their heads and to put coal in the cellar. But the woman was obviously a very bad manager. Much, too, of the weekly envelope had gone to the

installment man, Ellen thought, for the heavy furniture, and radio, for, doubtless, other things. She
had seen a fur coat in the hall. Mrs. Nelson's, no
doubt. A good fur coat bought, doubtless, on time.

A day or so before she was to take Gladys to the
Home, and after she had reported to her faithfully
what she had found out, and where she had failed,
Gladys, in a last spurt of hysteria, forced her way
into Smith, Lambert, Mason & Company's office and
demanded to see Nelson. There had been something
of a scene. Gladys was gotten rid of, tactfully, and
Nelson was, promptly, discharged. Gladys came
weeping with the story to Ellen, sitting there in the
sub-station until Ellen returned at noon. Ellen asked,
exasperated, "Why on earth did you do it, Gladys?"

The girl whimpered unceasingly. She was, she
said, afraid. Suddenly sick with a black terror at
what faced her; at the end of her rope. She had no
definite thought, no plan, only she had to see him,
she had to tell him what she thought of him, she
had to have that much satisfaction . . .

Now his firm knew—everything.

Ellen reported to Miss Renwick. "My fault . . .
if she hadn't found out his name, through me. But
I thought—I thought I could handle it, and that
she'd be reasonable."

"They never are," said Miss Renwick. "Cheer up,
there's no great harm done perhaps. We'll see."

Gladys went into the Home a day ahead of time. Ellen took her over on the ferry to the city in the bordering state, and saw her installed there, and promised to manage somehow to come and see her, and left her, resigned, all the fight gone out of her at last, and very much subdued. When she came out, she was assured, the baby would be taken care of, a job would be found for her somehow, and she could work out her own salvation. If any, thought Ellen, returning. And then—but there has to be—otherwise things haven't any sense, she told herself.

That night her telephone rang. She went, listlessly enough. She'd told Jim she was too tired to go out. But it would be like him to call and see if she would change her mind.

"Ellen?" asked Bartlett, over the wire.

CHAPTER NINETEEN

No, she was not too tired to see him.

He came that night, within the hour. He wouldn't stay long, he said briefly; it was, more or less, business. Coral managed things, took her little mother off into the bedroom, and shut the door, to discuss the furniture of the new flat.

He was friendly enough, restrained. The estrangement was still there. He came to the point at once.

Lambert was his client. And Lambert had come to him with the Nelson story, the use of his name. After discharging the man they had gone over his books. A long series of petty thefts, cleverly concealed. Now Bartlett had something to propose. Lambert had promised not to prosecute Nelson until he heard from Bartlett again.

"I had a talk with the fellow," said Bartlett. "It's all pretty clear. The champagne appetite, the beer pocketbook. He told me something about his family. He chose this means of escape, stealing a little, here and there, building himself a new personality, buying what he considered 'good clothes' and keeping them in his locker. Putting on the dog. Picking up a pretty girl and impressing her." He laughed a little. "I saw it somehow. Not that he isn't entirely culpable. It's just that he's a misfit. Wants to be . . . 'a big shot.' His own words. And hasn't a chance. Been sitting around ever since he left school, dreaming. He was with a shipping firm once. 'I couldn't stand it,' he told me, 'seeing the boats go out and me not on them.' Look here, Ellen, I have a sort of responsibility in this."

"What do you mean?" she asked him, gravely astonished.

"My name. He 'borrowed' my name. The way he 'borrowed' the money. I thought, perhaps, we could straighten things out. First of all, he'll have to have some sort of show-down with his wife. She has always, he told me, made him live beyond his means. And not to his own advantage."

"I've been there—to the house," Ellen told him. She described it.

Bartlett nodded.

"She'll be taught," he said, "how to run a budget.

I'll make good the loss to Lambert. Nelson can't stay on there, of course, too many people heard, too many know. I can get him a job somewhere else. He's a good bookkeeper. I know the place for him. He'll pay me back, a small sum every week. And that money will be put aside for the girl."

Ellen said, holding herself in:

"It—it's terribly decent of you. But why should you bother——?"

"I sort of got a slant on it," he said, a little embarrassed, "and it seemed to me that in a way it was up to me. Please realize, I am not condoning him—for what he did. I'm saying that I understand, a little. Perhaps if he'd had a different sort of home to go home to, perhaps if his job had held something of excitement, something not just deadly routine, it all wouldn't have happened."

She said, after a moment:

"That's a man's viewpoint, I suppose. I'm trying to see it. I think I do see it. All but Gladys' part in it."

She thought, Men are strange, the theft is more important to Frank than the other.

He said, "No, I see that, too. No excuse perhaps. Or, was there? A little opportunity for something he called romance, a chance to strut and preen himself and see adoration in a woman's eyes, instead of a sort of hatred; a chance to make someone—some woman—believe him what he wanted to be, what he couldn't ever be, what he'd dreamed of being. It wasn't that he was in love with Gladys. It was that he was in love with Gladys' idea of him. See that, can't you? And then, when things followed the law of cause and effect, when he was brought down to earth, when his foolish trappings dropped from him, he was just what I saw him today—a little ineffectual man, stubborn and resentful, afraid, somehow pitiful, the braggadocio all gone, a seducer, an adulterer, a thief . . . And I thought—there but for the grace of God——"

He broke off, exceptionally embarrassed, awkward; and rose to go.

"Then it's all right with you, Ellen? And the girl will get the money, I'll see to that."

"Yes, it's all right." She thought, "I mustn't cry, what a fool he'll think me!"

He said:

"I was pretty sore. Forget it. And what I said about O'Connor. You see——"

"That's all right," she said.

They stood there a minute, so much unsaid between them, and neither spoke. Had one of them spoken—Ellen said, desperately, "I told you that we've made all arrangements for Gladys——"

He listened, nodding. Held out his hand, "Goodbye," he said. "I'm glad you see it my way. You'll look after the girl, I know that. It just seemed to me if we could set Nelson straight things would be better, all around. I'm not," he added, "a reformer." He laughed shortly. "I'm not even inclined to good works. But somehow this got under my skin."

The door closed after him. She stood staring at it. Why didn't she call him back? Why didn't she call out to him . . . "You—you don't love me any more . . . you haven't, really, forgiven me." Or had he forgiven her, and in forgiving, ceased to care? That happened sometimes. What had she said to Pete? . . . in love there isn't any such word as forgiveness.

And what had Pete said to her—about jealousy, that dark and suicidal hell?

She had remembered that, the day Gladys had told her. It had been beyond all shame, all hurt love, the jealousy that she had felt. She had hated Gladys . . .

Her mother came out of the bedroom. She asked brightly, "Have you invited Mr. Bartlett . . .?" She stopped and looked around. She stated, with blank astonishment, "Why, he's gone!"

"Yes, he's gone," said Ellen, dully.

"Did you ask him, for Christmas?"

No, she had not asked him, Ellen told her; she had forgotten. She walked past her mother and Coral and into the larger bedroom. She shut the door. Nancy was out. She was alone, in the familiar room. She lay down on the bed, her hands clasped behind her head. If she could cry, she thought, she would feel better.

That chapter was closed. Gladys and Nelson who had wanted to be a big shot; and Frank. But life went on.

Christmas came; and went. There were flowers from Frank; a brief friendly card. He would be South, he wrote, with friends. That was all. Flowers fade.

Jim came, with his aunt, in the evening, to see the tree. He had gifts for them all. There was perfume for Nancy and Coral; there was a lavender shawl for Mrs. Adams. "Am I such an old woman?" she asked with amusement. "But thank you, Jimmy, it is lovely." It was, they assured her, and so becoming. There was also a ring . . . for Ellen.

He'd given her other things. Now, he took the little box from his pocket. They were standing alone together, by the lighted tree; the windows with their wreaths of green gave back a reflection, green and red and white . . .

"If you'd wear it . . .?" he asked.

But she shook her head. No, she would not wear it. He should not have bought it. "It will keep," he said, as cheerfully as he could, and put it back in his pocket. "It will have to keep. You'll like it, some day."

She thought, *No.* She thought of Coral. Coral hadn't a ring. It would be a long time before she would have a ring with a diamond shining in it—but Coral was happy.

She thought, "It might be easier to give in, he loves me, I'm really fond of him, he's cared for me all these years; everyone would be happy about it, especially Mother; it might be easier to surrender, to take second best . . ."

But she knew she wouldn't. She had something to sustain her, after all. She had her work. That mattered most. It would have to matter most now. She'd make it matter.

Christmas was over. The bread-lines increased. The lines before the registry offices waited patiently, in sleet and snow and rain, hour by hour. There were appeals, there were speeches, there was misery, there was suffering. This was an enormous country, it was a rich country. But the suffering went on. There were babies barely able to walk, dragging home crude wagons filled with sticks of wood. There were ambulances at people's doors, stretchers, neighbors saying . . . pneumonia . . .? Pete was desperate, overworked. "There isn't," he said on his rare hours off, "any end to this, the sickness from worry, from fear, from undernourishment . . ."

Ellen went into unheated rooms, the families huddled together; into houses where a single oil stove smoked. Ellen reported worthy cases to the gas company. The gas company saw that their service was not discontinued. Ellen tramped to the charity bureaus, Ellen reported cases, not of disease, but of starvation, which is worse than a disease.

It was a New Year. It would be a better year, they said.

She saw courage, in the bleeding raw. She saw a seventeen-year-old girl supporting a jobless father and brother, and a mother on sixteen dollars a week. She saw her, half delirious, lying on the bed she shared with her mother, "I've gotta go to work, I've gotta." Ellen saw a family die, leaving two; a girl of nineteen, a boy of twelve. "I have to look after the kid," said the girl, coughing. "I can't afford to stay out, sick."

All this and more. If she saw misery, if she saw tragedy, she saw gallantry. She saw the will to carry on, she saw the sacrifice and the stubbornness and the amazing fortitude of the human heart . . .

She thought, "What can I do, what can a thousand like me do, with our two hands apiece and our few hours in a day?" Not much, but it counted, it had to count. Every life saved, every job found, every family encouraged, every child given the treatment he or she needed, every lesson taught—it all counted. She thought of herself, for the first time, as an unknown soldier in a small army, an army that wouldn't, that couldn't give up, an army whose battles were unceasing, who had to go on . . .

"You're killing yourself," said Pete.

"Not me," said Ellen and laughed at him.

And then, one night, a ring at the door bell. She was alone with her mother. She went to the door, sick with hope, with fear that her hope was unfounded.

A very bitter night. And Bill, standing there, pulling off his cap with the warm ear-tabs; Bill in the horsehide coat and the sweater and the sturdy, scuffed shoes and woolen socks.

"It's me," said Bill. "Say, Mis' Ellen, the baby's awful sick and Ma can't get a doctor. I thought maybe——"

Mrs. Adams asked, "Why didn't you telephone the office, Bill?"

"It only just happened," explained Bill, "and I sez to my old—I mean, my ma, I says, 'Mis' Ellen'll come.' He's chokin'," said Bill simply.

Ellen went to the telephone and called Dr. Travers. He was out. She left an urgent message for him, and got on her things. It was something of a walk to Bill's, so they took a cab at the corner. "This is a swell cab," said Bill politely, "but it ain't as nice as Frank's . . ."

They reached Bill's house; he lived up three flights, in fairly large, fairly comfortable rooms. His mother, as red-headed as Bill, had the baby in her arms.

"It's—his throat," she said. "Croup like, but I never seen it so bad, no, not when Bill had it, when he was little."

Ellen looked at the baby. There were things to do and do fast. The first thing was to get Bill away, to isolate the gasping, choking child as soon as possible; to give an emetic; to improvise a croup kettle; to make compresses . . .

If it were membranous croup——

She worked rapidly, surely. The baby's mother helped her, not a woman to go to pieces, Mrs. Maloney. Bill and his father and Bill's little sister were banished. The tea kettle steamed. There were certain remedies in Ellen's black bag. If only Dr. Travers would hurry . . .

Now and then Ellen asked a question. No, the baby hadn't had diphtheria. Yes, Bill had had it, and the little girl, several years before . . .

The funny little tike with the top-knot of red hair was breathing a little more easily now. "God and His Saints be praised," said Mrs. Maloney. Ellen echoed her, silently, as she heard the heavy quick steps on the stairs . . .

It was membranous croup. She had done what she could; she had been prepared to do more, if necessary, if Travers hadn't come. But he did come. And

Mrs. Maloney held the lamp steady while he and Ellen did the things that were urgent and swift and delicate and sure. And presently the little boy slept . . .

And a long time afterwards, when directions had been left, and a nurse called, and everything attended to, Travers drove her home.

"Never had a better assistant," Travers praised her.

She was desperately tired; and yet her heart was very light. It was all so terribly worth while, no matter how tired you were, how discouraged, no matter if the hours came when it seemed a herculean task, no end to it, no proper beginning, and not much progress. Travers was talking about Pete. "He's the man for the job," he said. "I had hopes of Mel . . . but Mel's different. Pete knows these people, he loves them in his hard-boiled way, we're going to have a grand fight . . . and when I have to lay down the old arms, so to speak, he'll go on with it. That means a lot. He'll never be rich, I suppose," said Travers, with a chuckle, "but, boy, he'll be rewarded! He won't realize that till he's as old as I am."

Ellen went into the apartment. Her mother had made up the bed for her. "Don't come near me," said Ellen. "I've scrubbed up as best I can, but it wasn't enough."

She took off her clothes, dropped them in a solution, bathed herself, scrubbed, washed her hair . . .
"Ellen," said her mother, "you'll never get to bed . . ."

"There's the electric heater," said Ellen yawning. "I'll forego the luxury of hand-drying it, for once."

And the very next night, Bill came again.

No, not the kid, the kid was all right, there was a nurse there. Ellen knew that, one of the girls on the contagion service had been sent that morning. It was something that bothered him, Bill. He'd like to talk to Mis' Ellen, if he could.

Mrs. Adams smiled and went out to make cocoa. She was, Ellen discovered, so much happier when they let her do things. And Coral and Nancy were arguing, there in the bedroom, over the proper shade of green for gingham curtains for kitchen windows.

"Shoot," said Ellen encouragingly.

He wouldn't sit down, nor take off his things. He twisted his cap in his hands. His honest little eyes were distressed. He said, "You've been swell, Mis' Ellen. I—I gotta spill sumpin to you. Jees', I didn't mean nothin' by it. You see, that day I come here with Frank, well, when I come back, I see you— and that other feller——"

The grammar he was trying so painfully to acquire, fled. But no pleader at the bar could have been more eloquent. Ellen asked, "Well, Bill——?"

"Nuthin' . . . only . . . See, he was kissin' you
. . . or it looked that way. I—I thought, Frank's
crazy about her, see? she's his girl, but she's two-
timin' him I thought, he's such a grand sort of guy.
So I *told* him, see?"

So that was it. Ellen said, trying to smile:

"It's all right, Bill. Frank wouldn't mind, we're
just friends—and what you say wasn't, really, important."

"You're not sore at me, Mis' Ellen?"

"Of course not."

"Frank's sore."

"Oh, no, Bill, he isn't."

"Yes. I—I been to his office with the report cards.
He looks, and gives me the buck. He allers give
me a buck. But he don't have no time for me, he's
different, somehow, he don't care no more. I—oh,
what's the use?" said Bill, too stubborn to weep.

Mrs. Adams came in with cups and a bakery
cake. Bill's eyes widened. "Gee," he said, and was
persuaded to "take off his things and stay a while."
Chick was coming in for Nancy, they'd see that he
got home.

And so no more was said. Bill ate and drank, as
much as he could hold. And went home, or rather to
his mother's next-door neighbor, where he was staying until the baby was all well again. Ellen thought,
Poor Bill . . .

He was mistaken about Frank, of course. She herself wouldn't make that error of judgment again. He hadn't tired, he hadn't forgotten—Bill. He was busy, perhaps he was worried . . .

She tried to tell Bill so as, with Nancy and the very much entertained Chick, Bill left.

It was perhaps two weeks or more after that late one afternoon Ellen stopped at Bill's house to inquire after the welfare of her small emergency patient. The youngster was, his mother assured her, as fit as a fiddle. "When I seen you, holding him, and that terrible tube . . ." She shuddered and was silent. It was, Ellen agreed, not a pleasant process to watch, but it had done the trick. "We can't never thank you enough," said Mrs. Maloney.

She then said, "That Bill!"

"What's the matter with him?"

"Nothing but cussedness," said Bill's mother. "He's been playing hookey. Starts off to school as gay as you please, butter wouldn't melt in his mouth, with his lunch in his pocket, and a good lunch, too, now that Maloney is working regular, praise be to the Saints! But doesn't the truant officer come around again, sticking his long nose in the door. Three days, Bill isn't in school." She was dramatic. "Didn't Maloney strap him good for it? But it's no use talking to him, I thought this wouldn't be lastin', him goin' and comin' so quiet and good, after

Mr. Bartlett—a fine man if ever there was one—
got after him. I wish he'd git after him again,"
sighed Mrs. Maloney.

"Wait till I see Bill," Ellen threatened. She
smiled at the baby. "No, I won't hold him, or come
too near," she said, as Mrs. Maloney coaxed her
to "feel the solid heft of the rascal," "I go in and
out of all sorts of places, you know."

On the way to the door with her caller, Mrs.
Maloney said suddenly:

"Do you know who's moved in, the next house but
one, and has the upstairs? The Fontanas, the young
people, she that was an Esposito, you knew her,
didn't you? There was talk around," she went on,
dropping her voice in order, perhaps, not to shock
the baby with scandal. "I don't know . . . the
neighbors over on the block beyond said she went
away and came back and there was a lot of loud
talking and going-on, but she was married, and lived
with the old folks. Now they've moved in, but Fontana's lost his trucking business or whatever it was.
I don't know.

" 'Tis a hard world," said Mrs. Maloney, smiling
cheerfully while the little boy in her arms laughed
aloud, "but you've got to take it as it comes," she
ended philosophically. "Come in again, do," she said
to Ellen, "it does me a marvel of good just to see
you."

CONCLUSION

Going downstairs Ellen looked at her watch. She
would stop and see Gilda, for a minute, ten minutes.
If there was anything she could do for her . . .

She had not seen her since the marriage.

The woman who owned the small house directed
her upstairs, and sent her husky voice before her,
as warning, "Hey, Mis' Fontana, there's the nurse
here to see you . . ."

Gilda was waiting for her, smiling. "It was good
of you to come, I've been meaning to try and get to
see you."

Ellen went with her into the little flat. Two rooms,
spotless; two rooms bright with color, cheerful. A
canary, in a cage. Gilda's sewing. The smell of good
soup, coming from the tiny kitchen. "It isn't much
of a place," said Gilda, "I've tried to fix it up."

"It's sweet. Mrs. Maloney told me you were here. Gilda, how are things?"

"All right," said Gilda bravely. "Pasquale, well, he was unlucky, he hadn't much business, he lost the little he had, the truck, I mean."

"But——"

"Oh, it's all right, he's strong, he'll find work, he's out now, looking. But, we thought, we'd save and get another truck and a man to run it, and pretty soon, we'd have a—a fleet or something and be rich," said Gilda. "Mike wanted to help—go shares. Pasquale wouldn't let him, not till he had something to show for it, he said."

"He's good to you?" asked Ellen gently.

Gilda's great eyes were clear and grave.

"Yes, he's good," she said simply, "he does his best. We both do."

She said, a little later: "If you hear of anything . . . of course he—he isn't trained. But he's strong. He worked on a farm as a boy. I've been teaching him English nights . . . and other things. He's changed, some, I think," said Gilda, a little proudly.

There was a step on the stair, a man's step. "Perhaps that's Pasquale," said Ellen. But it was not.

The door opened at the moment the knock came on it. "Pasqual' here, Gilda?"

The speaker was in the room, a big young man, dark, good-looking. It was Jim O'Connor.

"He's not here, he's looking for work, Mr. O'Connor," Gilda answered. Her tone was exceedingly hostile. Jim looked at Ellen. That he had been very much taken aback at seeing her on his entrance was apparent. He said awkwardly,

"Hello, didn't expect to see *you* here. . . . Look here, Gilda, I'll go on, I'm late to an appointment. Tell Pasqual' that I think I have something in mind for him if he'll drop around the office tonight. I'll be there, working," he said. He turned to Ellen. "I've got the car outside. Shall I take you somewhere?"

The words were casual; the tone was insistent. Too insistent, Ellen thought instantly. For some reason he was displeased to find her here, and anxious for her to go. She smiled at him. "Thanks, I think I'll stay here with Gilda for a while."

"It's snowing," said Jim.

"I thought it would. But that doesn't matter. I'm through work but I have to go back to the office, on my way home."

He nodded, briefly, saying to Gilda, "Don't forget to tell Pasqual'——" and left. There was a little silence for a moment afterwards. Then Gilda, her oval cheeks flaming, burst out, "If only he wouldn't come, if only he'd give Pasquale a chance!" She was twisting her slim olive-tinted hands together in her lap. Pasquale's old-fashioned ring, a broad gold band, stood out against the warm flesh.

"Isn't that what he's going to do?" asked Ellen, puzzled. "I mean, Jim has influence down here, lots. In his work he runs into all sorts of people, he might easily find your husband a job."

She remembered asking Jim to have Fontana looked up at the time of that trouble about Gilda. He had kept track of them since. A little wave of warmth, of gratitude stirred her heart. That was pretty decent of him.

Gilda was staring at her.

"You don't understand," she said slowly. "I—have you known him long . . . O'Connor, I mean . . .?"

"All my life," said Ellen. But her tone was guarded. Something was wrong, terribly wrong. If she made the least false move Gilda would freeze up, would withdraw into herself. But Gilda was crying. Gilda was saying as Ellen, in the last few years had heard so many women say, "I have to tell you, I have to tell someone, it's killing me, I——"

"All right, Gilda," said Ellen. She took the girl's hands in her own, remembering another occasion. But this was Pasquale's wife who sat here weeping, her hands in Ellen's.

"You won't tell, you won't get Pasquale into trouble?" asked Gilda.

"No, I won't get him into trouble."

"The trucking business. He—he had that all right. But when he first came here, to the neighborhood, he met O'Connor. Pasquale didn't understand. It was a game to him, the racket. It was—exciting. He likes excitement. He's strong, he's young, dangers—that's a game to him, too. And he didn't mind if they *were* breaking the law. Laws didn't mean much to him—at home, it had always been a man's own law, first. You were your law. You understand. You know such people. And there was easy money in the racket . . ."

Ellen was cold with the realization which, coming to her slowly, was not to be denied. So many things began to clear, so many little pieces of puzzles began to fit in. Jim, denying he knew Fontana; Jim, at Fontana's table at the Napoli; Jim, and his new car, and his "big business"; Jim, and his careless ways, so easy with money; Jim, and Bartlett's warning.

She said, "Liquor, of course?"

"I don't know," said Gilda. She was calmer now. "Liquor, maybe. But something else. Something smuggled. Drugs, perhaps," said Gilda. "I've never been able to find out. Perhaps some imported goods, gotten through here without duty. I've thought and thought and tried to make him tell. He wouldn't, Pasquale's loyal, he laughs, he says, 'Never mind, I take care of it.' He had the truck, you see, and his little business. He was young," she said again, "and strong. He had friends . . ."

"It's Jim's business then, whatever it is?" asked Ellen slowly.

"Yes. He's . . . the organizer. He has men, working for him. He has ways of getting lofts and hideaways. He can take care of whatever it is they bring in, and of men, too, when they have to hide. He has—his real estate business, it's like a false front on a shop. The others do the hard work, the dangerous work. After . . . after Pasquale met me he wanted to quit. He told Jim O'Connor so. But he wouldn't let him. He said he was in it; he'd have to stay in it. But after—we married, he did quit. He went down to see O'Connor. He had a knife. He put it on the desk, he said, keeping his hand on it, 'I'm quitting.' He said, 'I'll keep my mouth shut, you needn't worry, but—I'm *quitting.*' O'Connor was— ugly. And while they were quarreling—it was at night—in the back room of the office—a man came in—his name was Brown. 'I'm Dan Brown,' he kept saying. Pasquale had never seen him before. He was like a crazy man, he told me. He kept screaming at O'Connor, 'You stay away from my wife—I'll see that you stay away from her.' He had a gun. Pasquale is bigger, stronger. He got it away from him. He said, he didn't want to be mixed up in a shooting. He said, he could take care of his own affairs but he didn't want to be in on anyone else's. He took the man out. He walked him, blocks, miles. The man, this Brown, talked, all the time. Pasquale didn't understand, much. Only that O'Connor had been hanging around his wife, making her unhappy and that Brown couldn't stand it. Brown kept saying, 'Now, now I don't know *what* to believe. In Christ's name, I *don't know what to believe.*'

"He walked all the fight out of him, Pasquale said," Gilda went on while Ellen sat there, still as if carved from wood, her heart the only living thing about her, she thought, leaping against her side, hurting. "And then he went back to find O'Connor. He was still there. He was drinking, he had been frightened. He told Pasquale that Brown's wife wasn't any good, and he'd done them a good turn since they came to the city; he said he hadn't had anything to do with her, really, only flirted with her a little, and she got sore at something he said and said she'd tell her husband. . . . That was all, he said. He then thanked Pasquale for what he had done. Pasquale said he hadn't done anything, perhaps he shouldn't have interfered. All he wanted now was for O'Connor to let him alone."

Gilda sighed.

"So, you see, he quit. O'Connor didn't urge him any more and he went on with his little trucking business. But trade was scarce. Sometimes he'd find his tires cut. Sometimes other things were the matter. Another man, here in this district, one of O'Connor's men, gave better prices. And for the last week or so O'Connor's tried to get him back. He said to him, 'See, you couldn't make a go of it. Better change your mind, I'll put you in the way of something good.'" Gilda began to beat her hands together. "I'm afraid he'll go back," she wept. "I'm afraid. And something will happen. Jail. Or he'll be killed, some night. I—he doesn't want to go back. But he keeps thinking of me. I'm going to have a baby. He keeps thinking of us . . . I'm afraid O'Connor's beaten him . . . and he'll go back."

Ellen said, through stiff lips:

"He won't go back . . ."

Gilda shrieked. She hurled herself at Ellen, caught her knees, huddled there on the floor beside her, all the restraint, all the ways of the new world fallen from her; a woman, Gilda, fighting for her man, for the father of her child. Whether she loved him or not was not important. She belonged; she was loyal . . .

"You won't tell—you won't get him into trouble?"

Ellen said: "No, I didn't mean that. Gilda, stop. Get up. Here, come over here, sit beside me. I won't tell. I'll find a way out for all of you, somehow."

"You won't—go to the police? About O'Connor?

If he's caught," sobbed Gilda, "he'll turn the other men up, all of them, to save himself, if he can . . ."

"I'm not going to the police," said Ellen. "I'm going to get you and Pasquale away. Into the country . . . somewhere. A house of your own, room for the baby to play in, to breathe in. Sunshine. Right away out of the city. We're going to do that somehow. Find work for Pasquale, and a place for you to live. Where you won't be bothered . . . any more . . ."

That was what she had to do; how, she didn't know. She went back to the office. It was past five o'clock. She had spent the last hour of her time with Mrs. Maloney and Gilda. But her calls had been finished. Miss Renwick was alone in the office, ready to leave.

Ellen explained her appearance. "I've come back to do some writing. . . . Tomorrow morning I've long reports. But there's a mental case I want to refer to Miss Allan, and some things I want to clear up, the report I have to take to the Charity Bureau and all . . ."

Miss Renwick nodded. "Then you'll lock up," she said, "when you're through."

Ellen would. Miss Renwick left presently. Ellen was alone in the bare utilitarian office, with its desks, its writing paraphernalia. The stenographer's machine was covered; the telephone, that instrument which sounded every moment of the working day, was silent. She sat down at her desk and tried to clear her mind. She must get this work finished, odds and ends of things that she had been meaning to get done for the last few days. She made a note of a child's name. The polio case across the street which had been going to the clinic. The orthopedic staff was looking after him, but she had met the mother on the street and had promised to see what she could do about getting clothes for the boy; he could return to school next term if he were clad, the city bus would call for him.

She picked up the telephone and called her house and Coral answered. "I'm at the office," Ellen said, "I'll be late this evening."

Then she was alone again, Coral's friendly pretty voice silenced. Terribly alone, somehow.

At six o'clock she was through. She pushed the papers aside, ruffled her hair with her hands. Gilda and Pasquale, who must be saved. Jim, who must be —warned. Yet could one warn Jim without endangering other people? What, exactly, was her duty in this instance? Her duty, she knew, and clearly, was to betray Jim. But how many others would suffer. Gilda hadn't known what forbidden things he dealt in, and if it were narcotics, Jim must be punished, no matter how other people were involved; for the good of the majority . . .

After a while she made up her mind. She said, "There's just one person." She said it aloud.

She called Bartlett's office on the off chance that he had not left. There was, for a long time, no answer. Everyone had left. She would have to wait until later and call his apartment after she got home . . .

"Ring them once more, operator."

Then Bartlett's voice, impatient, tired, "Well?"

She replied, laughing a little, "That tone will lose you clients, Frank."

The tone changed, perceptibly. But it was still guarded.

"Ellen?"

"Yes, Ellen. Frank, listen . . . Bill's taken to playing hookey. He—he thinks you're angry at him —something he told you—something he misunderstood. You're the only one who can persuade him to behave. His family would be so grateful—and the truant officer . . . too."

"The little devil——" Frank's voice was changing, surely it was changing, there was warmth in it, eagerness. She went on, bravely:

"He needs you, Frank. And—I need you. Awfully. There's something you can do for me——"

He said, over the wire, "There's something you can do for me, Ellen . . ."

She answered, after a long moment, "I think I

know. But even if I'm wrong . . . it doesn't matter
—I want *you* to know . . . I love you," she said,
and brokenly, "I love you——"

"Ellen—*Ellen*——"

He was shouting at her . . . she put a hand to
her ear——

"I'm down at the office," she said.

She heard the receiver go down on the other end.
She held hers until the operator said tartly, "Number
please . . ." and then put it down quite gently.
She was smiling.

In the downtown office Frank was hurling himself
into an overcoat, racing out, slamming doors, ringing
elevator bells to the consternation of the elevator
boy and everyone who saw him. He was rushing to
the place where his car was parked . . .

A dark night, clear and cold.

She was waiting there, there in the office. The
green shaded desk lights were on, the shades drawn.
She stood, waiting, leaning against the desk, in the
dark gray uniform with the blue of the tie at her
throat, and the magnificent hair tumbled. Her lips
were very pale against the pallor of her face and
her eyes were strange and lovely . . .

A car drew up outside, with a squeal of brakes . . .

Somewhere someone was singing. It was Accordion
Al, walking the dark cold streets, singing his interminable
song . . . "*Life is like a city street——*"

Frank was coming . . . she heard him, there just beyond the door; and in that split second her mind was divided. There was a part which didn't think, which could not, and a part which was concerned with Al and the boy who had been burned, who was well but who should, next year, have a skin graft . . .

The door opened. Bartlett said, "Ellen?"

There were no more thoughts; there were no words. She was in his arms, where she belonged. Close. Held safely, held strongly. He said after a long moment. "I was such a fool . . . I thought, if she loved me, that night when she came, she would have told me so, not wasted time in apologies. She would have said . . . 'I believed it of you but I loved you. I love you, now, that's all that matters.' But you didn't say it; and I thought you didn't care. I thought you cared for O'Connor. I thought——"

"Never mind what you thought," said Ellen.

And then after another interval, he was sitting beside her on the desk and saying sternly, "I'll attend to Bill."

"It wasn't his fault. Oh, I don't mean running away. That was yours, because he thought you didn't care what became of him. I mean, he *did* see me— and Jim. I—Jim had gotten out of hand, that was all—it wasn't—I mean——"

"Damn Jim," he said cheerfully, "I can forgive him anything now."

"Can you? And must we?" she asked soberly.

He looked at her, the tumbled hair, the flushed sweet face, the strong sweet generous mouth, not smiling now, the mouth which had kissed him, which he had kissed, the little stubbornly set chin.

"What do you mean, Ellen?"

"Must we—damn him?"

She told him of Jim, of Pasquale and Gilda. He listened, frowning.

"I told you I'd had him looked up. There were rumors. But nothing to go on. This Fontana . . . I think I can get a place for him. I wonder if he can garden, if he knows anything about farming . . ."

"He was," said Ellen, "a farmer's son. So Gilda told me."

"That's fine. There's a man upstate, a client of mine. He has something of a showplace, but it's practical, too. There's a cottage and a job and everything all ready. I'll long distance him tonight. It's as good as in our hands . . . But O'Connor——?"

Ellen said, quite suddenly:

"If it's drug traffic . . . oh, if it's *any* traffic, we've no right to—to think of anything. Of his aunt. Of the people he may drag into it. Of long friendship."

"Women are hard," said Bartlett after a moment.

"I suppose they have to be. No, there's another way. You'll let me handle it. I come in contact with so many people. I know what Bill would call 'big shots.' Politically and all that. Some of their hands are none too clean. As I see it this—whatever it is—it's a small racket, hasn't been big enough to bother anyone—yet. But there's a way of putting fleas in certain ears. You'll see. Ellen, don't look so dramatic. He won't be killed, I promise you that. He won't even be hurt—except maybe in his pride. But he'll be put out of business. Quietly. Effectively. And for good. I don't even think he'll stay here long, in this neighborhood. It will be made too hot for him. And it may teach him a lesson. The little fellows—they get theirs after a while. The big ones go free. That's the damnable part of it. But in this case it will work out all right. We won't need any publicity. If officialdom comes into it, it will come in so quietly that no one will ever know——"

She said: "I know you can handle it, Frank. The way that's best for everybody. I know it will be a right way, too."

He kissed her, smiling a little. And there was no more speech. "Frank," she said after a while, "look at the time."

It was after eight. The telephone spoke there at her elbow, petulantly. "For heaven's sake," said

Coral's voice, "are you dead or something? Mother's fit to be tied."

"I'm all right, I'm coming home," said Ellen.

"What's up? You sound funny——"

But Frank had taken the phone from her. "Hope you saved some supper for Ellen and for me. I'm coming home, too. Kill a couple of fatted calves, Pete's going to get a brother-in-law."

"What did she say?" Ellen asked him when he had hung up.

"Plenty. I didn't listen. Come on, darling."

At the office door she turned, seeing that the latch was on, seeing that it would lock after her.

"You won't be doing this long," he told her.

"No, I suppose not." She was grave, a little unhappy. "I'll miss it," she said honestly, "it's so much a part of me, it means so much——"

"I know. I thought, When she puts me before the work, then I know she really loves me. And you have," he triumphed. "But there'll be lots you can do," he said, "and we'll do it together . . ."

Driving home, he asked her carelessly:

"Are you marrying me for my money, Miss Adams?"

"I don't think so," she told him, giving it proper thought. "You haven't enough, have you . . .? I mean to make it worth my while?"

They laughed, idiotically, to the astonishment of

a large cop beating himself across the breast to keep warm, stamping his feet . . . whistling a tune. Accordion Al's tune——

"That's just it, I have."

"I knew," she murmured, really serious this time, "that you had a good practice or whatever you call it—but——"

"Oodles of money," he said firmly, "thanks to an uncle . . . about three years ago. Sitting there in banks and gilt-edged bonds. I never saw much sense in spending it just to *be* spending. And I was afraid that if I once got the habit I'd quit the law and loaf. So I sort of tried living on what I earned. That's over now. I'm marrying an extravagant woman."

"Who is she?" asked Ellen demurely.

He ignored this.

"Enough," he said, "for all of us. To see Pete through anything, and Coral. To make your mother happy and comfortable. To buy Nancy a couple of telephone exchanges . . . or at any rate I'm rather a large stockholder. To help Bill . . . and the others. That's what I meant when I said . . . we'll do it together. There'll be work for you, Ellen. It is work to know how to help people by spending and not hurting them. Besides," he said lightly, "I'm subject to colds and need a lot of nursing . . ."

She was trying to keep back the tears. And so she said:

"If you're marrying me to have a nurse in the family, forget it. Break it off, here and now. For if you as much as sniffle I'll have specials in, on eight-hour shifts, two at a time . . ."

And now they were home. Coral and Nancy had turned from the window and were saying: "There you are, Mother . . . for goodness' sakes, angel, stop crying . . . everything's simply gorgeous." And someone was rushing to the kitchen to start the coffee perking. . . .

But for a moment Ellen and Frank were alone in the close tiny intimate darkness of the car. Making their wordless, solemn vows, voicing, mutely, their ecstasy and their hope; a little interlude of rapture, of promising, and of pledging, before they should draw a little apart one from the other and go into the house, and take up the business of living, however altered, once more . . .